"Close your eyes, and no peeking."

"Okay," McKenna said, "just don't let me fall and pull us both into the water."

"Cowboy's promise," Coop said, feeling just a bit silly saying that, but it made her smile and her hand tightened on his as she closed her eyes.

He walked slowly into the bend, making sure she had her footing by the side of the stream, then at the right moment, he stopped. Letting go of her hand, he said, "Keep your eyes shut," then he moved to one side so he could see her face. "Okay, open your eyes."

He watched her hesitate, then her eyes opened. She blinked and whispered, "Wow," in a voice that was touched with wonder. The huge rock with a five-foot-wide split down the middle was just a rock, but it was beyond special to McKenna. She stared up at it, tipping her head back to look at the flat top, at least twenty feet above the stream.

Dear Reader,

Life gets hard, and even the best of us seeks some reprieve—even if it's only temporary. *A Cowboy Summer* is the story of Cooper Donovan, rodeo superstar, who wants relief from the chaos of his professional life. He heads to Wyoming, to his family's Flaming Sky Ranch. He wants to be alone.

McKenna Walker, a pediatrician in a neonatal ICU, has failed in love and is facing burnout on her job. When a friend offers her an isolated Wyoming getaway near amazing hiking trails, she accepts—hiking is stress therapy for her. She wants to be alone.

When they end up at the same place, they find fate doesn't ask permission but gives them a chance to find out that simply holding hands can give two people a completeness that they never thought they'd find.

I hope you enjoy their cowboy summer journey.

Safe ride,

Mary Anne

HEARTWARMING

A Cowboy Summer

—

Mary Anne Wilson

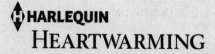

HARLEQUIN®
HEARTWARMING™

Recycling programs
for this product may
not exist in your area.

ISBN-13: 978-1-335-58502-8

A Cowboy Summer

Copyright © 2023 by Mary Anne Wilson

For questions and comments about the quality of this book,
please contact us at CustomerService@Harlequin.com.

Harlequin Enterprises ULC
22 Adelaide St. West, 41st Floor
Toronto, Ontario M5H 4E3, Canada
www.Harlequin.com

Printed in U.S.A.

Mary Anne Wilson is a Canadian transplanted to California, where her life changed dramatically. She found her happily-ever-after with her husband, Tom, and their family. She always loved writing, reading and has a passion for anything Jane Austen. She's had fifty novels published with Harlequin, been nominated for a RITA® Award, won Reviewers' Choice Awards and received RWA's Career Achievement Award in Romantic Suspense.

Visit the Author Profile page
at Harlequin.com for more titles.

For Tom:

Memories of holding hands
make my heart smile.

CHAPTER ONE

Wyoming, Mid-June

COOPER DONOVAN, aka Flaming Coop D, championship saddle bronc rider and the golden boy of rodeos, had his best-laid plans to get down to the main stable on Flaming Sky Ranch without anyone seeing him shattered by a voice screeching behind him: "Flaming Coop D! OMG, it's you! It's you!" His heart sank.

He hadn't even reached his horse's stall and was dressed like a ranch hand in a faded cap with the ranch's logo on it, along with torn jeans and a T-shirt that read "No Ride's a Bad Ride." He'd thought no one would look at him twice and that all the guests who'd come for the Junior Rodeo Trials this weekend would be in the arena where the action was.

One obviously wasn't. Coop considered not turning around, but he couldn't help it when the intruder said, "You don't know how happy you make me and my boy, Charlie. He wants to be just like you."

Bracing himself, he turned to find a thirtysomething woman dressed in jeans and a Flaming Sky Ranch T-shirt. Her hat was a newer version of the one he was wearing. He felt awful, but he didn't want to admit who he was, so he tried to deflect and distract. "Ma'am, guests aren't allowed back here."

She ignored what he said and took a step toward him, so he tugged his cap lower— that was about all he could do. "Coop, I'm just so happy to see you up close and personal. We go to as many of your shows as we can. You're so great."

He gave her his best fake puzzled look. "Please, the stables are private during any rodeo event."

"Sure, okay. I'm sorry, I got lost, then when I saw you here, I just had to tell you how much we love what you do and that you're such a good example for my boy."

He really felt like a heel, but if he confirmed who he was, he knew it would leak out, and he'd have to leave town. "Ma'am, I need to get back to my work, so please go back to the arena. I don't want to lose my job."

She faltered for a second, then looked embarrassed. He hated to see that. None of this was her fault. "I was just thinking if you were Coop that I could get an autograph for Charlie. I'm real sorry for interrupting."

He knew how important his fans were to his career, and he didn't want her to go away disappointed. He took out his cell phone and tapped his top speed-dial number. "Please, just wait a minute," he said to the woman, and then he heard his mother's voice on the other end of the line.

"Coop, what's going on?"

"Mrs. Donovan, I'm in the main stable grooming Blaze, and a nice lady's here. She and her son are big fans of Flaming Coop D, and she would sure appreciate an autographed picture and maybe a little something to go with it."

"I thought Abel had that section blocked off. Okay, what's the boy's name?"

"Ma'am, what's your son's name?"

"Charlie Denton."

The name sounded familiar to him, but

he had no idea why. "Charlie Denton," he repeated to his mom.

"Coop, that's Sandy Denton's boy. The family moved into town about a year ago. I think her boy's around eight. Tell her to find me at the main entry to the arena by the snack booth. I'll take care of her son."

"Thank you, Mrs. Donovan. I'll tell her."

He put away his phone and told Sandy Denton where to find Coop Donovan's mother. Her sudden grin and an excited, "Thank you, thank you. The Donovans are so wonderful!" made him feel even worse. But he figured her boy would be beyond happy with a Flaming Coop D autographed picture and whatever else his mother would give her.

As soon as she hurried off and he was alone, he saddled up Blaze and headed in the opposite direction from the main house and the arena. He went north until he found the switchback that led up to the old part of the ranch in the foothills. He'd come back home—actually, he'd snuck back onto the property in the evening—two weeks ago without being seen. He'd wanted to be out of sight to relax, regroup and to heal the ribs he'd bruised at his last show getting off the bronc who he'd just made angrier by getting in eight seconds on his back to win the ride. The injury was minor in the scheme of things, but he needed to focus and reset himself before he went back to training in a week, then onto the circuit again.

He needed no one to know about his location. But now, this lovely mom who loved her son would be going back and telling everyone about the ranch hand she met who looked just like Flaming Coop D. Maybe she'd start talking to her friends who would talk to their friends, and they'd figure out that he'd tried to pull one over on her.

Self-preservation had kicked in, and now he was riding to the one place he'd always felt safe and out of the way: the original house his Grandpa Maxima Donovan had built sixty years ago. In the years since, he'd spread the Donovan land down in the valley below and developed the hugely successful Flaming Sky Ranch. It was where Coop had been born and raised. Now, he couldn't chance staying in the valley any longer, so the old adobe house tucked away in the hills would be his safe place for the next week.

COOP WOKE SLOWLY to balmy air brushing his face and found himself lying on the uncomfortable wooden bench on the porch of his grandpa's old house. He opened his eyes and stared up at the heavy beams that supported the overhang above him. He must have been exhausted to have fallen asleep there and slept right through the night.

That had not been a stellar moment for him yesterday, but today Charlie would be wearing a brand-new Flaming Coop D hat, or maybe a shirt. Knowing his mother, the kid would probably be wearing both and clutching his autographed picture.

Coop was still wearing what he'd had on when he'd left the stables last night, all except for his boots and hat. He eased himself to a sitting position and spotted the cap perched on top of the boots on the single step up to the porch. He stood to retrieve his boots, ignoring the hat and sat on the porch step to tug them on. He raked his fingers through his unruly black hair with a sigh and decided against putting the old hat back on. He picked it up and tossed it toward the hitching post to his right. It landed perfectly on top. He'd perfected that toss when he'd been a kid. He hadn't lost it.

He touched his chest on his left side and pressed against his middle ribs. Nothing. No pain and no discomfort. His bruising was healed, and he was good every other way physically. He knew he could leave now and be fine to go back into the arena, but he didn't want to, not yet. He'd take the next week and spend that time up here, alone with no visitors—no matter how well meaning—and he'd do what he wanted to do.

A glance up at the eastern sky awash with early morning pastels was enough to cement his resolve. He had no appointments, no shows that he had to get ready for, no physical therapy, and no business meetings that demanded his attention. It was just him for seven days with Blaze. He felt a bit like the kid he'd been when he used to sneak up to the old place by himself. This was where he'd dreamed about being old enough to join the rodeo circuit and become a world champion like his dad.

With the tryouts being held again today, he couldn't risk riding back down there to the main house, where he'd spent the last two weeks, thinking he could become invisible to anyone he came across if he dressed like a ranch hand and kept his head down. But he needed fresh clothes and some staples. The old house had been cleaned out a long time ago. He'd call down to get what he needed brought to the foot of the switchback. No strangers wandered around there, and he could pick it up later.

The balminess of the morning breeze made the thought of a brisk swim in the stream-fed pond very appealing. He'd swim first, then he'd ride. He hadn't been riding on this part of the ranch for a very long time, and he wasn't going miss the chance right in front of him. He had nothing but time, and he'd make every minute he had up here count.

He heard his cell phone ring, and at first, he wasn't sure where the sound was coming from. He looked around and saw it under the bench. Stretching, he managed to get it without standing and looked at the caller ID. Luke Patton, a good friend and the local veterinarian, was calling. He picked up. "Good morning, Luke. You're up early."

When Luke answered, "I never went to bed," Coop knew the call was important.

"What's going on?"

"I've been up all night talking with Archie Newman, a vet over on the Utah border. Archie had some horses brought in from a raid on a breeding ranch over there a day ago. Two horses were too damaged to survive, and Archie had to put them down, but he thinks the other two might stand a chance if we could take them in here. He's tight on space and help, and he'll have to make a choice he doesn't want to make if he can't find a place for them."

Coop exhaled. "How bad are they?"

"The pictures Archie sent were horrific, but I think they stand a chance. Their treatment won't be easy or cheap if we take them. I didn't want to call you about this, but what I have left in the charity funds this month isn't going to be enough."

Coop never did get used to what so-called human beings could do to an animal. He tried to keep his voice low and even. "I can't give you much of my time, but I can support you financially. The thing is, I'm no mind reader, so you have to tell me exactly how much we're talking about."

"Sorry, Coop. I thought I could manage until I saw the photos Archie sent me and figured out what it might involve."

"Forget sorry. You took Blaze in when I found him half dead after being abused, and you worked a miracle saving his life. Don't *ever* apologize to me for asking for help so you can help other horses like Blaze. Just tell me what you need."

He heard Luke clear his throat. "Transportation, ASAP. It would take too much time to send my trailer to Utah to bring them back, and Archie asked everyone he knows but came up empty."

"Call Henry. My bet is he'll know someone who can transport them as quickly as possible from that end. He isn't just the best mechanic and body man around—he knows people who know people."

"Good call. I'll contact him."

"What else do you need?" Coop asked.

Luke laid everything out, then added, "I need it all on-site when the horses arrive." Then he gave Luke an estimate of the overall cost. It was a lot, but Coop didn't ask any questions. He trusted Luke completely.

"Tell you what. I'll arrange to have the money deposited into the Simply Sanctuary Horse Rescue account, then I'll put you on my private funds account and approve you to transfer what you need when you need it. That'll simplify everything. When you need it, take it. I'll arrange that as soon as I get off the phone."

"Where are you?" Luke asked.

Coop hesitated but told the truth. "Grand-pa's old place."

"How long have you been back?"

"A couple of weeks. I don't want anyone beyond family and close friends to know I'm up here. I needed a break from everything before I head back in a week."

"That's the place to be to pick up the pieces," Luke said.

"Yes, it is. Listen to me. Don't be too proud to ask for help."

"I'm working on that," Luke said. "Safe ride, Coop."

"You, too," Coop said and ended the call. In five minutes, he'd transferred the money to Luke's Sanctuary account and approved

Luke's use of his private funds. With that done, his next thought was to get Blaze ready, walk him down to the pond, swim until he shriveled up then ride off on a whim.

He went indoors to find something he could fill up with water to take with him and realized it had been almost three years since he'd stepped inside the house. It looked pretty much the way it had for as long as he could remember, except for a few improvements in the great room. A sturdy-looking iron-framed bed by the side window had replaced the sagging double bed that he and his brothers had used back in the day. He obviously hadn't made it there last night, collapsing on the old wooden bench instead. A forest-green couch that he remembered having seen in his parents' storage shed had found its way into the house to take the place of a sofa bed that had been pure torture to sleep on.

An old table under the front window near the door had been around long enough to have the names of most of the Donovan clan carved into its top. His was there twice. Once as Cooper Donovan and once as Flaming Coop D, carved when he'd been ten years old. His grandpa had admired it. "That boy's got dreams," he'd heard his grandpa say to his dad. The older man understood dreams. The Donovans' Flaming Sky Ranch had been his dream that had come true.

He went over to the tiny kitchen in a small nook on the other side of the door. A short counter along the sidewall held a shallow sink serviced by an old-fashioned hand pump for water. A two-burner propane stove sat beside a half-size refrigerator that he'd never seen before. He crossed to open its door and found a half-full bottle of water, ketchup, dill pickles and an unopened bottle of champagne. He took the bottled water out and dumped its contents into the sink. He had no idea how long it had been there, and stale water was one of his dislikes.

After he'd filled it from the pump, he looked up at the mirror that had hung over the sink for as long as he could remember. He'd sat there more than once to watch his grandpa shave with an old-fashioned blade razor. As a kid, he'd always thought how brave Grandpa Donovan had been to use that razor when he could have cut his throat trying to shave. The man had never drawn his own blood, and Coop had never tried to shave with a straight edge.

He didn't like shaving very much, so he only did it when he felt like it. He hadn't felt like it for more than a few days, and he didn't feel like it today. He worked the pump on the sink, captured some water in his free hand and splashed it on his face. Then he finger-combed his black hair back and noticed gray showing at the temples in the mottled mirror. He and Caleb, his identical twin, were born just minutes apart. He was the younger of the two, but he knew he looked older than his brother. His tan was deeper, his eyes had more lines at the corners, deeper brackets framed his mouth, and he'd bruised his ribs on a maneuver that any rookie would have made safely.

He turned away, grabbed the bottle of water and headed for the door. He heard his phone ringing when he stepped outside and spotted it on the step where he'd left it. By the time he got to it, the ringing had stopped. Looking at the screen, he was surprised to see the call had come from Caleb when he'd just been thinking about him. They'd had twin moments before, like when he'd try to call Caleb and Caleb would be calling him, so neither one got through. Or like the time in school when Caleb had broken his arm, and Coop had felt pain in his own arm at the same time it happened. Coincidences, maybe, but perhaps there was more to it.

Before he could call Caleb back, he heard a horse snort and looked up. His brother was riding across the dry pasture coming toward the house. Coop sat down on the stair and waited for Caleb to come to him. He was riding Blue, a big, strong horse with a steel-gray coat that showed hints of blue in the sunlight. His midnight-black mane and tail made his coloring even more striking.

Caleb dismounted and secured Blue to the hitching post that had the hat on it, then turned to Coop and grinned. "Hello, little brother. Why am I not surprised to find you up here? You're so predictable. You always did end up here when you ran away."

Coop chuckled at that. "It always worked, until you or Max came along to drag me back down to the main house."

"I'm not here for that. I'm just the messenger." Caleb looked cool and fresh in the black leather vest he wore over a white

T-shirt, along with jeans and tooled boots. His hat was from the Flaming Coop D merchandise line: brushed black leather with a gold braid around the crown and the brim slightly rolled. It looked good on him.

Coop motioned to the step by him. "Take a load off so I don't get a kink in my neck from looking up at you."

Caleb took his time settling by Coop, stretching out his long legs and removing the hat to rest it on his thigh. "Sure is pretty up here."

"Yeah, it is. Now why are you up here at this time of the morning when your whole family is usually still asleep?"

"Blame it on the usual suspect, Mom. As soon as I got here to help with today's setup, Mom took me aside and told me what happened yesterday and asked me to give you a message."

"She couldn't have just called me?"

"She was in a huge rush to get the tables set up, and I didn't mind the ride, actually. She said to tell you that Charlie was thrilled with his signed picture and a kid's hat and shirt. Fans forever. You played it well."

"I felt like a jerk, but I'm glad the kid's happy."

"You can be a jerk," Caleb said. "I remember when you—"

Coop cut his brother off. "Is that it? Or was there more to her message?"

"Mom said, since you're up here, stay up here until at least five this afternoon. It seems Charlie's gifts riled up some other kids who have literally been looking all over for you. The gates close at five, so the coast should be clear then."

"I'll go one better. I'm not going back down. I'll stay up here until I leave. I need to be up here. I need the peace this place gives me."

"I get that. Being famous is fun, but it can also be pure misery." He patted Coop on his knee. "Sit tight, baby brother. I'll go down and help Dad with the setup."

"Whoa, rein yourself in. I need a favor. I have a backup duffel bag in the room Mom uses to store my merchandise. It's black with a Flaming Coop D logo running along both sides. It's got my clothes and stuff in it, and I need some staples, too. I don't care what Mom sends, except I need good coffee grounds. Have someone leave them in the pump house at the bottom of the switchback, and I'll pick them up when it's clear down there."

"Sure. Give me a couple of hours." Caleb stood up and put his hat back on. "I'll text you when I've dropped the bag. Enjoy this place while you can."

"I've got every intention to do just that, but one more thing I need is my hat."

Caleb glanced at the cap on the hitching post. "I wondered where that came from," he said. "I'll make sure to emphasize your hat is needed desperately."

"You do that," Coop said.

Caleb went to Blue, and once he was up in the saddle, he looked down at Coop and touched the brim of his hat with his forefinger. "Safe ride, baby brother," he said, then turned and headed back the way he'd come to cut through the trees halfway between the house and the bluff where the land fell out of sight.

"Safe ride, big brother!" Coop called after him, then remembered something else. "Hey, my boots—don't forget my boots!" Caleb waved a hand in acknowledgment over his shoulder, then kept going until he disappeared into the thick stand of trees onto the dirt path that a lot of Donovans had beaten down over the years to get to the pond and the entrance to the switchback. Coop looked around, and that sense of peace and quiet he seldom felt anywhere else surrounded him.

Swimming then riding. Seven days like this would be very good. He smiled.

CHAPTER TWO

THE NEXT MORNING, Coop woke in the iron bed that had proven to be very comfortable, and he knew exactly where he was without even opening his eyes. Getting up, he didn't worry about hooking up the shower to the gravity tank that fed it, and figured swimming was just as good and a lot more enjoyable. He'd thankfully received a text from Caleb in the late afternoon yesterday that his packages were at the pump shed. The ride down to retrieve them went well, and even better, Coop finally had his own boots and hat.

He was going to start today the way he'd started his first day: swim a couple of laps in the pond, then float on his back for a while as he stared up at the true blue sky. He quickly dressed in jean shorts, along with a short-sleeved blue shirt and his boots.

When he arrived at the pond, he led Blaze over to one of three hitching posts at the top of the stairs that went down to the dock he and his brothers had helped his grandfather build years ago. He patted Blaze's neck, always impressed to the see how healthy and strong the golden red quarter horse looked. No one would ever guess that he'd almost died a year ago. Thanks to Luke, Blaze had been one of *Simply Sanctuary Horse Rescue's* successes.

He looked around at the vast clearing, its parameters defined by rocky bluffs to the west and stands of thick pines and deciduous trees way off to the north. Straight across past the pond was the entrance to the switchback.

To the southeast was a panoramic view of the valley below that could take a person's breath away. But he barely looked at it now as he strode toward his target, towel slung over his shoulders. The long, irregular body of water could loosely be called a pond or a lake, depending on who described it. It was fed by small underground streams that broke through the rocky land and was fringed with low bushes, plants and a lot of age-smoothed rocks.

He took the four steps down to the dock,

which was weathered but sturdy. Then he removed his hat, tossed it up toward the hitching post by Blaze and ringed it over the top to keep it safely out of the way. The water level was lower than it had been before a prolonged drought that had only broken a few months ago, but the pond was deep enough for what he wanted to do.

Dropping the towel on the bottom step, he stripped off his shirt with his cell phone in the breast pocket, then his socks and boots, leaving them all on the steps. Wearing the cutoff jeans for swim trunks, he took two long strides to the farthest edge of the dock jutting out over the water. He stretched his arms straight out in front of him, his hands pressed palm to palm, and dove in.

When he surfaced halfway to the other end, he flicked his head to get his long hair off his face and took several deep breaths before he started laps. He kept going until he felt a vague throbbing around the area where he'd bruised his ribs, but no actual pain. Still, he was ready to float.

He flipped over onto his back and stretched out. When he got bored, he challenged himself to see how long he could hold his breath underwater, something he'd done with his brothers years ago. He'd beaten both Caleb and his older brother, Max, regularly. This time, he was short on air, so he floated for a bit, then tried it again after he'd let himself breathe in enough oxygen. He went under, letting himself sink until he started to rise and surfacing with his back up, his arms outstretched, keeping his face under water. This time he stayed longer before he flipped over and breathed.

"Hey, mister, what are you doing? Do you need help?"

The intruding voice cut through his peace, and he righted himself to look back at the dock. He almost sank again when he saw a woman at the edge of the deck, looking as if she were having a panic attack. "Are you okay? Do you need me to help you out?" she called to him.

He shook his head hard to get his hair of his face and finally found his voice. "What are you doing here?"

She stood with her hands on her hips and a black backpack at her feet, where it could easily be kicked into the water. "What are *you* doing here?" she asked, calming down a bit.

He stayed where he was, while she was obviously waiting for his answer. "I think the real question is what are *you* doing here?" he finally said.

She looked to be in her twenties—younger than Charlie's mother had been—dressed in faded jeans, a blue tank top and heavy boots that looked as worn as his were. Her bright yellow sports cap with "Take a Hike" on the front hid her hair. Her heart-shaped face might have been attractive if she hadn't been glaring down at him. "Thinking I'm glad to know you aren't drowning or dead."

"I was enjoying myself until you started screaming at me. Why are you even here?"

"I'm staying here," she said with a slightly defensive lift of her chin.

He repeated her own words back to her. "Nooooo, *I'm* staying here."

Her eyes widened slightly as she let out a breath. "Oh, no. This can't happen. They must have double-booked or something."

"No, they didn't," he said as he finally stroked over to the dock. She moved back a pace as he pressed his hands on the deck, then looked up at her. "You must be lost."

She cocked her head a bit to the right as she studied him. "I doubt that."

"What do you doubt?"

"I know I'm not lost, and I know this is my place for the next couple of weeks."

He shook his head. "No, this isn't your place any more than I was drowning. Go on back up the stairs, and you'll have cell reception. Contact whoever you dealt with and figure it out. Go ahead."

She hesitated, then did as he asked. Meanwhile, he got out of the water, grabbed his towel while she had her back to him using her cell phone, and had his shirt on before she turned to come back down the stairs. He kept roughly toweling his hair.

"I can't contact him. He had an emergency and he's out of reach."

Coop rubbed his legs as water ran down them from his soaked shorts. It was hopeless and he gave up, tossing the towel onto the step by his boots. "Then go and find him, whoever he is, and tell him he blew it." He raked his hair back in an attempt to regain some semblance of order. "It's on him."

She hesitated, then went to grab the backpack, walked around him to the top step and sat down. She put the backpack by her side. "I can't do that. Sorry. I'll just sit here and wait until I can contact him."

That wasn't in the picture. "Uh, no, you won't."

She looked up at him, and he could see her eyes were a pale green with hints of gold around the iris, a different color but pretty. "I won't bother you. Go ahead and keep swimming or go for a ride, and I'll stay here and keep trying to make contact to prove I'm right." Before he could tell her that she wasn't ever going to be right, she finished by saying, "I could be wrong, but I know I'm not wrong."

He would have laughed at that ridiculous logic if she hadn't said it without any hint of a smile. "Wow, that's a mangy dog's circle."

She squinted up at him. "A what?"

"You know the way dogs circle and circle and circle when they're chasing their tails and never get anywhere? You could be wrong, but you aren't wrong, because you're never wrong, so you can't be wrong, because..." He let that trail off.

"Okay, I get it." She exhaled with obvious exasperation. "I should have said I *know* I'm right."

He looked down at her. "I can make a call and clear this up right now."

She shrugged at that. "Then be my guest."

He pulled his cell out of his shirt pocket, but when he looked down at it, the screen was blank. It was dead. "Can I use your phone? Mine's dead."

She was still holding her phone but hesitated. "You give me the number, and I'll put in a call for you."

He'd had enough. "Oh, come on. Let me call, and I'll put it on speaker so you can hear it."

She hesitated, then used her fingerprint to unlock the phone before she handed it up to him. He put in his uncle Abel's number, and it went straight to voice mail. He almost left a message, but it would take too long to explain the situation. So he gave the phone back to her. "Never mind. He's not picking up."

She put her phone back in the side pocket of her bag. "That was a bust," she muttered.

"Come on," he said and reached to free Blaze's reins from the hitching post.

She made no move to stand. "I can wait right here. But you can leave. I'll enjoy the view, which is simply unbelievable, and make my call later."

"No, I'm going up to the house, and I'm asking you to come with me. You don't have to go inside, just give me time to charge my phone enough to make a couple of other calls." Then he realized his charger was still plugged in down at the house. He'd totally forgotten it. He'd have to borrow her phone again, and he wondered if her goodwill had been used up on his first call.

He retrieved his hat, put it over the saddle horn, then started off leading Blaze and realized right away the woman wasn't following him. A glance over his shoulder showed her standing by the top step holding her backpack by one strap but not moving toward him. "Come on, darlin'. Keep up."

"I'm not in the habit of strange men calling me *darlin'*, and I don't intend to go anywhere with a complete stranger, especially not to a house in the middle of nowhere."

She folded her arms across her chest with more than a touch of defensiveness.

"Then why were you on the dock screaming at me?"

She sighed. "Hindsight being what it is, I should have let you drown, but I took an oath to not do that to anyone. You're just lucky, I guess."

Sarcastic much? He kept that thought to himself. "Lock yourself in your car or truck, and you'll be safe while we get this straightened out."

She nodded to him and magnanimously gave him permission to do what he was going to do anyway. "Lead the way."

He started off again and didn't look back. If she came, she came; if not, he'd have to wait to get ahold of his uncle, the ranch manager, to get him to take care of her. Uncle Abel kept the house cleaned and repaired; he'd let him be the one to get this woman off the ranch. That way, there wouldn't be a headline in the paper about Flaming Coop D throwing a pretty lady off his land. He cringed at that visual. "So, how did you drive onto the property when the gates are kept locked?" he asked without a glance back at her.

"I didn't." When she responded, he could tell she was pretty close behind him now. "I didn't realize I didn't have the key for the gates until I got here. So I texted my friend to let him know I was locked out. When he didn't respond, I climbed over the fence and walked that long road up to the house."

So she wouldn't be locking herself in her car, yet she'd still come with him. That was good, because he didn't want a scene. "Why did you come down to the pond?" he asked as they walked out of the trees.

"I went inside, found that the kitchen sink was damp, and I figured someone had been there recently who shouldn't have been. So I went looking around and spotted the dried grass pushed down from someone walking this way, and I followed the path and found you in the pond playacting at drowning."

"You're a regular Sherlock Holmes," he murmured.

"You sure fooled me," she said. "I was told I could use the place because it was empty, and I really needed a place to stay. That's why I'm here."

She was half right, the part about the place being empty. A ringtone—"I Feel Good"—sounded and startled him. He turned and watched her open her phone.

She looked up at him. "I have a text. It was sent almost fifteen minutes ago, but I just got it. This proves I'm supposed to be here." Then she read it aloud to him.

"'Sorry, forgot about gate key. Under flat black rock by east gate post. Hope you have a great time up there. I promise you won't regret it.'" She smiled up at him, a victory smile. "I told you so. Problem solved!"

If he hadn't known about the black rock by the gates hiding the key, he would have laughed. But he did know, and that meant whoever had texted her had known and sent her up to the old ranch on purpose. Again, he took off walking with Blaze, who was being very patient with him going so slowly.

"Well?" she asked coming up beside him as they neared the adobe house. One look at her, and he knew she was not only expecting him to apologize but to be the kind of cowboy who'd ride off into the sunset. She was wrong on both counts.

"Well, what?" Coop asked as he secured

Blaze to the hitching rail by the porch, then took the single step up to sit down on the long bench. The woman stayed on the step looking over at him. She was pretty enough—no makeup that he could see, an almost boyish figure, long slender legs, and her green eyes were interesting. Those eyes never looked away from him. He wondered about her hair, all neatly hidden under the yellow hat with just wisps of auburn showing.

"This is where you say, 'Sorry, have a great day,' and leave." She looked too smug.

He held out his hand. "Let me see the text."

She brought it up again and handed her phone to him. "See for yourself. I'm quite good at reading."

So was he. He read it, then glanced at the sender's name and phone number at the top of the screen. He was surprised by the picture icon. He stared at a likeness of an old friend of his, Dr. Boone Williams, a man he'd grown up with and who ran a medical clinic in Eclipse, the nearest town to the ranch. He tried to get his mind around why Boone would have sent this woman up here.

Finally, he handed her phone back to her. "I have to go in and get some dry clothes on. I'll get right back to you."

McKenna Walker had her back turned to the house when she heard the door open and shut. She spun around to see that her nemesis had changed into a pair of worn straight-legged jeans and a chambray shirt with the sleeves rolled up. He had to be over six feet tall, and he looked striking, with dark hair and eyes. His features were sharp, but together they made a good-looking man. He was lean and strong and gave off heavy cowboy vibes as he took up his original spot on the long bench.

"So, who are you and why are *you* here?" McKenna asked him straight up.

He studied her for a long moment before he said, "I'm an old friend of the best doctor in Eclipse."

It took her a second to put him and Boone together, and finally, she realized he had to be a Donovan. This was their land, their home, and he had been swimming in their pond. She felt warmth in her cheeks from embarrassment and quickly started apologizing. "Oh, gosh, no, yes, of course. You're one of the Donovan brothers, aren't you? Boone talks about you three all the time. I should have known, but I never... I'm sorry. Really sorry. I really did think you were drowning, by the way. But I am beyond sorry for the way I acted all high and mighty, like you were trespassing or something." She finally made herself stop babbling and waited for him to say something.

He shrugged his broad shoulders. "Hey, you either rope it or you don't. What I want to know is, which Donovan son do you think I am?"

She assumed that was cowboy talk for "Let's forget it," so she would. But she didn't have a clue which of the three sons he was as she realized she could check one off the list. "I know you aren't Caleb, so you have to be Max or Cooper."

His dark eyes narrowed. "Why not Caleb?"

She had an answer for that. "Boone once said something about Caleb being injured during a bull ride, that he had a limp. You don't have a limp."

"Down to two. Now, who am I?"

"You don't know who you are?" she asked, the corner of her mouth lifting up.

"Despite being an identical twin, I knew who I was around two years of age."

She left her backpack on the step and went up to sit by him on the other end of the bench. "Okay, I can narrow this down by asking you one question, with maybe a follow-up, and no lying on your part, either."

She wished she could take the lying comment back, but decided to leave it when he said, "Okay, no lying. Ask away."

"Did you ever sit on the hip of the roof of a hay barn to watch an eclipse? Yes or no?"

He took his time raking his fingers through his damp hair before he finally said, "Yes."

"This is way too easy," she murmured, feeling very satisfied with herself. "Boone told me that Max never did climb onto the high part of the roof, so that means—"

He cut her off. "Before you guess wrong, darlin', you should know that Boone couldn't always make it to watch the eclipses with us, and Max definitely did get on the roof once when Boone wasn't there. I know that for a fact."

"Shoot," she said. "I have to assume you're telling me the truth."

"You bet. That information's solid."

She found herself smiling, kind of enjoying the game he was putting her through. "I've got it. Don't evade, distract or deflect. Answer me this. What was the secret ingredient in the chili contest at the fire department's barbeque in Eclipse six years ago? Boone told me who won it because of the secret ingredient."

He shook his head ruefully. "Sorry, it's a secret. I keep secrets. It's a cowboy's honor kind of thing. So I can't tell you that."

"You're Cooper Donovan," she said emphatically.

He looked genuinely surprised. "What?"

"You're Cooper Donovan, the rock star of the rodeo crowd, famous beyond measure and a real favorite of female fans."

He obviously didn't like her summation of who he was, but that's what Boone had told her. "You think that's me?"

"I know that's you." She held up her forefinger. "Boone told me that a twin had won that cook-off, but I forget which twin he mentioned."

"Why does that mean I'm Coop?"

"Caleb limps and you don't, as I said, and Caleb shared the secret ingredient with everyone eventually. Cowboy honor or not, you could have told me the ingredient without breaking any promises. He said it was brewed coffee."

He actually laughed at that. "Boone has a habit of telling stories, doesn't he?"

She nodded. "Yes, he does. I love that about him."

For some reason he frowned, then his face cleared. "Let's hope he never writes a tell-all book."

She waved that away with a flick of her hand. "He's far too busy to do something like that. Speaking of Boone, he was under the impression that no one lived up here now, and he talked to the ranch manager who was also under that impression. Boone said that the man took care of the house up here, and he knew everything about it. Now you're here, and neither you nor I know what's going on." She finally said what she probably should have said as soon as she learned he was a Donovan. "I think I should be going. You obviously want to be here, and you're living in the house."

"I'm staying up here for a week."

"You mean you don't live here all the time?"

"No, just when I need to get away. No one really knew I was up here until this morning, not even my uncle Abel. Then you showed up in person."

She sighed. "Big mistake there. I'm sorry for barging in like that. I didn't expect to come across anyone, and at first, when I saw you in the pond, I thought maybe it was just a cowboy thing—that you'd been riding around and stopped at a random watering hole to get clean and cool off."

He shook his head. "Why would you think that?"

"I guess I've watched too many old Western movies in the middle of the night. I love them. Things were so simple back in the old days. Although, honestly, I've never known a real cowboy. Boone sure isn't one, or at least since I've known him, he hasn't been acting like a cowboy."

"Well, now you do know one. For almost sixty years, this has been private land. If someone wants on it, they ask permission. No drifters just passing through, or squatters. That's why they build fences."

"You're lucky to own this. So, I guess I'll go into Eclipse and find Boone. He wanted me to stay with him at first, but I'm here to hike, and the good trails are so much closer to here. I was even hoping I could get Boone to come here to relax. I really have missed him."

"So, you and Boone have a long-distance relationship?"

"Oh, no, a long-distance friendship. We met when I was in his group my first year of internship at medical school. When he changed specialties, he asked me out, and we went on a couple of dates before we figured out that we made better friends than anything else. He's dear to me, believe that, and I love him, but that's it. I'll head to his office, and we'll figure out my plans together."

"So, you're a doctor," he said. "What kind of doctor are you?"

"A good one, I hope," she replied with a smirk.

"I meant, what's your specialty?"

"Pediatrics. I work in the neonatal intensive care unit. It's for babies who're born too early or born with problems that need correcting."

"That's heavy," he said.

"It can be," she said. "Hiking's been like a form of therapy for me. There's no interruptions, no arguments, no crying. And I can hear myself think. That's why I came out here. I figured it'd be the perfect place to recharge." She paused and wistfully looked around. "It certainly seems calm and peaceful here."

He nodded slowly, as he appeared to contemplate what she'd said. Then he spoke up. "I need a favor from you before you leave."

"Absolutely. I owe you one for busting in like I did."

"I don't keep score of what people owe me. I just need to ask you to not tell Boone or anyone else that I'm up here."

"Okay, I won't ask why. That's between you and him, but what do I tell him about me not staying here? He won't believe I hated it or that I was afraid of being so isolated. Neither would work. He knows I'd love to be here, and being isolated is a plus in my book."

"Thunderation," he muttered.

She narrowed her eyes at him. "What did you say?"

"*Thunderation.* Why?"

"Do you watch a lot of old Westerns, too? That sounds like something an old cowboy would say."

"I've been around old cowboys my whole life. I guess I just picked things up along the way, both at home and on the circuit. It means—"

She cut him off. "I know what it means and that you're probably using it so you won't start cussing. I like that, actually. My parents told me that when a person swears a lot, it's because they have a limited vocabulary."

He almost smiled at her. "I won't argue that, but about Boone, I've changed my mind. Just tell him the truth and ask him to keep it to himself, period. I'd owe you one if you'd explain it to him."

She almost groaned when she remembered something. "Good thing you don't mind Boone knowing, because I just remembered I sent another text when I first realized I wasn't alone. But I'm not sure he even has it yet. It seems my texts aren't always delivered in real time."

He seemed to be trying to be patient with her and she really appreciated it. "What did you say in it?" he asked.

She took out her phone, opened it and scrolled for a moment before she turned it toward him so he could see the screen. He read it to himself.

Call me! I'm not alone up here!!

She drew her phone back. "I tend to overuse exclamation marks. I'm so sorry."

"You didn't say Cooper Donovan was here."

"That's true. He probably wouldn't even think that since your uncle didn't think you'd be up here. I can text him now and tell him I'm fine, and that I'll explain it all to him when I see him. How's that?"

"It can't hurt."

She quickly put in the text, then looked back at him. "It's done. I hope he gets it soon. I'm curious about why it's so important for you that no one knows you're up here, but I figure it's pretty obvious. Boone told me how your fans and the press follow you wherever you go. Is that it?"

"You're close enough." He sat forward, resting his forearms on his thighs. Then he said, "I need to be up here. I came home for a break, to get away from my work, and the last thing I want is someone knowing I'm up here and spreading it around. I don't want people fighting to get a picture or trying to interview me. It's that simple. My land, my privacy. I value both, and when I'm on the circuit, the PR is part of my job. I do it, but I won't do it up here. For the next week, I'm staying up here alone. Period."

She understood getting away from work. She was running from hers, hoping to get perspective and go back to trying to help the babies without being worried about messing things up. "I guess I understand, and I won't ask about anything else."

"Thank you," he said, giving her a sideways glance. "Appreciated."

She tried to shift the conversation completely. "Boone told me about Split Rock Canyon. He said it's within hiking range from here. There's a legend about a couple jumping off the huge rock their deaths because they couldn't be together. It sounds very *Romeo and Juliet*—so sad but also romantic."

"What about it?"

"It's on your land, right?"

"Yeah, it is, but if you're looking for romance, you won't find any there. I figure the whole thing is a conglomeration of old tales that have been passed down over the years. We used to go up there in the summers. We never found anything fancy about it. First, it's not a legitimate canyon. It's a small gorge worn away by a stream that runs through it. At some point, the rock broke in two from erosion, and the gap between the two parts was wide enough that the stream split, and the water flowed around one side and through the break. It never converged on itself again. The two streams flow down and out of sight at the lowest point."

"Canyon or gorge, Boone said it's worth a trip."

"I guess it's worth it. Maybe someday Boone can take you up there. He came with us on a lot of our trips."

"He'd never be able to get time off for that. But I was thinking, since Boone's tied up until later today, maybe I could hike from here to the canyon or gorge or whatever. When I get back, Boone should be around, and I'll leave you to yourself to do what you want to do up here."

"You don't even know where to go to find it," Cooper said.

She shrugged that off. "No, I don't, but you do."

He looked taken back. "I'm not hiking anywhere. I'm here to take it easy. Hiking would be work for me, and I'm not working up here."

His horse whinnied, obviously getting impatient to be off on their ride. McKenna turned to look at the animal. "I have a deal," she said as she reached to retrieve her wallet from her backpack.

This intrigued him. "What kind of deal?"

"Let me rent your horse, then I can explore around here while I wait for Boone."

"No," he said abruptly.

"Boy, you aren't an easygoing cowboy, are you?" She tried to tone down her sarcasm with a smile. She put her wallet away in her backpack and stood up. She'd stayed too long. "I'm really sorry for intruding almost as much as I am for not being able to stay here."

Coop shrugged. "Every road has its potholes."

She gave him a narrow look. "Are you calling me a pothole?"

"No offense intended, just another old cowboy saying. I thought it kind of fit the situation."

She slipped one strap of her backpack over her shoulder again. "Forget it," she said. "Enjoy being here. I really mean it. It seems to be a good place to just breathe."

"It's a good place," he said.

"I guess I'm not going to see the canyon."

"I would say you're guessing right. Besides, that story about the lovers' leap is pure hogwash."

"Did you just say *hogwash*?" she asked.

"I sure did, darlin'. I could've said claptrap, hokum, twaddle... My grandpa used all those words when he was talking about something he knew was nothing but nonsense."

She laughed softly at that explanation as she turned for one last look around. Then she glanced back at Cooper, who'd been watching her. "You know, this could be cute if you cleared the weeds and planted some flowers. It would be really nice to sit here and watch the sun set or an eclipse or a meteor shower."

"Cute?" he asked. "Them thar would be fighting words for my grandpa."

She smiled and he smiled back at her. "Okay, I won't mention flower planting around here again."

"Say, Doc, what's your name, anyway?"

"McKenna. McKenna Walker."

She sighed softly, then stood straighter and pointed to her cap. "Okay, I'm taking a hike out of here," she said. With that, she adjusted her backpack, using both straps now. "Enjoy this beautiful day, Cooper."

She took her time walking away, her smile gone as soon as she turned from Cooper and headed toward the dirt drive to follow it to the gates and to her car parked outside them. She felt sad but kept going. Things happened the way they happened, and it wasn't in the cards for her to be on Donovan land too much longer.

When she was almost to the drive, her phone chimed, announcing an incoming call.

She stopped, took it out and looked at the screen. When she saw the caller, she spun around and jogged back to Cooper, who hadn't moved. "It's Boone!" she said as she leaped up onto the porch. "He's calling me."

McKenna handed her phone over to Cooper. "Talk to him," she said breathlessly. "You explain everything."

"I will," he said as he took the phone and put it to his ear. "Surprise, Boone!"

CHAPTER THREE

"Coop?" Boone asked with obvious confusion in his voice.

"That's me," Coop said.

"What are you…?" Boone's voice trailed off, then he asked, "Why do you have McKenna's cell?"

"Because she's with me at the old ranch. It seems you told her to come here on vacation."

"You're back home? Abel told me the place was empty. Now you're there?"

"Yeah, and so's McKenna. She'll be heading over to your place as soon as we hang up." He glanced at her, more than aware she was following his every word. "She needs to settle some plans with you about her hiking."

"Why didn't Abel call and cancel if you went up there?"

"He didn't know I came up here from the main ranch yesterday on an impulse. I needed to get away from things down below, and when I got here, I decided to stay until I head back to work in a week. Then your doctor friend showed up. She can't stay."

He didn't miss the way McKenna flinched at his blunt statement.

"Can't you stay with your folks and let McKenna have the house?" Boone asked.

Boone had cut right to what wouldn't work. He was a good friend and deserved an answer to that question. "I was, but I can't now. The junior rodeo tryouts are going on down there, and fans are swarming all over the place." He explained how he'd stayed under wraps and how he'd been spotted in the stables. "I'm sorry, but I'm staying."

"Can McKenna hear me?"

Coop looked at her still standing just a few feet from him, her head down as if she were mesmerized by her boots. "Yep. Why?"

"Because I'm going to talk about her, and she hates that."

"Most people do, Boone," he murmured.

"I'm serious, Coop."

"Okay, hold on." He looked at McKenna. "I'll be right back," he said before he walked down off the porch and away, stopping halfway between the house and the old stable farther west. "Okay, it's clear."

"I'm worried about McKenna. She really needs to be there and do all the hiking she wants to do. She's a great doctor, but she's been going through a rough patch in her life—personal and professional—and I was hoping that her being up there would help her find herself again."

Coop glanced back at McKenna, who'd gone up to sit on the porch bench, but she was watching him. "And?" he asked, looking away from her.

"Is there any way you could let her stay there?"

For the second time in two days, Coop felt like a heel, but he couldn't go back down to the main house. "Sorry, I can't." He looked up. McKenna hadn't moved. "Okay, let's be blunt. I need this place right now. I'm dragging, and I came back to fix that. I still have a week before I have to report back. Listen, I wish her well, but I need to be here alone."

"Okay, okay, that's fair. It's just…" Boone was quiet for a moment before he said, "Never mind, I'll have to figure it out for her."

"Give me a break, Boone. The obvious solution is her going to stay with you. There's some hiking close to your place on the riding trails. She'll be happy. You'll be happy. I'll be happy."

"I know I'd be happy having her here, and obviously you'd be happy not having her there. The thing is, she needs some time to herself to regroup."

Coop muttered. "She's your girlfriend— it only makes sense for her to be with you."

"She's not my girlfriend, but she's a dear friend who's in trouble, and I'd do anything for her."

Coop hadn't really believed McKenna's explanation of their relationship, but he knew Boone well enough to know he never embellished a situation to make it sound better or worse than it was. It was exasperating to be put into a position he'd had no part in creating and one in which he looked like the bad guy. "You've got that huge house, but I guess I could sleep in the stable here," he muttered with protective sarcasm.

"I already have company, Coop. I'm vetting two candidates to see if one of them would be a match to join me at the clinic."

"A medical convention," Coop said flippantly. "She'd fit right in."

"She wants solitude, not a lot of medical talk, but if you can't do it, you can't do it. Let me talk to McKenna."

Coop went back to where she was sitting. "Is everything all right? Does he understand?" she asked as he sat down and handed her back her phone.

"Boone needs to talk to you."

She took the phone. "What did you say to Cooper? He doesn't look happy at all."

She watched him as she spoke to Boone, and he couldn't make himself smile to save his life right then. McKenna sat back and listened, then closed her eyes. "No, I don't want to. I'll figure this out and get back to you." A pause, then she said softly, "I know, I know. I can handle this. I'll be okay, and I'll let you know where I land." She listened again, then said softly, "I love you, too."

She sat there silently, then finally opened her eyes and stood up. Reaching for her backpack, she slipped the strap over her right shoulder and exhaled before she spoke to Coop. "I'll be out of your way as soon as I can climb back over the gates and get to my car."

"You're going to Boone's?"

"No, he has some possible candidates staying with him who might work at the clinic. I'll find a place closer to Cody that can work for what I need."

Boone's words came back with a vengeance. *She's been going through a rough time...up there she'd be able to find herself again.* He gave up. He couldn't just turn her away, and he thought about giving her a possible option, even if it wasn't perfect for either one of them. At least he wouldn't look like a bad guy and feel like one, too.

"Listen to me. I'm going to be here for a week, and then I'm leaving to go back on the circuit. If you want, since you're Boone's friend and all, how about you find another place to stay for my time here, and when I leave, you can come up here and have the place to yourself. You can do all the hiking you want then."

She was silent at first, her eyes holding his. Then she exhaled. "Do you really mean that?"

"My word on it," he said. "I don't give that unless I mean to keep it."

Her eyes seemed overly bright for a moment, as if she were fighting tears that he really hoped she wouldn't let show up. "Thank you…thank you so, so much."

He held out his hand to her. "Is it a deal?"

When she put her smaller hand in his, the warmth and softness in her touch stopped him in his tracks for a moment, then they shook, and the contact was gone.

"Okay, it's a deal," she said and smiled at him.

McKenna hadn't seen that offer coming at all, and it had taken her a moment to realize that Cooper had actually handed it to her. This was his land, his house. After Cooper left, this would be all hers. It was more than fair of him. She just needed to find a place to stay for one week.

His smile faded, and he looked serious. "One more thing before you leave. Can you promise me you won't tell anyone about our deal or that I've been up here?"

That was ridiculously easy to agree to. "I have no idea who Cooper Donovan, the rock star of the rodeo world, is. I've never heard of him."

That brought a rough chuckle. "There's no rock stars around here, darlin'." His expression turned self-deprecatory. "I honestly try to leave that in the show ring."

She doubted he could do that even if he tried. "Then we're all good, because I don't know much of anything about rodeos. No offense, but the only reason I've heard your name is because Boone mentioned you. Sorry."

"Don't be. That's just fine." She watched as something seemed to pass over his face, and then he said, "So, when you go hiking, how long are you gone for, generally?"

She was a bit confused by his question. "Well, personally, I like full-day hikes. When I reach my goal, I spend time there to just enjoy it, then head back. I pretty much try to leave around dawn and come back before dusk."

"And is that what you planned on doing every day when you got here—hiking the various trails around here for the whole day?"

"Yes, that's right. Although, I'll probably

go into town a few times and see Boone and maybe shop. But otherwise, yes, I'll be hiking all I can. I know that I won't have a chance like this again for a long time. Work tends to never stop for me, but I have this break now."

He pulled on his chin. "So, theoretically, if two people were here at the same time, and one was gone all day, and the other was here all day, they'd barely see each other."

"I guess so," she said, not certain what answer he wanted. "I don't understand what you're getting at."

He hesitated, then surprised her again. "Boone's been a good friend of mine for years, and I think I need to do him a favor."

"What favor?" she asked cautiously.

"I'm trying to say, I think we could make it work if you stayed here for the whole two weeks. You'd do your thing, and I'd do mine, and I trust you to tell no one I'm up here if you go into town or down on to the big ranch for some reason."

McKenna wasn't at all sure she hadn't imagined what he'd just said. "You're telling me I don't have to go to a hotel for the first week."

"Yes, I am," he said. "Do you want to do that or not?"

She didn't know what had changed his mind so dramatically, but she wanted it very much. "Yes, yes, I do, if you'll let me."

"Why would I make you that offer and not let you do it?"

"I… I just…"

"Look, the house is tiny, basically one big room, and there's only a couch and bed to sleep on. I'll take the couch and you can have the bed, but if you're not comfortable with both of us sleeping in the house, there's a tack room in the barn with a cot in it. I've slept out there more than once. So you choose whatever way you'd be the most comfortable. Also, if I'm out there, you'd have full privacy and never have to see me. It's up to you."

She had the ridiculous urge to throw her arms around Cooper Donovan and tell him she'd sleep in the stable and he'd never have to see her. But all she managed to say was "We can both use the house as long as there's room for two people."

His dark eyes held hers. "Then you agree to it?"

She nodded.

"Well, we both want peace and solitude, so we go our own ways, and that is it."

"I absolutely agree. I just don't know how to thank you."

"Don't worry about that. You concentrate on hiking and get settled in the house while I go on a long ride. I might see you tonight, but I might not. This is all yours, Mac."

"No one calls me Mac," she said and regretted it as soon as her words hung between them. She'd just received the perfect gift from him, something that was going to make her next two weeks fantastic, and she'd chosen to correct him over something that didn't really matter. Quickly, she tried to walk that back. "I'm sorry I said that the way I did. That was a kneejerk reaction."

Thankfully, he accepted her apology without any hesitation. "Sure, okay. McKenna it is."

That had been about the dumbest thing she'd done in a long time, and it had to be with this particular man. All she could think to say was "Thank you."

"One question. Why would you have a kneejerk reaction to being called Mac?"

She'd never explained that to anyone, probably because no one had asked her before. But she felt like she owed him. "My parents insisted on full names, no nicknames. So I don't have a nickname."

"Oh, I see," he said with one dark eyebrow raised. "If we speak to each other for whatever reason, why don't we put personal subjects off the table? That would make things a lot easier. Right?"

"That's fine by me." She surely wasn't going to tell him how stupid she'd been in the past about relationships. Boone was the only one she'd ever told, and she'd known he hadn't understood why she decided she was over trying to have a relationship. She was simply no good at them; they were a dead end for her.

"Okay, that's the way it'll be," he said with that half smile of his.

As he stood up, she said, "I might be gone when you get back, maybe on a short hike, or maybe to pick up some things in town that I forgot."

"Just remember not to—"

"I don't know a Cooper Donovan. I'm no rodeo fan. Don't worry about that."

"Kind of hurts my feelings that you're not a fan, but everyone around here will know you don't know me the first time you call me Cooper. Any fan or press person would call me Flaming Coop D or Coop D or just plain Coop."

"Cooper it is, so I won't slip up."

"That works for me," he said as he went down to his horse, got in the saddle in one fluid motion and put his hat on. "Are you going to the general store in Eclipse?"

"I'll go there if I can get bedding and a few dishes, also a couple of food items."

"Go to the general store. They have all of that and more."

"That's where I'll go."

"Good, and when you meet the owner, Farley Garret, watch what you say. Farley's a great guy, but he's the hub of gossip in town. He's like an old town crier passing out the news. He knows everyone and what everyone is doing, or not doing."

"And they say women like to gossip, huh?"

"Farley's the exception to that. Just don't give him any ideas, okay?"

"He'll get nothing out of me," she said. "I promise."

"While you're there, could you pick me up some coffee? I was supposed to get some, but that didn't happen."

"What brand?"

"I don't care what brand you get, as long as it's not instant. I prefer a fresh grind that doesn't have some flavor added to it."

"Okay," she said. He shifted in the saddle as if to take his wallet out of his back pocket, but she stopped him. "Put that away. It's my treat."

He smiled at her. "Okay, then," he said. "See you when I see you." He turned his very patient horse and road off in the direction of the trees with the pond beyond them.

McKenna sat on the old bench feeling both relieved and excited that she was here and staying for two whole weeks. It had all worked out, and she didn't quite understand why Cooper had shortchanged himself by making it two weeks. He'd lost his isolation for his week, and she'd gained it for herself. It didn't make sense, but he seemed just fine with it.

All that truly mattered was he had gifted her two weeks. She'd stay out of his way and get in all the hiking she wanted. After a very shaky beginning at the pond with Cooper, it was all good—very good—now.

IT WAS ALMOST one in the afternoon when McKenna drove back from Eclipse and through the now unlocked gates onto the access road toward the old adobe house. Everything she needed had indeed been available at the general store, and Farley Garret had waited on her personally when he'd found out she was Boone's friend. The man was well into his sixties, dressed like some garish Western performer, with a purple silk shirt studded to overload with silver, the same silver that showed on his white boots and a white tall crown hat. He was beyond friendly, going with her as she roamed through the store and helping her find what she needed. They'd stopped by a major display of Flaming Coop D merchandise: boots, hats, clothing, accessories and even stuffed horses and bulls.

The backdrop to the display was a giant poster of Cooper in the middle of a ride on the back of black horse with its rear feet bucked up high and its front feet angled into the sand.

"That's our boy," Farley had announced as he'd come up from behind her. "Born here and grew up at the Flaming Sky Ranch just north of here. A great young man and real rodeo star."

She'd asked, "What's his name?"

"Flaming Coop D. You must have heard of him, at least from Doc Williams. He and the Donovan boys have always been good friends."

She had chosen her words carefully. "I'm from Boston, and Boone and I talk mostly about medicine."

"You're probably the only one around here that never heard of Coop." He had chuckled at that. "Too bad he's not around. I'd introduce the two of you."

She'd asked a question for her own curiosity. "So, where is the rodeo star?"

"I'd sure like to know where he took off to. He did a great ride in a rodeo a few weeks back—took first, of course—then he dropped out of sight. Probably taking it easy or enjoying himself." Farley actually winked at McKenna. "He's real popular with the ladies, if you catch my drift."

She sure had. "I hope he's having a good time wherever he is."

That had brought a chortle from Farley. "You can bet the ranch on that."

As she crested the rise in the dirt access road, she saw the house and smiled. She parked the SUV rental near the porch step, got out and scanned the area. Nothing stirred except the dried grass as a warm breeze skimmed over it. "Cooper!" she called out. When there was no response, she opened the car door and started taking her purchases into the small house.

Cooper must have still been out riding, so she set to putting her things away. She'd bought a light comforter and pillows to use on the couch, where she'd decided to sleep, so Cooper could have the bed. All she'd found in the house were a couple of folded sheets and two very flat pillows stacked on the bed. With the groceries she'd bought to add to what she'd originally brought up with her, she felt settled and pleased with herself as she went back outside to sit on the porch bench.

The peace in the air was almost tangible, and she just wanted to wrap it around herself. Boone had been right to urge her to come up here, and he'd taken care of all the planning while she'd arranged her time off. Her last night at work before she'd flown out of Boston had been hard and frustrating. She'd been asked to give a second opinion on a new arrival, a thirty-week preemie, and by the end of her shift, she was still unable to reconcile her findings with the other doctor's.

That had bothered her a lot, but being told to go home and not stick around for the lab results when her shift was over by the head of the NICU had hurt. She'd felt as if she'd failed the child, and she hated that more than anything. She'd been called a perfectionist more than once, and Boone had told her that trait was a blessing and a curse for a doctor. He understood.

A noise drew her out of her thoughts, and it sounded like someone driving up the access road. She looked toward the top of the driveway as a large black pickup truck crested the rise and came toward the house. The single-horse trailer it was towing had a logo on its side: flowing flames came out of the hooves of a black silhouette of a racing horse. The words "Flaming Sky Ranch" in gold letters ran along the bottom.

She stood as the truck slowly made a wide turn to park right behind her SUV with the passenger-side door facing her. Heavy tinting made it impossible to see who was driving until the passenger window slid silently down. Cooper was looking out at her.

"What are you doing?" she asked.

"Boone called and said you'd love to have a horse up here to ride since you're staying. I picked out a horse for you, and he's a good ride."

She'd called Boone to let him know she'd be staying for the two weeks right before she'd gone into Farley's store. Apparently, he had called Cooper after they hung up. "Wow, thank you so much for doing this," she said.

The horse whinnied in the trailer and Cooper motioned to her. "Get on in, and I'll give you a ride so I can introduce you to Bravo."

She didn't have to be asked twice and hurried to get into the high cab. They drove past the house and up to the stable with some empty pens near it and a small corral.

He pulled to a stop past the stable to align the back of the trailer with the sliding doors. When Cooper got out, McKenna followed suit and went around to the back of the trailer. Cooper crossed to open the doors, then came back to where she stood. "Step back, and I'll get Bravo out, then I'll get his stall set up."

After taking a couple of steps back, Mc-Kenna watched Cooper open the back door of the trailer to pull out a metal ramp. "While I put the supplies away along with his tack, you stay out here with Bravo and talk to him so he can get used to you, okay?"

"Sure," she said.

With the rear door out of the way, she was able to look directly into the trailer and finally see Bravo. He was tossing his head from side to side, barely missing contact with Cooper, who was in the process of approaching him. He was a deep sorrel with four identical white socks, and his mane and tail were dark brown. The only other white on him was a blurred shape between his eyes that almost looked like a cloud. He appeared strong but seemed uneasy.

"Can I do anything to help?" she asked.

"I've got this," Cooper said as he eased the animal down the ramp, then toward McKenna. He handed her the reins. "Just keep him here and talk to him. Keep your voice low and steady."

While Cooper unloaded supplies, she stayed out of his way with Bravo, who was very still now except for his dark eyes darting back and forth. McKenna slowly reached a hand to touch his neck and stroked his silky coat, feeling the solid muscles under it.

"Hi, there, boy," she cooed to him, and he shifted, drawing back for a moment before turning more toward her. That's when she saw the scarring at his mouth. It looked healed, but she'd never seen anything like it before.

When Cooper finished unloading, he came out, then slid the ramp back in place and shut the trailer up before he turned to her. "How's he doing?"

"He's tense, but he's being okay." She grimaced as she looked at the poor animal's mouth.

"Hey, are *you* okay?" Cooper asked as he came closer to her.

She had to swallow to get out her response. "His mouth. What happened to him?"

Cooper stroked the horse's muzzle as he answered McKenna. "His owner didn't like the way he felt riding and took it out on him. He had other wounds, but his mouth injuries made it almost impossible for him to eat. He's healed up really well, and we have special bridles for him that are specifically designed to be gentle. He's responsive, easy to control—just don't jerk him if you can manage it."

"Absolutely." She found herself struggling with the burning of unshed tears behind her eyes. She hardly ever cried, even as a child, but the more frustrated she'd become at work, the more she had to fight tears. *Burnout* was a word she hadn't said out loud, but Boone had used it on their call before she left for Wyoming. She blinked rapidly, then asked, "What happened to the person who did this to him?"

"We can talk about that later. I have to get the trailer back."

Bravo went docilely into his stall, where Cooper had laid fresh straw over the cement floor. There was a flake of hay in a metal holder attached to the top rail, and a large bucket of water was available for him. He went to the water first, and Cooper stepped back and out to close the half gate and secure it. When Bravo stopped drinking, he backed up into the far corner of the stall.

Cooper was beside her. "He's a quiet horse, but I've ridden him, and he's a good mount. He's very safe. I don't want you to think he's unruly in any way, because he's not."

"Thank you so much for bringing him up here," she said.

"My pleasure. So, it looks like your bedside manner as a doctor carries over to horses, too."

"Scared is scared, and both animals and children respond to gentleness and kindness. They sense it." She kept her eyes on the horse.

"Well, you're good. He's already having thoughts that maybe you're not going to hurt him." Bravo stayed in the far corner, keeping the most distance he could between himself and the humans. Then Cooper said in a low voice, "He's on the move, but don't look. Let him get closer."

As Cooper spoke, McKenna waited, hoping Bravo would get close enough for her to touch him. Then he was there near her arm that rested on the top rail. She felt the heat of his breath and she didn't move.

Cooper spoke again. "I think he's falling in love."

"I'd be honored," she whispered. "Can he do treats?"

"Apples and carrots."

She slowly lifted her hand, making sure he could see it, then brushed it lightly over his muzzle. Bravo snuffled. "Okay, Bravo, tomorrow you'll get an apple." The animal snuffled again before moving back toward the corner.

"I'm leavin', darlin'," Cooper said.

"Thanks again."

He went out, and she heard the truck start up and pull away. Bravo was watching her.

"We'll have a good time together," she said, making a promise to him and to herself.

CHAPTER FOUR

DAYLIGHT WAS STARTING to fade when Mc-
Kenna stepped out of the house onto the
porch and sat down on the long wooden
bench. She was pleased with the house as
she settled in. She was sure pleased with
Bravo and was looking forward to a couple
of rides if she could fit them in. She was
already feeling less tense. The peace and
quiet were working like magic. The fresh
air was cooling off, and it carried the scent
of earth and dried grasses with it. Stretching out her legs, she sat back with her head
resting against the adobe wall.

Cooper still hadn't come back, and she'd
been wondering if he'd found another place
to stay, or maybe he'd just left the area al-
together. As she sat there watching the sun
dipping lower and lower toward the horizon, she heard something off to the east,
then she saw the man and the horse. Coo-

per on Blaze. She smiled as he came closer and stopped by the porch step to look down at her. "How's it goin'?"

"Great. I love this place."

"It's easy to love, that's for sure," he said. "I'm going to take care of Blaze, then I'll be back. How's Bravo doin'?"

"When I left, he was starting to nibble on the hay. I thought that was a good sign."

"It sure is." He nodded, then nudged Blaze to keep going in the direction of the stable.

She stopped herself from following him and sat down on the porch step. It was a lot more comfortable than the bench was. She stayed there until she heard rustling, then footsteps approaching from the far side of the house. Turning, she saw Cooper stepping up onto the porch. "So, what're you up to?" he asked.

"Just enjoying watching the coming night." She figured he'd keep going into the house, but he didn't. Instead, he crossed to sit down by her. "I was thinking that a rocking chair or a swing or maybe a glider with cushions would be perfect for sitting out here," she said to him.

"Anything with a pillow would be." He

settled, stretching his long legs out and taking his hat off to rest it crown down on his thigh. "My grandma used to have a rocking chair out here, and no one could use it but her. We were relegated to the bench Grandpa made. That's why he built it long enough to seat at least four kids and two adults. I usually sat right here. It was more comfortable."

As he spoke, she noticed how defined his cheekbones were and observed fine lines at the corners of his dark eyes. "You sound tired," she said and stood.

"Where are you going?" he asked looking up at her.

"Inside, so you can have your peace and quiet we agreed to, and—"

He cut her off. "Hold on. I never said that there couldn't be any civil conversation when we're both here at the same time."

She looked down at him. "If you're sure—"

"I wouldn't say it if I wasn't."

"Okay." She smiled. "How about I go make us a cup of coffee, then."

"Oh, by all means, darlin'. I could use some coffee."

"You relax, and I'll brew it and bring it out here."

"That sounds like a plan, but before you go inside, I'd like to get something straight about this situation."

He sounded as if he wanted to redefine their agreement, and so far, the changes had been in her favor. But she'd probably agree to just about anything to keep their deal intact. "What's that?" she asked.

"It's simple. I take my coffee black, period. If you make what you think is fantastic coffee and add flavoring or special creamer, I'll take a pass."

She almost laughed at his sober pronouncement, but she controlled herself. Coffee must be very important to him. She knew that condition from her days as an intern when coffee had kept her going.

"Absolutely, nothing fancy. Give me five minutes, and I'll bring you the best coffee you ever had."

"I sure hope so, darlin'," he said.

Once inside, McKenna started the water heating, then went over to the linens she'd bought. She picked up two of the new pillows, still in their plastic packaging, and took them to the front door.

"Heads up," she called out to get Cooper's

attention. He turned, and she tossed one of the pillows over to him. Then the second one followed. "One for me, and one for you so we can sit on the bench, but leave the plastic on so they don't get dirty." Then she ducked back inside and finished brewing the coffee.

COOPER HAD SHIFTED to the bench and was using one of the pillows when McKenna came back out. The other pillow sat beside him. He looked at McKenna as she held the coffee out to him. "Bless you, Dr. Walker, for the pillow," he said as he took the steaming mug from her.

"Be careful, it's hot," she said. She used her free hand to toss her loose auburn hair over her shoulders as she sat next to him. He was thankful the yellow hat had been discarded for now. Cautiously blowing into the mug, he finally took a sip, followed by another before he looked back at McKenna. "That hits the spot."

She looked pleased and that pleased him. "A question?" she said.

"Sure."

"The shower doesn't work, not a drip of

water's coming out, not a single one. Is it broken or shut off or something?"

"It's shut down. It's a gravity feed setup, and the valves that control the flow are shut. I'll try to get it going tomorrow."

"I'd appreciate it. Hiking can get messy."

"Go for a swim if you want to. The water's warming up, and it's soft water."

"One more thing?"

"Why not?"

"What were you really doing in the pond when I got there?"

He knew that had to come up sooner or later. "Okay, straight word. I was practicing holding my breath. Honestly, I was doing it because I was alone, then I wasn't. That's where it all went off the rails."

She chuckled, and he thought that he liked talking to her. This was definitely not the way he'd planned on spending his evening when he woke up this morning, but he was surprised at how much he was enjoying it.

"So, are there any questions you have about the area before you set off on your own tomorrow?" he asked her.

"Are their bears around here?"

"They're around, mostly closer to Yellowstone and farther west near Jackson Hole. But we've had our share. If you see one, try to keep at least a hundred feet away from it and don't run. Slowly back up to get out of its area. You'll need to get bear spray from the ranger on duty at the gates, and if the bear gets aggressive, use it. It only sprays for about six or seven seconds, so aim well. Attach it to your belt or waistband so you can get it out quick."

"Okay, I'll definitely pick up some bear spray," she said.

"They keep track of wild animals in the area at the ranger station. They'll warn you when you get there about trails they don't want you on for that day. Believe me, most animals will run away from you, not at you."

"I'll talk to Boone's friend, a ranger who's supposed to be at the back gates, when I get there."

"Danny Stucky?"

"Yes. You know him?"

"Sure. I've known him all my life, pretty much. He's been a ranger forever."

"That must be a small-town thing, everyone knowing everyone. You probably started kindergarten together. You and little Danny Stucky."

"No, you'd be way off on that."

"You said you've known him all your life."

"I have. He brought his boy, Jimmer, to school on the first day. Mom took me and Caleb."

She looked surprised, but all she said was "Hmmm."

"What does that mean?"

"Excuse me?" she asked.

"You said, 'Hmmm.' That's not a word."

She put her mug down and shrugged. "It should be. I use it a lot when I'm talking with my patients or their parents. It gives me time to consider what I'm going to say before I say anything."

"What were you going to say about Danny?"

"It wasn't about Danny. It was about Boone. It's just...the way Boone was talking about him, I guess I thought he might be trying to set me up with him or something." Coop thought he saw a faint brush of color in her cheeks. "I just imagined him being younger."

"Does Boone try to set you up with a lot of guys?"

She grimaced. "This is personal, but you're good friends with Boone, so I'll explain, if you really want to know about the two of us."

Coop did want to know, but he didn't want to sound too anxious about it. "It's up to you if you want to talk about it."

"Boone wants me to be happy, and although we don't live near each other, he keeps tabs on me. He tries to give me pep talks. I mean, Boone's single, but if I tried to set *him* up, he'd kill me. He cares about me. That's it."

"So, he tries to set you up with guys?"

"Yes, but I don't do well in relationships, and he knows that. He's always encouraging me to keep trying, but after my third relationship ended in disaster, I told Boone that I'm not doing it anymore. My ex, Dalton— who was perfectly lovely—told me that he was breaking up with me because he didn't think I knew how to love someone. He wanted someone who at least liked him enough to make time for him to find out if it could be love."

Cooper shrugged. "It sounds like you're better off without him."

"Oh, I meant it when I said he was lovely. It was all on me. He was right. For a short moment, what he said crushed me, but I got over it faster than I should have. I bet you believe in soul mates, don't you?"

"I don't know. Maybe. I'd probably call my mom and dad soul mates. I can't imagine them ever not being together."

"My parents sure weren't soul mates, not even close. I'm not even sure they liked each other. But they bonded over their professions. They're both into medical things. They've also been divorced for ten years. The most important thing to them is being perfect. They sure couldn't do love. I think I'm like them." She shrugged. "Maybe it's in my DNA, but I'm tired of trying to figure it out."

He studied her. "Did you just stop dating?"

"Yes, my work's demanding, and I need to focus on being the best I can be. I've had some things happen lately that really woke me up to that. You don't get good by settling, and I never want to settle when it comes to my job. So it is what it is." She smiled wryly at him. "Way too much information, huh?"

"I asked for it."

"I agreed to tell you. Maybe we'd better not do that anymore, unless you want to confess something about your love life."

"That's not gonna happen, darlin'. I'm kind of like you. I have to be in the moment when I'm working, and a beautiful woman can certainly be a distraction. Not that I don't date, but I'm pretty selective when and who I'll date."

"I guess it would be a problem if one of your dates was a kiss-and-tell kind of girl?"

"You hit it."

Although his need for no distractions while training and competing was a no-brainer for him, he couldn't help thinking it was too bad she'd cut herself off like that. "So, you'll never date again?"

"If I ever did, I'd have to date a doctor who understood that life. Unfortunately, I'd end up with a marriage like my parents', which would be pretty awful."

"That guy Dalton sure did a number on you."

"I really hurt him. I thought we were fine

going out to dinner once a week, talking on the phone some. We went to the theater once. We were both really enjoying it, and then I got called away on an emergency. Maybe that was the last straw for Dalton. I felt more terrible about hurting him than about anything he said to me."

"What if Boone asked you to marry him? He's a doctor, and he seems to understand you, and he certainly understands what it means to be a doctor. You two might be a good match."

"We went on two dates and realized we were better at being friends, and it turns out, we were right. Haven't you ever had a female friend you loved but weren't *in love* with?"

"Actually, yes, I had one once. We really matched up well, and she was with the rodeo. It went okay until marriage came up for discussion. That's where I stopped. We both agreed we weren't ready for it. We would have stayed friends, but she moved to Florida."

"There you go. It happens. What I never understood is why men think a woman can't be friends with another man without it being something more. Can you explain that?"

He was getting in too deep. "I plead the fifth on that," he said. "And don't try to read my mind."

"I don't have to be The Amazing Kreskin to know what you're thinking."

"Who's that?"

"Just one of the best mind readers in the last century. He was brilliant."

Coop could say one thing about McKenna, conversations with her were never boring. "I'm glad you're no Kreskin."

"Should I tell you what I'm guessing you were thinking?"

"No, I don't want to wrestle that steer right now."

"Say, what?"

"It means I don't want to deal with that because it's a losing proposition for me. Besides, thoughts should be the property of their owners and not some stranger who makes a wild guess." He released a breath and stood up. "I'm going to head to the stable to check on the horses and make sure the gates are locked, and then I'm going to make myself a sandwich. Would you like me to make you one, too?"

"No, thanks. I'm okay. I ate earlier."

"Okay, then," he said. "Enjoy the night, and don't forget to get bear spray from old Danny."

CHAPTER FIVE

Coop took his time taking care of the horses, and by the time he got back to the house, he thought McKenna would have gone to bed. But as he got closer, he knew he was wrong. McKenna was sitting on the porch step, her arms around her knees and her head back looking up at the sky. "Beautiful, isn't it?" he said as he sat down by her.

"Absolutely," she said. "I can't even describe it."

"My grandma Eagan, my mom's mom, wrote poetry, and she found words to describe it. I sure never could."

"I couldn't either," she murmured.

A three-quarter moon was rising in the east, its light starting to touch the landscape with a silvery hue. "Gonna be a full moon soon. I think there was an eclipse earlier this year. Meteor showers are the best show around here in December or January. Although there wasn't much of a show this past year."

"I wish I knew the names of the constellations," McKenna said, still staring up at the heavens. "All I know is the Big Dipper."

He pointed in its direction. "There it is right there."

She shifted to look where he was pointing. "I see it," she said in a soft whisper.

They sat silently in the night, and Coop couldn't remember the last time he felt so peaceful. Then McKenna sighed softly. "Thank you."

"For what?" he asked, glancing at her to find her looking at him.

"Letting me stay here. You didn't have to do that."

He hadn't had to do it, but now that he had, he knew he'd been right to let her stay. Just sitting and stargazing with her reminded him of how much he had loved being at the house as kid. The sense of wonder he heard in her voice brought that all back to him. "I'm glad we came to a deal," he said.

"I am, too. When can you tell me about what Bravo went through?"

He didn't want to get into that on a night

like this. "I'm going to go inside and make that sandwich. When I get some time, I'll tell you all about Bravo and about Blaze, too. They're both rescues. You need to get to sleep to be ready for tomorrow."

She stood and asked, "Who usually rides Bravo?"

"Mom. Caleb's wife, Harmony." He stood, too, and held his hat in his hand as he cleared his throat. "Although she has a horse named Runt that she's in love with. She rides Bravo when Runt is being shoed or having his teeth done. When Luke Patton, our town vet, comes here, he takes Bravo out for a ride to help condition him to expect kindness and not misery."

Something struck her. "Is Luke the one who rescued Bravo and Blaze?"

"Yeah. He operates a horse rescue from his property called Simply Sanctuary. It's a really special place."

"But you were also involved in rescuing Blaze?"

He slanted her a sideways glance. "He was my first."

"You just found him somewhere and took him home?"

That brought a humorless chuckle from Cooper. "In a way."

"Tell me how you found him."

He wanted to not go into it, but he had a feeling McKenna would insist sooner or later. "Okay. I'll try to make this short. I was traveling from the Las Vegas area up to Colorado for a rodeo a year ago. When I'm driving, I tend to take back roads with my crew instead of freeways and congested highways. I'd just left a small town near the Colorado border and stopped at a convenience store to get some cold drinks.

"While Dixon, one of my crew, went inside to get the drinks, I was stretching my legs and looked across a two-lane highway. There was a horse in a dry pasture leaning against an empty hay shed. The longer I looked over at him, the more I could see he wasn't leaning for comfort—he was leaning to stay on his feet. I went over to get a better look, and I could see his matted coat stretched tightly over his bones."

McKenna watched Cooper as he swallowed and shut his eyes for a fleeting moment, then he pressed his hands to thighs. "He was starving to death, had open wounds from being whipped and flies everywhere. I jumped the fence into the pasture, and when I approached him, he turned his head slowly in my direction. I had never seen such hopelessness in an animal's eyes before."

He startled McKenna when he slapped his hat against his thigh. "The guy in the store knew the owner and got him to come down on the pretext that someone wanted to buy the horse. He showed up while I was on the phone with the sheriff. I mentioned my older brother, Max, was the sheriff of Clayton County, and that sped things up. All I had to do was keep the owner there until the law arrived. Luke agreed to take Blaze if I could get him transported as soon as possible to Eclipse.

"We knew if he died, it wasn't because we didn't fight to help him. But he survived the trip, and now…you've seen him. He's thriving. He's a great horse, and a healthy coat is covering his strong muscles now."

MCKENNA HADN'T TAKEN her eyes off Cooper since he began telling her about Blaze. He'd shown tension, anger and frustration while he spoke, but right then, he smiled at the happy ending. He looked like a kid who'd gotten exactly what he'd wanted from Santa Claus for Christmas. Purely happy.

"That's incredible," she said, realizing she'd come close to tears listening to what the animal had gone through.

"Luke literally saved his life."

"Just tell me what happened to the owner."

He exhaled harshly. "He got punched in the face and broke his nose. Then he was arrested, put in jail, and they gave him the longest sentence they could when he went to court."

"What was his sentence?"

"He got a year with another year of probation and a fine of a thousand dollars."

"How did he break his nose?"

He flashed a smile. "He accidentally ran into my hand when I asked him why he did that to Blaze. He shouldn't have said he didn't want him anymore and he wasn't about to pay to have him put down, but he did. The sheriff told him to try not to bleed in the back of his cruiser."

He exhaled. "I need to eat."

"I'll come with you so you can tell me about Bravo."

McKenna followed him inside and sat down at the table, but he seemed hesitant to talk about Bravo. She didn't understand why until Cooper finally spoke. "This is between us, okay?"

"Sure, okay."

"I should say that after Blaze, I got together with Luke and offered to help him financially. He was operating on a shoestring, and I owed him for saving Blaze. Soon, the word got out, and he started receiving calls from all over the state."

Kindness seemed to be part of Cooper's makeup. Behind the rodeo star was a man who helped abused animals and who let strangers stay when he wanted to be left alone. "It's sad that there's even a need for a rescue like that but great that your friend offers help."

"Luke does the medical side, and I'm not home very often, so I try to support him any way I can from a distance. Right now, he needs more space, which isn't available near him. He's on a small piece of land on the fringe of Eclipse, and a lot of that's taken up by his normal veterinary work. He gets overloaded with rescues, but he takes in as many as he can."

"You found Bravo, too, right?"

Coop finished making his sandwich and brought the plate over to the table. "I found Bravo near the New Mexico–Texas border on my way to San Antonio. He was tied to a heavy post by the side of the road, and a big burly guy was beating him with a whip and screaming at him. I really don't remember exactly what I did or said, but Dixon told me later that I jumped out of the truck and ran at the man, grabbed the whip…and the next thing I remember is a cop fighting me to get the whip out of my hand.

"The guy had blood on his shoulders. I guess I got in a few good lashes before they stopped me."

He gave a smile with no humor in it, as if he couldn't believe what he'd done.

"I'm not proud of myself. Long story short, I ended up with Bravo being released to me, and we got him back here, and Luke worked his magic. It was touch and go, but Bravo pulled through. It's been eight months and he's doing great."

McKenna's stomach knotted, much the way

it did when abused children were brought into the ER. "I hate to ask why the guy treated him like that."

"I don't know. I was past caring. I was pretty mad that the penalty in the area was a slap on the wrist, but the idiot headbutted one of the deputies who was trying to put him in the squad car. That earned him a two-year sentence for assaulting an officer and resisting arrest."

"I think you and your friend Luke are real heroes."

When she glanced at him, he was shaking his head. "Anyone would have done the same."

"I don't think so. No one had done anything about Bravo or Blaze until you did."

"They're both safe now," he said, taking the last bite of his sandwich and pushing the plate aside. "That's what counts." He nodded at her. "I'm going to head to the stable again—I forgot something there. You should get your sleep so you can enjoy your hike tomorrow."

It was clear enough that he wanted some time alone. "Okay." She yawned. "I'm tired.

It's been a big day. Good night," she said as he headed to the door.

She heard Cooper's voice before the door shut behind him. "Good night, darlin'."

WHEN MCKENNA DROVE away from the adobe house the next morning at dawn, Cooper was still asleep in the bed. She went west on Twin Arrows and was surprised to find the entry gates for the trails were only a two-mile drive. Just as dawn started to invade the shadows on the land, she parked on a cleared patch of ground to one side of the gates. After twisting her hair to confine it under her yellow cap, she put on her back-pack, locked the car then went to the gates. The air was cool and fresh, and she was ex-cited about what lay ahead of her. But she needed to get past the gates that were se-cured with what looked like a brand-new padlock.

"Hello!" she called out. "Hello?"

The ranger station on the other side of the barrier was shut, and the hours were posted on the door: "Open from dawn till dusk, weather permitting. Everyone *MUST* check in!"

"Hello!" she yelled again.

This time the door opened, and a man stepped out. He was tall, lean and darkly tanned, wearing jeans, heavy boots and a uniform shirt with a forestry patch on the chest. He put on a Western hat over gray hair that matched a full mustache, then hurried over to her smiling all the way. He wasn't bad-looking, but if he was a day under sixty, she'd be very surprised.

"Greetings," he said in a deep voice.

"I'm so glad someone's here. I didn't want to have to climb over the fence."

"Some do, but it's not a good idea," he said and opened the lock with a key on a ring that held at least a dozen other keys.

He stepped back and swung the gates open. "Come on in, ma'am," he said with a sweep of his hand. "I'm Ranger Stucky, and I'm the one you need to contact with any questions about the land, the trails, the weather or the state of the union." He had his patter down perfectly.

So, he was *the* Danny Stucky. "Good. First, I need to purchase some bear spray."

"Absolutely, although there haven't been any sightings for a while. But it's good to be prepared."

He motioned her to walk with him. "This is your first time, right?"

"Yes, sir, it is."

"Then the bear spray's on me."

"Oh, thank you."

He let her precede him into the ranger station, which had been divided in half: to the left in the large room was an office area; to the right, a wall of hiking accessories and tools, with shelves full of packaged foods meant for backpacking. He motioned to a table by the door that held a small computer on it.

"You check in here, and make sure you give a name for someone we can call if you get sick or something, and also put in your cell phone number and where you're from. Include any medical conditions you might have."

"Of course," she said and typed in the information.

He came over when she finished, scanned her input then turned to her with a smile. "You're a friend of Boone Williams and you're a doctor, too?"

She'd put Boone down as her contact. "Yes, I am a doctor and an old friend of Boone's." She'd leave it at that.

He was smiling at her. "You don't look like no doctor I ever had."

"I've heard that one before," she said. "Do you have a map of the trails?"

"Sure do, ma'am," he said and reached around her to take a glossy brochure off the shelf above the computer. He handed it to her. "It's got every trail covered—length, time, difficulty rating. If you have any questions, you come and find me."

"Thank you so much," she said, ready to go outside and figure out what trail she wanted to explore.

Danny followed her out, then touched her arm. "I'll show you our display," he said and urged her toward what she'd thought was a table of some sort but turned out to be a massive tree stump.

When they got close, she saw that a rough map had been carved into its broad top, the various trails marked by different colors of paint. She made a show of studying it, but she'd already decided on the trail she wanted to hike first when she'd looked online: Rising Mists. Danny approved. "Medium difficulty, full day and it intersects with another shorter trail."

She was ready to get started, but Danny didn't move. "So, you seem pretty young to be a doctor," he said.

"I'm old enough."

"I'd say you're in your late twenties."

"Close enough."

He was getting annoying, especially when he asked, "You and Boone, are you dating? Engaged?"

"He's a very good friend."

Was he actually hitting on her? Over sixty and getting her stats?

"He's a good man," Danny said. "He and my boy, Jimmer, they've been friends since school time. Jimmer's an artist, you know. Does wood carving and paints things and builds furniture. He makes a real good living at that, and he's got a nice little display space near the general store in town. You might want to go over there and say hi. He'd make a good guide around the valley, if you need one."

So that was it: Danny was shopping for his son, just getting the facts to pass them on. She was sick of matchmakers. "I might do that," she said, politely lying with a straight face. "Right now, I'm really excited about today. Thanks for your help," she said and went to find her trail and start walking.

At first, she was feeling a bit annoyed by the ranger, but as soon as she put some distance between herself and the station, she forgot about everything except what was ahead of her. The beauty of the landscape was unparalleled, and the farther she went, the more her tension evaporated.

Even after spending extra time at the trail's summit, she arrived back at the ranger station around three o'clock, at least two hours earlier than she'd anticipated. It felt good being out in the fresh air, walking through a part of the country that not a lot of people knew existed. She signed out without running into Danny Stucky, until she arrived at her car in the parking lot.

The man was there putting a piece of paper under the driver's-side windshield wiper. He must have heard her approaching and he turned, grinned at her, and pulled the paper back to hold it out to her. "They're calling me over to another location, so I thought I'd leave this for when you got back."

She took the paper from him and unfolded

it. In strong print, she read *Jimmer Stucky* and a phone number.

"When you're in town, call Jimmer and maybe go to lunch."

She refolded the paper and tried to be polite. "I probably won't be in town other than to visit with Boone."

"Ah, the good doctor. Well, maybe you three could share a meal and get to know each other."

"Thanks for the thought," she said and hit the button to unlock the rental.

"Say, where are you staying around here?"

"A place Boone found for me." She could see more questions coming, and she didn't want to deal with them. "I'm exhausted, but the hike was wonderful. It was one of the best trails I've ever been on. Good work," she said and quickly got inside the car. She closed the door right away, but that didn't stop Danny from coming and rapping on her window.

She slowly lowered it. "I really have to be going."

"Will you be coming back tomorrow?"

"I think so," she said, then tried to form a smile as she slid her window back up. Without looking at Danny again, she backed up and turned toward the way she'd come that morning.

Ten minutes later, she was stepping up onto the porch of the adobe house. She peeked in the windows to see if she could spot Cooper, but there was no sign of him, so she went inside. She left her backpack by the couch and headed to the bathroom. The shower was still waterless, and she needed a shower. As she stepped back onto the porch, she heard the neigh of a horse coming from the area over by the pond. She'd take a chance that Cooper was down there and set off in that direction.

She took the same route she had the day before, cutting through the tangle of brush and trees. She heard the sound of splashing from up ahead and smiled to herself. When she stepped out of the trees, she saw Cooper doing laps with strong strokes, heading to the dock. He made it, slapped his hand hard on the deck, then pushed off and headed back for another lap. She acted impulsively and ran down past Blaze to the dock. Stepping over Cooper's discarded clothes, she dropped down in the middle of the weathered wooden planks and crossed her legs as Cooper turned to head back.

When he was almost to the dock, he looked up and saw her. His surprise showed. He stopped and stared up at her before he slowly sank down out of sight under the dark blue water.

She waited for him to come up, and when he did, he reached out to grip the deck. Shaking his head to clear his hair from his face, he looked up at her. He was silent for what seemed forever before he finally spoke. "What are you doing here?"

"I have a very important question for you, and I couldn't find you until I heard Blaze whinny."

"I thought you weren't going to be back before dusk."

"So did I, but I was wrong. I got off the trail early and headed…back here." She'd almost said she'd headed back home but caught herself. She loved it here, but it would never be her home.

"How was the hiking?"

"Blissful," she said. "But I came down to ask you about the shower. There's still no water, not a drop."

"Sorry, I forgot about it."

"It will work, won't it?"

"It should. If not, there's always water down here."

"How do I turn it on up there?"

"You don't. I'll be up there as soon as I finish down here, and I'll get it working for you."

"I'd appreciate it. Oh, I met Danny Stucky. I've gotta say, he's an attractive man for being so old. Maybe Boone was onto something. He's got that great mustache and thick gray hair, a deep voice and an even deeper tan… He's in great shape, too."

"Wow, did he ask you out?"

She rolled her eyes. "No, he didn't, but he's trying to set me up with his son, Jimmer. Did you know Jimmer's an artist, does wood carvings and builds furniture, and he makes really good money doing it? Danny even gave me Jimmer's number for when I go to town so we can have lunch. It's horrible. I feel as if I have a tattoo on my forehead that says, 'I need a date!'"

Cooper swiped at his hair and narrowed his eyes on her. "Nope, no tattoo."

"Good. By the way, who calls a kid Jimmer?"

"Danny and his first wife Connie gave him that nickname, and it stuck. I think his real name's James. He's a nice guy. Maybe you should have lunch with him."

"I thought I made my thoughts on dating clear enough last night when I burdened you with my tale of failed relationships that you wouldn't even think about suggesting that to me."

He moved to grab the edge of the dock with both hands. "I remember now. Sorry." His voice didn't sound as if he were sorry at all.

"I remembered what you said about not letting on that you're up here. So when Danny asked where I'm staying, I cut him off at the pass. I told him Boone had arranged my accommodations."

"Nicely played."

She got to her feet and walked over to the edge to look down at Cooper. "I was going to go for a short ride before it gets dark, but suddenly, I just want to take it easy. I guess it's been too long since I've been hiking, and I can feel it in my legs and back."

Now he pressed his hands flat on the dock. "Can you move so I can get out of here?"

"Of course. No telling what's swimming around your feet in the water," she said as she moved back.

"Nothing I can't handle, darlin'," he said, and in one smooth move, he leveraged himself up and out of the water. He was wearing soaked denim shorts as he had yesterday and was dripping all over the place. Quickly, he went to the bottom step, grabbed his towel and briskly started drying himself. With his back to her, McKenna saw a raised pale scar on his tanned skin. It appeared to have been healed for a while, and it was long enough to run from just under his right shoulder blade at a downward angle to his spine.

She had no idea why it hadn't struck her before how dangerous his work was. It wasn't just sport to ride on crazed animals bent on shooting you off their backs and through the air.

Looking away from his broad back, she said, "I'm really not in any rush for a hot shower." She moved to slip past him and started up the stairs.

"You won't get to ride that pony around here until later," he called after her.

She stopped midflight, not getting what he was trying to say, and without turning around, she asked, "What pony?"

"The hot shower pony. There's no hot water unless you heat it on the stove and fill up a watering trough. That's a lot of work, bucket after bucket. That's why most people back in the day only took a bath once a month."

She finally turned around. Cooper had his denim shirt on but not buttoned up, and he was toweling his hair. "Then I'll have a cold shower, as long as there's running water, whenever you have the time."

He balled up the towel, then seemed to toss it right at her, and she reached out for it, but it sailed off to her left landing on the top of the other hitching post by Blaze. "I practiced that move a lot when I was a kid."

"You have skills," she said. "Yet there's seriously no hot water."

"I told you there can be," he said as he smoothed his hair back from his face, then sat down on the middle step and reached for his socks and boots.

"Cold's fine," she said, ready to leave him alone. "I'll see you around."

She started to walk toward the trees to get to the house. Why hadn't she given more thought to what Cooper did for a living? He had to have other scars besides the one on his back; he'd probably been injured plenty of times. No wonder he'd wanted to be alone on the old ranch before he returned to his so-called normal life.

What he'd told her about the Simply Sanctuary rescues and now seeing his scar made something clear to her: this place was a sanctuary for him when he needed it. He'd given up part of that by letting her stay.

She'd been enjoying talking to him and eating with him, but she'd change that for his sake. From now on, she'd keep her distance to make good on their deal. It was the least she could do.

CHAPTER SIX

COOP HAD BEEN surprised when he looked up and saw McKenna sitting on the deck obviously watching him. He hadn't expected to see her today. But there she'd been, smiling at him. Now she was walking away from him and he headed up the stairs. He reached for Blaze's reins, then led the horse back toward the house with him. As he broke out of the trees on the far side, he saw McKenna reach the house, but she didn't stop.

He headed after her and saw her going into the stable. By the time he approached the open door, McKenna was sitting on the baled hay across from Bravo's stall. She was on her phone, and he heard her say, "I shouldn't have accepted it. My mistake." She was silent for a long moment before she spoke again. "Boone, listen to me. I was wrong. Enjoy that, because we both know I'm rarely wrong, and it's even rarer for me to admit to it." Pause. "Not funny. I'm serious. Call me back as soon as you figure it out." Another pause. "Of course I still love you."

She ended the call and lowered the phone to her lap. Sitting there with her head down, she looked sad. He made more noise than he had to by pushing the partially open door back all the way. McKenna heard it and glanced over at him. "You're putting Blaze away?" she asked.

"Yeah, I guess so. We rode a lot today." He went to tie Blaze's reins to the large ring on the center support post of the stable. "I thought I heard talking when I got to the door."

"Yes, I was talking to Boone about something. He's in a crush at the clinic, so he couldn't talk too long."

"He works too much," Coop said as he went to get the brushes and rags to clean up Blaze.

"I think I'll take a ride after all. Maybe toward Split Rock Canyon."

Coop frowned. He didn't want her to ride there alone. "I know this land. I can ride anywhere and make it back in one piece. However, you *don't* know this land. You don't have a clue where the canyon really is, so common sense means you wouldn't start out at this time of day trying to find it." That sounded reasonable to him.

She agreed without argument. "You're right. I couldn't find it unless I fell into it."

He was relieved. "Good, then that's settled. No ride to the canyon."

"Don't get out over your skis. No ride right now, but I'm thinking of doing a half trail in the morning and coming back around noon, then going to find the canyon. Or I could do the canyon in the morning—that might be better—then tackle the half trail in the afternoon."

"That sounds like a plan, but where are you going to go to look for the canyon?"

"I don't know, obviously, but you could draw a map for me—I'm good at reading maps."

He could do that in his sleep. "Sure, why not?"

"That's great." She stood up. "I'm going back to the house to leave you to your solitude. If I make dinner tonight, I'll leave some in the fridge for you. Help yourself whenever you feel like eating."

He realized he'd kind of been looking forward to an evening meal with her. He'd enjoyed being in the house and seeing McKenna across the table from him last night. But he wouldn't argue. She needed her space. "Thanks."

She nodded. "I'll bring down some carrots or apples for the horses later."

"Sure, the horses would love it. As soon as I finish with Blaze, I'll take a look at the shower hookup."

"I'd appreciate it," she said as she approached Bravo's stall. The animal ambled over to her with no hesitation. As she stroked his muzzle, she said, "I'll be coming down here around dawn, and you be ready for a ride." He snuffled softly. "Good, I'm excited, too."

"I didn't know you spoke horse," Coop said.

She patted Bravo on his neck, then turned to Coop. "I don't, but I work with children who can't explain why they hurt or are sad or angry. But you get to recognize the emotions in their eyes. I think horses are kind of like that but different. Bravo looked pleased, and I'll take that for what it's worth. Now,

I'll get out of your way," she said and started for the door.

Coop wondered why she was being so distant. He didn't think she'd be mad about the shower, or maybe she was. She probably understood the horse more than he understood women. With her being pretty much a stranger, he was at a loss about what was going on with her. But that was personal and none of his business. He just felt uneasy for some reason.

BY THE TIME Coop was walking back to the house, dusk was falling. He'd found a broken line on the feed tube to the shower from the water tank, and he'd had to hunt around in the stable to find out if there were any spare parts left there in the tack room. He found a part that would do, then spent more time modifying it to make a good seal on the line.

As he approached the house, the lights were on inside, their glow spilling out onto the porch. He spotted McKenna right away, sitting on the porch step again. He was almost to her when she must have heard him coming. Turning to him, she smiled, then went back to watching the sky come to life

with stars, the glow of the moon just showing on the horizon.

"I found a map online of the sky over Wyoming this month and it shows the position
of all the viewable planets."

He sat down by her. "It can be quite a
show, especially if you're used to city lights
blotting out most of the display."

She glanced at him. "Did you get the
shower going?"

"I hope so. There was a feed line problem,
but I think I fixed it. If not, I'll call Uncle
Abel to come up tomorrow, and he'll get it
done."

"Okay, I'll go in and try it so I can get to
bed early. Leave the map to the canyon for
me on the kitchen table, and I won't have to
wake you up in the morning."

"You don't need a map."

"Excuse me?"

He'd made a decision about her riding to
the canyon by herself before he'd left the stable. "When we were kids, Mom and Dad let
us roam all over our land, but it was always
understood that we didn't go off on our own.
At least one other person had to be with us."

"I'm an adult, and I can read a map, if

you'll make one. If you won't, I'll call Jimmer and agree to a lunch date with him if he'll make me a map."

For some reason, Coop didn't doubt she'd go for lunch to get the map. He chuckled roughly at that. "He'd make a good map. He is an artist of sorts. But don't bother him. I'll go with you."

Her eyes widened. "What?"

"I think it's a good idea. You can't wander around out there, map or not, and expect to find it."

"You can't do that. What about our agreement?"

"It was my idea. I'm the one who offered it to you, and now I'm willing to suspend the agreement for as long as it takes to get to Split Rock, explore it and get back here. If you agree, then we'll do it. If you don't, then we won't."

"You're serious?"

"Absolutely. Do you agree?"

She hesitated, obviously considering his offer before she finally said, "I agree."

His wins staying on the back of mean horses for eight seconds had almost been easier than getting McKenna to agree to let him tag along with her. He wouldn't be taking a victory lap, but he did have to control an impulse to do a fist pump. Instead he said, "We'll leave at dawn."

WHEN DAWN BROKE the next day, McKenna and Cooper were riding away from the stable toward Split Rock Canyon together. It still didn't quite seem real. She'd been confounded by Cooper's offer the night before since it meant giving up his solitude to get her to the canyon. If there had been no agreement between them, she would have asked him if he'd go with her. Life was strange sometimes. Two weeks ago, she never would have believed she'd be in Wyoming, riding a horse, headed toward a place with a history that might have been woven out of whole cloth—and riding with a rodeo star. She smiled at that, and Cooper apparently didn't miss it.

"You amused about something?" he asked as they road to the west.

She glanced over at him at him at the same time he looked at her. His hat shadowed his eyes, but she didn't miss the raised eyebrow. "I was just thinking that life has a way of going off on a path that you never saw coming."

"That's deep," he said.

She wouldn't argue with that, but she did have a question. "Why are we going this way? I know it's two miles to government land ahead, and the canyon's supposed to be on your land."

"It is. We're going about a mile this way, then we'll veer to the north. You'll understand when you see it."

"Okay, just checking. How long will it take to get there?"

"Are you like one of those kids who repeatedly asks, 'Are we there yet? Are we there yet?' and spoil the trip?"

"No, I'm the kind that gets an answer and accepts it...usually."

"We Donovan boys were experts at triggering Dad when he was driving us to junior rodeo competitions. He'd finally say that if one of us asked that question one more time, when we went through the only drive-through on our route for food we'd get nothing."

"Did he ever follow through on that threat?"

"First, that wasn't a threat. Dad never

threatened us. It was a promise, and he kept it because one of us did it again."

She looked over at Cooper. "Which one?" she asked.

He slanted her a look. "Guess."

"You did, didn't you?"

"Maybe you are a mind reader," he said. "In my defense, Caleb and I were getting on each other's nerves, and the way I asked it was, 'How soon will we get there so I don't have be around him anymore?' and when the drive-through came up, Mom and Dad got coffee and burgers, and we got bottled water. The burgers sure smelled good, too."

She laughed. "I think I'd like your dad."

"I'm sure you would." Coop drew Blaze to a stop, and McKenna pulled Bravo back. "This is where we go northeast."

He'd said she'd understand, and she did as she scanned their surroundings. Dense stands of trees were lined up like soldiers on duty to the west and rugged land rose beyond, but in front of them was a rocky clearing. Some of the rocks would be called large, and some were so huge that the trees behind them were barely visible. She couldn't see how far the clearing went.

"This is the way we do this. I'll go ahead, and you follow. I know where the horses might have problems with rocks hidden by the dead grass."

"Sure, okay," she said, and Cooper pulled ahead.

He led the way, zigzagging through what felt like a maze. But the horses never faltered on the slight incline of the land. "How much farther do we have to go until we hit the canyon?"

She didn't realize what she'd said until Cooper glanced back at her over his shoulder. "Lucky for you, drive-through burgers aren't on the table on this trip."

She laughed at his quick reaction, then said, "Like father like son."

"A lot more than I ever expected to be," he said as they kept riding.

"I bet you had a lot of pressure on you to join the rodeo and become a champion."

"Not from anyone but myself. Mom and Dad were there for support when I made the choice, but they never once told me I had to carry on the Donovan name. They never said that to any of us. But they're proud of me, I know that. I also know they're starting to wish I'd name a retirement date, but they'd never mention it unless I asked them for their opinion."

"Are you thinking about it?"

"I think about hanging up my saddle every time I face my competition for an event and most of them are younger than twenty-five, some even under twenty. There I am, thirty-five."

"That's not old."

"In rodeo years, I'm almost a grandpa."

She remembered the scar on his back, something she'd tried to forget. "I imagine doing what you do takes a toll on you."

"You might say that."

She let that go when she looked ahead and thought she saw trees growing shorter until she realized the land they grew on was angling downward. "Cooper?"

He stopped and looked back at her. "You okay?"

"Fine." She pointed ahead of them. "Are those trees growing shorter as we get closer, or is there a downward incline coming up?"

He didn't have to look before he answered her. "You caught it. The ground ahead slopes downward."

"Oh, we aren't going there, are we?"

"Actually, you found the canyon—at least the entrance."

She didn't understand. "What?"

"Come on. We'll have to leave the horses up here, but getting down to the canyon should be easy for a real hiker."

"Okay, where do we leave the horses?"

He dismounted. "We'll walk them to the canyon's opening and tie them there."

She quickly got down and went with Cooper toward the slope. After securing both horses to a low, heavy-branched tree, Cooper went closer to the drop. When she was beside him, she looked down at something she hadn't imagined. It wasn't a drop-off or a cliff of any sort; it was an incline that went down about twenty feet to what looked like a solid wall of trees, tangled growth and rocks.

"Where do we go into the canyon?" she asked.

"Dead ahead." He turned to her and took her hand in his. "It's very uneven walking," he said.

Then they started down. It took all of five minutes to get to more level ground.

Cooper let go of her and stepped in front, put out his hand, curled it into a fist, then punched forward through the dense growth. His hand went right through the barrier, then he pulled back and smiled at her. "You're here. All we have to do is tear down the vegetation to expose a broken arch that lets us into Split Rock Canyon."

"Okay," she said, closing the gap between them. When she made a fist, Cooper grabbed her hand to stop her before she could duplicate his punch.

"No, don't do that. I knew where the arch was. If you hit the arch, you could break your hand. Sorry for showing off. I didn't think of that until right now."

He was still holding on to her hand, and she didn't pull away. "I'll rip, not punch," she said, then glanced at his hand on hers. "I'll need two hands for this."

He let go right away. "Yeah, we both do," he said and reached to get to work.

It took a little time to pull away the brittle foliage that could have been there for years before the arch was partially exposed. It was made of stone that had pitted and cracked over time, and the vines and grasses had been growing in its spaces. Her heart was actually beating faster from anticipation and excitement.

"Listen to me before we go through. There's rules you have to follow, and please don't question them or me."

She was getting used to him issuing rules that actually made a lot of sense. "Absolutely."

"First, I go in front of you, and you follow in my tracks. Don't go running ahead. If I tell you to stop, you stop right where you are. If I tell you to run, you take off and don't look back. If I tell you to be still and not make any noise—"

She cut him off. "I'll be very still and not make any noise. It's so beautiful around here."

A lot of things were beautiful right then, and Coop wasn't thinking about the canyon at all. McKenna seemed to light up the world around him. He cringed at that thought—a poetic turn of phrase that was not like him at all. But he meant it. "Okay, enjoy the beauty. We've got a short walk down to the creek, then we'll follow it to the split rock."

"Wow, I can hear the water already. This is really an adventure."

"I guess it would qualify as an adventure for someone from Boston."

"It most certainly does." Her smile was still intact.

He ducked to lead the way through the old arch and into the gorge. McKenna was right there with him, and he took her hand. She curled her fingers around his, and he felt relieved.

He gave her time to scan their surroundings. The gorge was long and narrow, barely forty feet between the sidewalls of pitted rock and vegetation struggling to survive in its cracks and crevices. The creek wandered along below them, and a sweet fragrance lingered in the air.

"This is overwhelming," McKenna said in a half whisper, the tone that he'd expect to be used in a church.

"I'll go ahead," he said, letting go of her hand and starting down into the gorge, breaking a trail in the scrub on the rocky ground. "This place used to be called Singing Wind Gorge by the natives. Its name was changed before I was born. When the wind sweeps through here, it makes a whistling sound, so the first name fit."

"Too bad they changed it," McKenna said from close behind him.

"I don't know who signed off on it, but Split Rock stuck."

"That's a shame." Her voice came from farther away, and he immediately turned to check on her.

She was crouching by the creek, holding her slender hand in the clear water, sweeping it back and forth. When he cleared his throat, he caught her attention. "When I told you the rules, I should have added, if you want to stop, just let me know."

She stood and came over to him. "You really need to make a book of rules before you bring anyone else down here so they can study them." She was enjoying what she was saying, her green eyes almost twinkling with humor.

"Suggestion taken," he said, then turned to keep going.

He heard her crunching the grass as she followed right behind him.

He finally stopped when the bend in the creek was close. He turned to McKenna,

who was so close he almost bumped into
her. "When we go around that bend, you
won't be able to miss the rock." He held
out his hand. "Close your eyes and take my
hand."

"Why?"

"Just do it. Trust me." She put her hand in
his. "Close your eyes, and no peeking."

"Okay, just don't let me fall and pull us
both into the water."

"Cowboy's promise," he said, feeling just
a bit silly saying that, but it made her smile,
and her hand tightened on his as she closed
her eyes.

He walked slowly into the bend, making sure she had her footing by the side of
the stream, and then at the right moment he
stopped.

Letting go of her hand, he said, "Keep
your eyes shut," then moved to one side so
he could see her expression when she saw
the rock. "Okay, open your eyes."

He watched her hesitate, and then her eyes
opened. She blinked and whispered, "Wow,"
in a voice that was touched with wonder.
The huge rock with a five-foot-wide split
down the middle was just a rock, no more

and no less, but it was something beyond special to McKenna. She stared up at it, tipping her head back to look up to the flat top at least twenty feet above the stream.

"The creek is named Snake Creek, and it eroded the center to cause the split ages ago. The two halves of the creek never flowed back together. Sort of symbolic of the two lovers who were separated and could never be together, I guess."

"So, the story really isn't true?" she asked, never taking her eyes away from the rock.

He wished he was a good liar, but he just wasn't. "No, it's not. It's just a fable that's been handed down from generation to generation."

"Oh," she said, then took out her phone and began to take pictures. "It's beautiful up here, wild and wonderful."

She turned her camera toward the creek. "The water's so clear you can see every stone at the bottom."

McKenna was obviously thrilled by the whole thing. He wished he could get that sense of wonder back. The last time he'd come close was on a ride he'd made in New Mexico, setting a new high score with his win on one of the toughest horses ever. He'd hardly been able to absorb it before the moment was gone and he was facing another ride.

She tipped her head back and put her hand up to the brim of her yellow cap to protect her eyes from the glare of the morning sun.

"You need a full-brim hat out here," he said. As she stood, he took off his hat and held it out to her. "Try this and you'll see what I mean."

"Okay." She tugged off her cap, letting her auburn hair fall loosely around her shoulders and handed it to him, then put his on. It was a bit too big for her, but she did look good in it. "I need to get one of these hats next time I'm at Farley's."

"If you're done with your pictures, we should start back."

"Not yet," she said, turning to him. "I want to climb up there and see the view. I bet it's spectacular. It's climbable, isn't it?"

He'd done it more than once himself, but it hadn't been to take pictures. "Yes, if you're careful. But if you want the best way up, you need to cross over the creek to get to it."

"My boots are waterproof, and the creek looks pretty shallow. Lead the way."

He pushed her hat into his pocket and reached for her hand. "It's slippery, too."

With their fingers laced, he led the way through the shallow stream and stopped by the sloping side of the huge rock. He pointed out the crude steps that someone had laboriously chiseled into the rock.

"It isn't easy, but it's the only way to get to the top. Can you manage it?"

McKenna took pictures of it, then turned to Coop. "Sure, no problem," she said and pushed her camera into her jeans pocket. "I want a picture from up there to prove to Boone that I made it."

"He'll be impressed," Coop said. "I'll take a few from down here to show him, too."

She turned to the rough stairs. "Here goes," McKenna said, and before Coop knew it, she was starting up the side of the massive rock, hand over hand, one foot at a time.

He stood back watching her. "Careful," he called. "Check and make sure it's clear of snakes before you step out."

"Sure," she called to him as she kept climbing.

He was impressed, even if the rock had a convenient slant inward. McKenna stopped at the top, hesitated, then called back, "No snakes."

"Good. Don't go near the back of the rock. Your shoes are wet and it's slippery. It's a bad fall from there."

"Got it," she said before she disappeared from sight.

He moved to get an angle where he could see the top and McKenna. There she was, near the south side, and when she saw him, she grinned. "This was *so* worth it!"

She had her phone out, snapping pictures almost in a circular method so she got every angle of the view. He knew what it looked like: the mountains north and west, then the open view of the valley to the south. It really did feel like the top of the world. He pulled out his phone and took a couple of pictures of McKenna, but his hat was shading her face, and he called out to her. "Take off the hat so Boone can see your face."

She immediately removed it, and he took pictures of her standing up there, her auburn hair lifting softly in the breeze as she grinned from ear to ear.

"Got it," he called out.

She put his hat back on, then spread her arms wide, tipped her head back and twirled around. He snapped more pictures, then stopped when she neared the front edge and sat down, dangling her feet. "What did you all do when you came up here?"

He wasn't going to do a confessional with her. "We had fun, darlin', and we got out of our chores because no one could find us."

Her chuckle drifted down to him, and when he realized how much he was enjoying the sound, he said, "Time to go. There's no more to see."

"Oh, shoot," he heard her say, but she got up and disappeared from view.

He was at the bottom of the rough steps just as she started down. "You're good at this," he said as she finally planted her boots on the ground and turned to him.

"I love it. If I lived here, I'd explore all this, every inch of it."

He thought he and his brothers had probably done that in the past. "It's a great place to live," he said.

She looked over at him. "This has been

so great. I really appreciate you doing this for me."

He had an idea there wasn't a lot he wouldn't do for her if he ever got settled in his life, but by then, he was pretty sure, despite her protestations about not looking for love, she'd be with someone who adored her. He didn't hesitate taking her hand again going back to forge the stream, then heading out of the canyon. The hike back was slow and quiet, and Coop never let go of McKenna's hand until they were stepping through the worn arch and past the pile of cleared brush they'd made. Both horses whinnied softly when they saw them appear.

McKenna stopped for a minute, looked around, then glanced at Coop. "If things were different, this would be a great place for a picnic, wouldn't it?"

"If things were different," he said, then mounted Blaze while McKenna got up on Bravo.

When they arrived back at the house, Coop dismounted, and as McKenna got down, he took Bravo's reins and secured him and Blaze to the hitching posts. "When are you going hiking?"

"As soon as I get something to eat and freshen up."

"I'll take care of the horses, and then how about I make us eggs and bacon? They're quick, and you need lots of protein."

"You're catching on," she said. "But I can make them."

"No, you do what you need to do, and I'll cook. Trust me, I do a mean eggs and bacon. Then you can take off afterwards."

"If you don't mind, that sounds wonderful."

He didn't mind at all.

DANNY WAS BY the gates when McKenna arrived for her hike, and he was pleasant, smiling for no reason she could understand and talking about how insects had taken down one of the old trees. He walked her all the way to the top of the trail she chose, then she understood everything when she turned to say goodbye to him.

"Say, Doc, I was wondering if you're gonna be busy tonight."

The man was as clear to see through as freshly cleaned glass.

"I'm just going to shower, eat and go to bed."

His smile stayed in place. "Jimmer and me, we're gonna go to the Over the Moon Diner in town, and we be honored if you'd come along with us or meet us there."

"That's a lovely invitation, but the farthest I'll go after hiking today is back down the road, and then I'm staying put."

She'd spoken quickly to get Danny to go away, but she knew she'd blown it as soon as the words were out of her mouth. Any hope that Danny wouldn't put two and two together evaporated when he said, "Dang. You never told me where you're staying."

She decided the truth was the best option because she felt pretty certain that Danny could find where she was staying on his own, anyway. "I'm down the road on an old ranch. It's close enough to walk if I had to, and it's so peaceful."

"The only place that close to here is the old Donovan place."

She tried to look a bit confused. "It's something like the Flaming Sky, I think. Boone made the arrangements for me. I just use it for my base."

"You know that their son's a big rodeo star? Jimmer's a good friend of Coop Donovan and his twin brother, Caleb."

"I don't know anything about rodeos." She hitched her backpack higher. "I'm off," she said and turned to go.

"Have fun, Doc," Danny called after her.

McKenna walked faster away from Danny. "See ya later."

CHAPTER SEVEN

McKENNA GOT BACK to the house four hours later just as rain began to fall. Cooper was gone, so she sat out on the porch and watched the rain. She caught its scent in the air along with damp earth and a freshness that it brought with it. She stayed there until a wind came up and drove the rain toward the house.

She got up, grabbed the pillows and went inside. After taking a cold shower, she dressed in pajama bottoms and an oversize white T-shirt. She kept expecting Cooper to show up, but he never did. She ate her dinner of pasta and marinara sauce by herself, then lay down on the couch and stared up at the shadows over her.

Her day had been great, the ride to the canyon, a wonderful adventure. She'd loved it. Then the hike. Taking Danny out of the mix, she'd loved it, too. The half point had been a ridge with a beautiful view.

Lying there on the couch, she finally let herself remember more than just the ride that morning. There was Cooper offering to go with her and the time he'd held her hand on the way back from the rock. They'd laced their fingers together as if they'd been doing that for a very long time. She'd liked it, that connection, and it made her uneasy.

The sound of her phone ringing cut into that thought. She didn't recognize the number, but she answered it. "Hello?"

"Doc, is that you?"

She recognized Danny Stucky's voice and didn't do what she wanted to do: she didn't hang up on him. "Who's this?"

"This is Ranger Stucky."

"Oh, hello."

"I hope I'm not interrupting anything, but I'd guess you've noticed the rain. We're not sure how long it's going to last or how hard it will get, so I'm calling to let you know, you'll be notified by phone in the morning by six o'clock whether the trails will be open or closed."

"Thanks for letting me know."

"I was wondering, if they're closed tomorrow, maybe you'd have time to do something with Jimmer."

She rolled her eyes. "If I'm not hiking, I'll be with a friend for the day."

"Oh, local guy or what?"

"Boone, you remember Boone?"

"Of course. Okay, you have fun, and you'll get a call around six."

He hung up, and McKenna gave up. She'd have to tell him something to make him go away. Maybe she could tell him she was celibate. She laughed at herself as she got up, went over and turned off the lights, then came back to lie down and try to get some sleep. But no matter how hard she tried, she couldn't fall asleep. She finally got up, found the pack of cards she'd bought at Farley's, and went to sit at the table and play solitaire.

She'd barely finished taking the jokers out of the pack and shuffling the deck when she heard footsteps on the porch, then the door opened. Cooper hurried in, closing the door behind him. When he turned, McKenna smiled at him. He looked like a drowned cat as he headed across the room.

"Later," he called over his shoulder and

went into the bathroom. He left a trail of water on the floor in his wake.

She heard him moving around, then water running with the usual rattle of the pipes. She waited until he finally came back out and walked over to the table. He was in jeans and a loose black shirt with his hair combed straight back from his face. He sat down opposite her, and she finally asked, "What happened to you?"

"I moved a bale of hay when I was checking on the horses, and I lost my balance and fell."

He touched his left side around the middle ribs, and she didn't miss his slight grimace. "Are you hurt?"

"Just mad at myself."

"You just got back and went down to the horses?"

"No, I've been at the barn since around four. You weren't back, so I went to check on them, and I got a few calls I had to take. By the time I was ready to come up here, it was raining. I figured I'd feed them early and not have to come back later."

She noticed him starting to rub his side now. "So, that's why you were lifting hay?"

"Yeah, that's why."

"I wish you'd tell me the truth."

He blinked at that. "What truth?"

"That you did get hurt and you're not going to say a thing about it."

"I told you—"

"Why did you grimace when you touched your ribs, then? And now you're rubbing them."

His hand stopped moving, but he kept it where it was. "I hit something during the fall, probably a post."

"Can I look at it?"

"No, I don't need a doctor. I told you, I'm fine."

She shrugged. "I've never had that happen before."

"What?"

"My offer of a house call being refused."

"Very funny," he muttered.

She picked up the pack and started shuffling again. "Everyone knows cowboys play cards, so I assume you do."

"I've been known to from time to time."

"I bought these cards at Farley's. They're rodeo cards, and look what's on them." She flipped a card toward him, and he picked up a king of hearts, looked at the front then the back, and flipped it back over to her.

"I didn't know we sold playing cards."

"With your logo on the back and everything. I bought them to take to work with me when I go home."

"You play cards at work?"

"You'd be surprised how you can divert a child's fears by playing Go Fish or Old Maid with them. Sometimes I work in the ER, and about a year ago, I had a seven-year-old patient who fell off his bike. He'd been riding without a helmet, and his head was bleeding a lot. We had to keep him for observation overnight."

She smiled softly. "His name was Atlas, and he was tiny for being seven years old. In the middle of the night, he woke up thinking he'd die, so I sat with him. We ended up playing cards, and thankfully it was a slow shift, so I kept him occupied. His game was poker. I'd never played it, but I agreed to it, and he said he'd show me how to do it.

"The prize for the winner was a candy bar out of a vending machine by a waiting room. He left with seven chocolate bars, the big ones. I left with nothing. I kind of figured out he was a ringer when he told me that a single king beat three queens."

Cooper laughed at that. "You never told him how wrong he was?"

"No, he needed to win, and I honestly had never played poker, so I thought maybe he was right. He went home with candy and a smile, despite the bandage wrapped around his head."

He shifted in the chair, and she caught him grimacing again.

"You're being silly," she said.

"About what?"

"Not letting me check your ribs."

"They'll be fine."

"I don't have a lollipop to bribe you with, but I can make some of my extraordinary coffee for you if you'll let me have a look. It won't take too long. I promise."

She was worried she'd gone too far and made him mad, but surprisingly, he asked, "How can you do it? You don't carry an X-ray machine with you, do you?"

"No, I don't, but I have two hands that are remarkable at finding swellings, tenderness, even broken bones just by touch. They're amazing. I also have my black bag out in the car."

He folded. "Okay, take a look."

"Wait here. I'll be right back."

Thankfully, he did as he was told, and when she returned with her bag, he was sitting in the chair. His hand was still on his ribs. As she put her bag on the table, she glanced at Cooper. "I need to turn your chair away from the table so I can get in front of you."

"Sure," he said and stood up slowly.

She reached for the chair and pulled it into position.

When he was seated, she moved over to stand in front of him. "I'll just get your shirt back off your shoulders."

He put both hands on his thighs and kept quiet while she moved the shirt to expose his chest. She undid the buttons then eased the shirt back off his shoulders. "No need to take it all the way off," she said.

She'd learned early on in her internship to never show any reaction to anything when she was looking at a patient for the first time. Her mantra was, "Be calm, be calm, be calm." She'd found out the hard way that children could read an adult like a book when they were afraid of what was going on. Cooper wasn't afraid, but he obviously saw that fraction of a second when she looked at his chest before she looked away.

"Go ahead and just say it," he said as she met his dark eyes.

She'd noticed his muscular shoulders and an impressive six-pack under smooth tanned skin. But what caught her off guard were his scars. His back scar was just the beginning. "I'm sorry. I just didn't expect…"

As her words trailed off, he finished for her, "Me to have personal tattooing on my body?"

She tried not to look back at his chest that had a pale scar she could tell had been there for a while, cutting across his chest to just below his breastbone. Another ragged-looking scar, two or three inches long, showed on his left shoulder cap. Three puncture wounds near that had no more than a year or so of healing.

"That's what you call those, personal tattoos?"

A wry smile held no humor. "Oh, you want it in doctor speak? Okay. I have had an assortment of lacerations, contusions, tears and punctures. Over a hundred stitches here and there. I've been very lucky. The worst I've had is when a horse rolled on me and broke some ribs and caused sternum damage. Oh, I've dislocated my shoulder twice, had a broken collarbone and a fractured wrist."

She avoided looking at the scars again and kept her eyes on him. "How many scars are there?"

He started to shrug, but he stopped right away. "I don't keep track of that stuff."

"Oh, yes, you do. Even young boys can tell you how many scars they have."

He lifted one eyebrow, then said, "Okay, maybe a dozen."

"Is that all?" she asked with exaggerated skepticism in her voice.

He exhaled. "Okay, thirteen. Those you can see and a couple on my legs—oh, make that fourteen, one on my back where I was thrown and hit a post with a nail in it. It tore my back. I always forget about that one, because I never see it. Do you want to see it?"

She didn't want to see it again. "I don't think so." He might be a rodeo superstar, but it looked as if he'd paid his dues along the way. "Now that that's settled, why don't you get on the bed and at least be comfortable?"

"Nope, I'm good here."

Stubborn. "I need to wash my hands." With that, she crossed over to the kitchen and pumped water over her hands. She dried them quickly with a hand towel, then went back to Cooper.

She looked at his chest, laser-focusing on just the left ribs. Something wasn't right. There was no reddening or visible bruising that she'd expect from a blow to the area. Cooper was a walking billboard for scars. She looked right at him. "If there's more to this rib thing than what you're telling me, you need to let me know."

"Like what?"

"Come on. You might have had a hay bale fall on you, but there's no sign that you took any impact on that side."

"You're good," he said.

She knew she'd been right. "I really need to know what's going on."

"Okay, that's fair."

She crouched in front of him and gently touched his left side, starting at the middle ribs to work her way down. "If it hurts when I'm prodding, let me know. Meanwhile, tell me what happened."

"You got it, darlin'."

"Okay, I'm listening. Tell me your story."

She felt him tense when she pushed lightly with her fingertips between his ribs. "I came home mostly to get away from the rodeo circuit and get my act together before leaving again. But I also came back because I got hurt on my last ride. It was relatively minor. It's right where you're pushing now."

She could feel a slight swelling between the ribs, but there was no discoloration of the skin. "Okay."

"It's important for what I do to not give off any appearance of weakness in public. So, I came home. I literally snuck onto the ranch unseen, and no one knew I was here until I shot myself in the foot. That's a metaphor, darlin'."

"Yeah, I got that." She stood up to do something she thought was best for the situation. "I know you hardly know me, but you trust Boone, and he trusts me. So, for your own peace of mind, before you tell me how you did it and what your diagnosis was, give me a dollar, and anything you tell me will fall under patient-doctor privilege. That means my lips will be sealed for the small price of a single dollar."

He narrowed his dark eyes on her. "I've heard lawyers do that, but a doctor?"

"We do it, and since I'm here and the only doctor available is snowed under with work, I'll take a dollar and you'll become my patient."

He shifted to take something out of the watch pocket of his Levi's, then held his hand out to her palm up. A silver dollar was in the middle of his calloused palm. The old coin showed wear from the hands that must have held it over the years. "It's my lucky piece."

"I can't take that."

"Why? It's real silver. Besides, I don't carry paper money on me, and I'm sure you don't take credit cards. Take it."

She let him drop it in her hand, and she closed her fingers around it, the metal still holding his body heat. "Okay," she said. "I'll keep it until you trade me a paper dollar for it, and it's yours again. Deal?"

"Deal," Coop said, and he wondered how

many deals he'd end up making with the doctor before he left. Three so far, and his lucky silver dollar wasn't in his jeans anymore. McKenna was putting it in a side pocket on her medical bag.

She crouched down in front of him again. "Go ahead and finish your story while I check some things."

He'd almost forgotten where he left off. "I was last to ride in the saddle bronc finals, and I'd made my time, eight seconds. Two pickup riders came alongside to get me off in one piece."

She was pressing on his ribs, then shifted to put her palm against his chest over the same spot. "Take as deep a breath as you can and let it out slowly. If you feel pain, especially sharp pain, stop right away."

He did as she asked, had no pain, then she went back to feeling his ribs one at a time. "Go ahead. Keep talking," she said.

"I thought I was safe to shift off the bronc. That's when the closest pickup rider offered an arm for me to grab to help me off, then let me down onto the ground away from the bronc. I made a rookie mistake, and somehow I ended up safe on the ground, but I hit my ribs hard on the way down. I actually didn't know I'd bruised them until I was back at my hotel room, where I twisted to pick my hat up off the bed. That was painful."

He thought she said, "Ouch," but wasn't sure. "What was your diagnosis?"

"Bruised ribs, I think six and seven. They didn't wrap me, but they told me not to lift anything for two weeks. I was given medication that helped, and I wanted to be out of sight, so I took off and ended up here."

She looked up at him. "Okay, from what I can see and feel, there's a slight softness between the sixth and seventh ribs, but no instability. No sign of a break and no bruising, so you must have irritated it when you moved the wrong way. You picked up the hay bale with no pain, right?"

"Yep," he said.

"Then you're good. Just favor that side for a few days, take the medication if you need it, and that's that."

She stood up and reached to take a stethoscope out of her open bag. "One last thing— just to be cautious, I want to listen to your lungs. Breathe normally."

She listened, moving the chest piece over his ribs, then leaned in toward him to check his back. He felt her warm breath brush his bare skin, and he closed his eyes. He'd had a lot of doctors before, but never one like Dr. Walker.

"That's it." She stood back.

"Well, what did my dollar get me?"

"You're in good shape," she said and put the stethoscope back in her bag.

"Good to know," he murmured as he stood up and looked out the window. "It's still raining. Does that mean no hiking through mud tomorrow?"

"I don't know. Danny called me earlier to tell me the decision to keep the trails open or closed them down will be made by six in the morning, and he'll call me."

"That's good of him," he said.

"Yeah, I thought so until he ruined those good thoughts."

"He offered up Jimmer to keep you busy if hiking's out?" he asked as he did up his shirt.

"Basically. I'm just trying to ignore him."

"You get to sleep, and I hope you can hike tomorrow."

"Me, too," she said.

He went over to the door and opened it. "I'll be outside for a while."

"Goodnight, Cooper."

He stepped outside, and as he closed the door, he said, "Goodnight, darlin'."

The rain had stopped, and when he felt the bench, it was dry. McKenna must have taken the pillows back inside, but he wasn't going to get them. He'd sat on the hard bench ever since it was put on the porch, and he'd survived. He sat down and took his phone out of his jeans pocket. He opened it and went to his photos. He pulled up the ones from the canyon and sat back, slowly scanning through them.

Every one of them had McKenna in it, and in every one, she was smiling. He lingered on the one he took of her standing on the flat top of the rock, her arms thrown wide open, her face tilted to the sky. Her auburn hair was streaked with gold from the sun, and she looked as if she were embracing the world.

He hadn't realized how much he'd missed this place until he'd made his escape up here; he felt more complete here than anywhere else. Then Dr. Walker had shown up, rattling the plan he'd made so quickly to stay at the old place alone. But gradually, that unsteadiness she'd brought with her surprise appearance at the pond had started to smooth out, especially up at Split Rock. He could almost feel her hand in his, and he knew that wasn't a good sign.

Whoa there, cowboy. Keep to your deals with the doctor. No more altering them for a single moment.

The next four days would be by the rule book he'd never written. He ran his hands roughly over his face.

Just four days.

THE NEXT MORNING at six, a text came with a list of the trails that were each tagged as open or closed. The trail McKenna wanted to hike was open, so she got ready and left quietly in order to not to disturb Cooper. She drove away from the ranch feeling leery about seeing Danny, and she drove away from the ranger station around three o'clock smiling because she'd avoided seeing him all day. She'd also had a fantastic hike to a high ledge where you could see the Grand Tetons and Yellowstone National Park.

She felt great when she arrived at the ranch despite her mud-caked boots, at least until she stepped out of the car and started to walk up onto the porch. That's when the pain hit her: cramps in her calves and lower back. She'd thought she'd avoided that misery when it hadn't hit her after her first or second hike. She needed to sit in a Jacuzzi and let the jets massage her legs and back. But since that was out of the question, and she couldn't stand in the shower long enough for that to help, she knew what she was going to do.

Cooper wasn't there when she went inside to change quickly into her swimsuit and threw a long-sleeved denim shirt overtop. After grabbing a towel, she pushed her bare feet into her sneakers.

She managed the short walk down to the pond, and once she was on the dock, she quickly took off her shoes and her shirt. Her yellow cap was next, and she shook out her hair, then put her phone in her hat on the step. Aquatic therapy was great for sore muscles, and she figured the pond would at least help some. She crossed to the edge of the deck, and looked down at the calm dark blue water. Not giving herself time to reconsider what she was going to do, she dove into the pond.

It was colder than she'd expected, but she slowly began to swim laps. It was soothing to her, and gradually the aches began to fade. By the time she was ready to get out, the aching was gone. Finally, she leveraged herself up and out of the water, retrieved her towel, ran it through her hair and placed the towel around her shoulders to keep her damp hair from dripping down her back. Then she sat on the edge of the dock, dangling her feet in the water.

A deep voice behind her startled her. "Darlin', you don't know what's under that water." She quickly turned, and Cooper was standing at the top of the stairs looking lean in jeans and a plain white T-shirt, with the brim of his hat shading his eyes.

"Oh, hey," she said, turning around and shielding her eyes against the sun. "I came down here because my legs were aching, probably from the combination of riding Bravo to the canyon and my hiking."

He took the steps down to the last one, then sat, resting his forearms on his knees and looking up at her as she stood. "So, how was it?"

"The water's cool, but it eased the muscle inflammation. How are your ribs doing?"

"I forgot about them until you asked. They're good."

"Did you come down here to swim?"

"No, I wanted to let you know I'll be moving up to the stable for the rest of my stay."

That came out of nowhere. "Why would you do that? The roof's leaking."

"It's fixed. We both came up here to get away. Now we both can."

She'd worried at first about him going on the ride with her, but he'd acted as if he really wanted to go. She hadn't pushed him at all. "You don't have to do that. If it isn't working out for you, we can go back to our original deal, me leaving then coming back when you're gone."

"No, you sit tight. I'll make the move."

The only thing she could figure out that might have caused him to decide to relocate to the stable was the way she'd insisted on checking his ribs. She'd gone too far, pushing him to let her do it, and she'd ruined everything.

"How are you going to shower or cook there?"

"You get the house in the evenings, and I'll get it during the day, so we'll each have what we need." He looked as if he was ready to say something else, but he didn't. He stood, took two steps at a time, then walked away.

McKenna decided to give Cooper time to get what he needed from the house before she went back to change. She'd been blindsided, for sure, and was embarrassed by what she'd done. She'd never needed to examine his ribs.

"Bad, bad call," she muttered to herself.

She knew she was overreacting, and it wasn't as if he'd kicked her off the land. She basically had what she and Cooper had agreed to the first day. Cooper just wouldn't be around in the evening or when she left at dawn to hike, even if he was asleep. She hugged her arms around herself and closed her eyes. One thing she was thankful for was that this didn't happen before the trip to Split Rock. At least she hadn't messed that up.

Despite the warmth of the air, she was shivering and put her shirt on. She wasn't certain how long she'd been standing there feeling sorry for herself, but she had to get back to the house and put on some dry clothes. She walked alone, taking her time, and as she approached the house, she was hoping Cooper would be gone. When she opened the door, she didn't have to call out to let Cooper know she was there. She could feel the emptiness of the space right away.

Then she looked around, and she saw the bed had been stripped. That made his decision final in her mind, and she hurried to where she kept her clean clothes on the side table by the couch and changed into jeans and a T-shirt in record time. All she took with her when she went outside was her phone. Without an idea where she should go for a walk, she decided to go down to Twin Arrows and choose which direction to go when she got there. It didn't matter, as long as she didn't go back to the house until dusk.

CHAPTER EIGHT

COOP SAT ON the cot in the tack room, an eight-by-eight extension on the back of the stable. He was wondering if he could have handled telling McKenna he was going to stay down there at night any worse than he had. First, he'd been surprised to find her in a bathing suit dangling her feet in the pond, with her auburn hair wild and damp. Then he'd spoken and she'd stood. That's when he'd known he had to sleep in the stable. As he spoke, he'd seen her shock, then a look of embarrassment that he couldn't figure out as he explained what he was going to do.

He wished he could have told her it was for his sake that he was making the change and not because of anything she'd said or done. It was what he'd done, thinking about her most of the day, even while Uncle Abel had been on the roof of the stable patching up the hole with him.

Then the what-ifs came. What if she'd come back to do some more hiking when he had another break from competition? What if she'd think about quitting her job and joining Boone at the clinic? What if he cut his schedule back so he could make a trip to Boston now and then?

When his cell rang, he glanced at the screen. It was ten o'clock and Luke was calling. He answered right away. "Hey, Luke."

"Are you still at the old ranch?"

"Yep."

"I need your help."

Coop got the details, said he'd be there as soon as possible, then realized he had no way to do that. He couldn't ride there, so he'd have to get his dad or his mom to come and get him and drop him off at Simply Sanctuary. But that'd take too much time. Then he realized how he could get there. He stared at his cell, then did what he had to do. McKenna had given him her number to send his photos to her, and he called her.

When she answered, her voice was soft, as if she'd been asleep. "Hello?"

"It's me, Coop. I need a huge favor right away?"

"Your ribs, are they—?"

"No, I need to borrow your car. Luke needs me. He has a horse emergency, and he can't do it alone."

"Sure, you can take the rental."

"Leave your keys on the seat." He was already walking out into the main area of the stables and putting on his hat as they spoke. "I'm on my way."

When he jogged up to the rental car and opened the door, McKenna was sitting behind the steering wheel. "What are you doing?"

"Get in and I'll tell you."

"No, you—"

She cut him off. "Get in. You're wasting time."

He hurried around to climb into the passenger seat and closed the door. "Okay," he said.

She started the car, then backed up and headed toward the gates. "You take care of the gates," she said.

He thought he was the one who usually gave orders, but it saved time for him to open the gates. She came to a stop, and he climbed out to pull them back, then he got back into the car. "We'll leave them open."

When she drove out onto Twin Arrows, he said, "Why are you doing this?"

"Luke needs help and you're going to give it to him. I'm coming along because you aren't covered on my rental insurance, but mostly because I want to help Luke, too. I know I'm a so-called human doctor, but I might know enough to give him some help."

He sat back in the seat and watched her as they approached the highway. "I'm sure he could use all the help he can get."

"Another reason for me driving is you don't need someone seeing you fly through town at this time of night. So, when we get there, you put your seat back and lie down."

Another order, and she was right again. "I never even thought about that. Good call."

Once they were on the highway heading south, he kept his eyes on McKenna. The woman just got better and better. She'd obviously been sleeping when he'd called, and in the time it took him to get to the house, she'd gotten ready and out to the car. Maybe that was a doctor thing, always being ready for an emergency. Granted, she was wearing pajama bottoms with what looked like images of fried eggs floating on the black fabric and had on a white hoodie that read, "You Had Me at Hiking!" slashed in deep green across the front. She'd been ready to go.

"So, if it's okay, can you tell me what's going on before we get there?" McKenna asked. "I don't want to get in the way of what he's trying to do."

He exhaled and told her what he knew. "A rescue has an emergency, and Luke's there alone until at least midnight before someone's coming in to take over for him. The horse had been doing well, but it seems to be having an anxiety attack. Luke can handle that, but it's the medication and taking care of the wounds that he needs help with." He kept talking. "His options are limited, and I'm sure I was the last one on his list. I'm going to do some horse handling for Luke."

"Oh," she said softly, her eyes straight ahead. "How bad was the horse when Luke got it?"

"Bad. He just took him a few days ago, and he's worried that the stress might make the horse unmanageable."

"Then what happens?"

"There aren't many options," he said and saw her tighten her hands on the steering wheel. He remembered her reaction to Bravo's mouth. "But Luke doesn't give up easily. He battles for the horse to the end."

"I understand," she said in a low voice.

"If you don't want to go in when we get there, you can stay in the car."

She looked at him. "No, I'll help if I can."

He was pretty sure McKenna Walker was better than just a good doctor. She was probably more like Boone—a doctor who really cared about each patient and never stopped trying to help.

McKenna turned onto a side street in Eclipse and drove slowly past homes that looked old and snug among tall trees, with only a few lights burning in the windows. At the far end of the narrow street she saw a large sign framed in white lights hung between two tall wooden posts that supported a pair of three rail gates: "Cowboy's Heart Equine Service, Open from 6 am to 6 pm." Under that it read, "Simply Sanctuary Horse Rescue, Open 24/7." The gates were open, and they drove through onto a gravel driveway.

A building ahead was darkened but had

a red neon light in the window that labeled it his office. Holding stalls were lined up to one side of it.

"We need to go by the office and make a right turn," Cooper told her.

When she made the turn, brilliant security lights flashed on along a wider driveway that led up to two similar buildings ahead. Both had holding pens outside with an oval riding ring between them. The right one was lit up inside. As they got closer, more security lights flashed on around the area as the ones they'd already passed went out.

As McKenna pulled up to the main doors and shut off the car, one of the doors opened, and a man came out silhouetted by the glow of lights behind him. Cooper got out right away and headed toward him. She hurried along after, and when she caught up, she heard a snatch of their conversation. "She wanted to come to help." Coop turned to her; his eyes shadowed from the bright lights overhead by the brim of his hat. "McKenna, meet Dr. Luke Patton."

The veterinarian was an inch or two shorter than Cooper with a muscular build and was wearing jeans, boots and a white

T-shirt. It had a large red heart on the chest, with one word printed in a simple font: "Sanctuary." With his sandy blond hair that could have used a trim all mussed, the man looked exhausted but smiled when Cooper said, "Luke, meet Dr. McKenna Walker."

"Human or animal?" The vet quickly asked McKenna.

"Little humans. I work in the neonatal ICU in Boston." She saw him try to hide his disappointment. "I also work in our pediatrics ER. I can do meds, if you fill me in, and I can monitor if you give me the base line."

Cooper spoke up. "She has a great bedside manner and hands out stickers for the good kids."

Luke chuckled at that. "Okay, then let's get inside and start."

McKenna followed the men into the larger building that was only half of a stable toward the back, with a hayloft overhead. The front of the building looked to be fashioned for very large patients. A table that she was sure would have held a huge horse was up against the front wall, along with a giant version of a transfer sling used to move patients.

Before she could ask Luke what they'd be doing, he answered her questions.

"I'm dealing with a horse that's fragile, both physically and emotionally. I can't put him out completely. It would put too much pressure on his internal organs to lay him on his side or back." He spoke as he crossed to the other side that had two wide stalls and one that was totally padded. She caught a glimpse of a horse in one stall that was a muddy gray, its head swinging nervously from side to side. "So, I'm going with twilight and local numbing injections for pain, so he'll be out of it, but not completely."

Luke stopped by a bank of locked medicine cabinets over a stainless-steel counter with triple sinks. "He came with no background information a couple of days ago from near the Utah border, not even a name, so for now, I'm calling him Barney. He's self-harming, but not intentionally. He was badly abused, and he just sees every advance and every discomfort as a prelude to being beaten. His instinct is to run. Tonight he felt threatened when a delivery came a day early, and the driver used his blast horn to let me know he was here. Barney tried to run through the rails of a holding pen and tore up some work I'd done on him when he first came here. It needs cleaning up, some restitching, and he'll never stand for it. Coop really knows horses, and not just riding them, either. He's got a real connection. I'm hoping he's strong enough and good enough to keep Barney passive for a couple of hours."

Cooper brushed past Luke and McKenna to walk over to the stall with the horse. McKenna started to follow him, but he stopped her when he said, "This is between me and Barney."

He didn't make any attempt to touch the horse but started talking in a low, even voice—words she couldn't make out—but the horse seemed to understand.

Luke tapped her shoulder. "Come over here, and I'll explain things to you while Coop works with Barney." They went to the long stainless-steel counter, and he told her what he was going to attempt. It seemed clear-cut to her. He also told her how Cooper had made it possible for Barney to get to Sanctuary for help just days ago.

When she turned, she was surprised to

see Cooper leading Barney out of his stall slow and easy. The horse had what looked like a huge gauze pad on his left rump that had to be four feet by four feet. There was blood seeping through it. Cooper nodded and Luke moved over to the open end of the padded stall.

"In and back," he said as Cooper led Barney toward it.

The horse went without any resistance.

For two hours, the three of them worked so smoothly together that anyone would have thought they'd been a team for a long time. When Luke had put his instruments in the sterilizer, he turned to Cooper, who was over with Barney, watching him.

Luke looked even more tired than he had earlier, but he was smiling. "His vitals are steady, and everything's cleaned and stitched."

McKenna was startled when Cooper came up behind her and put his arm around her shoulder, pulling her against his side. She kind of needed that contact, so she didn't pull back. "What are the odds, Luke?"

"The odds are one hundred percent I'm going to do whatever it takes to save him.

He's doing good now. I'm so thankful you two were here."

Cooper's hold on her tightened slightly before he said, "I'm glad Boone talked McKenna into coming to my ranch. Timing's everything."

IT WAS JUST past midnight when Luke walked Coop and McKenna out to the rental car after his relief had shown up. Coop looked at McKenna, who was talking with Luke about some medication. He didn't understand what they were saying and didn't try to. He was impressed with McKenna. Boone had told him she'd had a hard time back in Boston and needed to find herself. He'd seen her expression when she'd first caught a glimpse of Barney's wounds: the pain in her eyes had been palpable. For some reason, he'd felt protective.

Once they got going, he could see a change in her. She hadn't faltered once during the process. He could tell she was in her zone; whether she was helping a child or a horse, she had the heart of a healer. Boone had told him once that when he set out to hire new medical staff for his clinic, that was his top criteria. Coop actually understood that now.

He tried to catch what Luke was saying. "No, I don't have scales to weigh horses, but I have the Henneke Body Condition Scoring System, and that gives me a good idea of body weight. It's math and I understand math."

"We need to break this up and get home," Coop said. "It's getting late."

"I'll get back in there, but once again, thank you both." He stepped back inside and said, "Safe ride, friends," before the door shut.

Coop reached to open the passenger door for McKenna. "I'll do the driving this time," he said.

"What about the insurance?" she asked.

He closed the door before going around to slip behind the wheel. "I'll be responsible for any extra cost, no matter what."

"Okay," she said. "Luke was sure glad for your help."

"I'm just grateful for what he does for those horses. I'll help out in any way I can."

Coop seldom told anyone about this part of his life, but as he spoke, he had a thought come to him: when he retired from the circuit, he wanted to work more closely with Luke at Simply Sanctuary. He wanted to help him expand and be able to rehabilitate more damaged horses.

"If I lived around here, I wouldn't mind helping Luke some." McKenna spoke softly. "What he's doing is incredible."

"You'd switch to being a veterinarian?"

She chuckled softly at that. "No, I wouldn't. Pediatrics is what I love doing. Boone's asked me more than once to come out and partner with him at the clinic. He's kind of given up on that, but if I ever partnered, I'd be practicing pediatrics."

That took him a bit by surprise. "A lady from Boston would come out here to live and practice medicine?"

"That's not going to happen," she said. "Boone understands."

He did, too, but the idea of McKenna being around had been one of his what-ifs.

"There's kids out here, believe me. It seems everyone I grew up with has kids, except my brothers. Well, that's not quite right. Caleb just got married to a wonderful woman who adopted a little girl, Joy, and he's in the process of legally adopting Joy, too. So, I'm an uncle, and I think I'll probably be an uncle more than once. Caleb and Harmony joke a lot about having six kids." He exhaled. "Once Caleb got the idea of a family, he took to it like a donkey to strawberries."

That brought out laughter from McKenna, and it made him smile. "You're calling your brother a donkey? I guess being called a pothole isn't so bad after all."

His own laughter came, and for a moment, he felt some sort of connection with McKenna that he'd never had with anyone before. He backed away from that. A sense of humor was a good thing in his books, but whether she had that or not didn't matter. "Darlin', you need to meet our donkey, Morris. Kids love him."

"I don't think I've ever met a donkey," she said right when lightning sliced through the night sky. The next thing he knew, McKenna was saying in a half whisper, "One thousand one, one thousand two…" and when she got to one thousand six, thunder rumbled around them. He looked at her and saw her hugging herself with her eyes closed. "That's close," she said.

"No, it's not all that close." Coop spotted their turn off onto Twin Arrows and slowed. "Don't worry about it."

Lightning flashed again. All she got out was "One thousand one, one thousand two" before a lightning flash lit up the world, and she flinched.

Instinctively, Coop reached over to touch her arm. "Hey, it's okay. We're almost home, and I promise that the closest lightning ever came to the old house was a tree that it split in two way past the stable."

"Oh my gosh," she breathed. "Did it burn?"

Boy, he'd said the wrong thing. "I think it smoked, but it didn't turn into a torch or anything. Grandpa Donovan used to say that thunder is the sound of God moving furniture around in heaven."

He'd hoped for at least a chuckle from her at the ridiculous explanation, but she seemed serious when she asked, "You believed that?"

"No, I didn't, but I didn't tell him that."

"At least your grandpa told you something he thought might distract you. My parents tried to explain the phenomena to me, but all I heard was 'Lightning comes from the ground up,' and that scared me even more, especially when they wouldn't let me sleep in their bed and told me I'd have to sleep on the floor." She chuckled, but it was a hollow sound. "That got me to go back to my own room, where I hid under my blankets and plugged my ears and kept my eyes shut."

The next instant, the lightning was back, brighter than ever, and the thunder was there a fraction of a second behind it. He heard McKenna take a sharp breath, and he was thankful they were approaching the gates.

"We're here," he said, glad they hadn't closed the gates when they'd left for Luke's, and he wouldn't close them now. He drove onto the access road and said, "Thunderstorms usually come in July," just for something to say.

"June? This is June," McKenna said in a low voice.

"We've had snow in July before. Wyoming weather never really surprises me anymore."

He pulled up and stopped with the passenger door parallel to the porch. He turned to McKenna, ready to tell her to get out, but another flash of lightning came that lit up the darkness around them, overlapped by a deep rumble of thunder. It illuminated her with her eyes scrunched shut, and she wrapped her arms so tightly around herself that her knuckles were white.

He hurried out of the car, ran around and pulled her door open. Then he reached inside, and he awkwardly got a hand under her legs and one around her waist. He wasn't quite sure how he did it, but he managed to lift her up into his arms, and she held tightly to him as she buried her face in his chest. He kicked the door shut, then hurried up onto the porch and went directly to the entry.

Once they were inside, he went to the couch and sat down, shifting so she was sitting in his lap.

He felt her start to pull back, but when lightning blazed again and thunder came with it, she pressed even closer to him.

"Darlin', it's okay. It's passing over us fast. I don't even know if it's going to give us much rain."

"Are you sure?" she asked in a small voice.

"I'm sure. We'll stay in here until it's over. We're safe in here," he said.

The rain had barely started before it stopped, and it seemed as if McKenna were holding her breath, waiting for lightning and thunder to come again. It was a lull, a sort of quiet in the middle of the storm, until the lightning showed again followed by rumbling thunder. Both were less intense and growing farther apart. "Okay, it's getting farther away, so it's all good. Are you okay?"

She nodded, and her hair brushed his chin. "Okay," she breathed.

He waited for the lightning to come again, but it never showed up, and the thunder rumbled way off in the distance. "It's over," he said. "It's gone."

He felt McKenna touch his chest. Then she pushed herself slowly back and looked up at him. Her face was pale, and she shivered. "I'm so sorry," she whispered, then must have realized she was still sitting in his lap. "Oh, gosh." She moved abruptly, half tumbling out of his arms and onto the cushions. She scrambled to sit and pressed back against the arm of the couch.

He watched her without reaching out to help her. Holding her had been to protect her, to reassure her, too, but it was better now if she wasn't that close.

"I'll get a fire going," he said, but she stopped him before he could get up to do it.

"No, we don't need it. You should check on the horses to make sure they're not spooked by the storm."

He hesitated, reluctant to leave her alone, even if it was just for the short time it would take to get to the stable, check and come back. "If you're sure you're all right, I'll go and look."

She closed her eyes for a moment. "You don't have to come back. That's where you want to be. Isn't that what you said?"

"I did." He stood up. Nothing was going right. "You get some sleep."

He was out the door quickly, but he didn't leave right away. He sat on the bench and waited until he was pretty sure McKenna had to be asleep, and then he walked to the stable.

The horses stirred but settled quickly, and he crossed into the tack room. When he went to the cot and sat down, he got up right away. The roof was still leaking despite Uncle Abel's attempt to fix it, even when there wasn't much rain that fell.

His sheets and blanket were wet, and he figured he had two choices: go back up to the house and sleep there, or sleep in a stall on the hay.

CHAPTER NINE

McKenna woke to a quiet morning: no rain, no thunder, not even enough wind to rattle the windows. Everything was fine until she remembered her breakdown during the storm. She'd received a text that all but three trails were open, but for the first time, she didn't get up and hurry to any of them. She just lay there staring up at the ceiling and wondering how she could face Cooper again...*if* she ever saw him again. Some people had acrophobia, and some people had claustrophobia, but she had to have astraphobia, the fear of thunder and lightning. And it had shown up in front of Cooper.

She closed her eyes, feeling like staying in bed all day, and then she remembered that the sun was coming up, and Cooper would be back soon to claim his time at the house. She made herself get up and started toward the bathroom door.

"Good morning, darlin'. I was wondering when you'd wake up."

She was suddenly wide awake, as she spun around and saw Cooper sitting at the table. "I'm sorry. I didn't know how late it was. I'm going to get dressed and leave."

He looked annoyingly awake—and he looked *good* in black jeans, a gray open-necked shirt and black boots. Better than good.

"I'll get out of your way as quickly as I can," she said.

He stopped her before she could reach for the handle on the bathroom door. "Forget that. The roof's leaking again at the stable, and I'm canceling my offer to sleep down there. I tried the hay last night, and I won't do that again."

She went over to the table and sat down across from Cooper, careful not to show how relieved she was to have him here again. "You should have come back up here instead of sleeping in the hay."

"It wasn't that bad," he said and leaned forward to reach for the deck of cards. "By the way, my game is Stud Poker. What's yours?"

That was easy. "Five Card Draw, jacks or better."

"You sound like a real player."

"No, I'm not very good at it, but it's one they play in old Western movies. The story is that Doc Holliday favored it."

"Those old movies again, huh?"

"Don't knock them till you try them," she said. "Speaking of trying something, how about some coffee?"

"I thought you'd never ask."

She got up to start the hot water, then figured she'd go all the way. "How about breakfast? I'm going to make some power pancakes."

"I can use more power."

McKenna figured that Cooper would bring up her lightning episode sooner or later, and when he hadn't said one thing about it, she decided to acknowledge the elephant in the room. "I apologize for my... meltdown last night."

His dark eyes studied her for a moment. "No reason to be sorry for being afraid of thunder and lightning."

"It's called astraphobia, and I've had it since I was a kid, but I usually don't melt down like that. I'm very embarrassed that it happened."

"Hey, darlin', stop worrying about it. It's done. The thunder and lightning are over. You shouldn't be so hard on yourself."

She'd been told that more than once by people who didn't know her parents. They expected her to be hard on herself so that she'd excel and follow in their footsteps in the medical world. Putting pressure on herself was a bad habit she hadn't been able to break.

Part of the reason she had decided to come out here, after all, had been because she felt she hadn't been able to help the little one on her last day of work back in Boston. She'd failed, and failure wasn't an option.

"I should have been able to stay calm. I'm not a little kid anymore."

"It's over with," he said. "But there's something I want to talk to you about."

"What?"

"It's those pajama bottoms. Where did you ever get them?"

Her face broke out in a grin, and she ran her hand over the soft black fabric on her thigh. Fried eggs with broken yolks floated all over them. "From a friend of yours."

He made a scoffing sound. "No. Not Boone the perfect, the one voted most likely to be on the cover of a famous men's magazine in high school? I don't believe you. That Dalton person probably gave them to you."

"Nope, Boone. He started gifting me a pair for my birthday every year, and I have five pairs so far, all of them as ugly as it gets. This is the latest pair, and it's actually a lot better than some of the others."

"I can't imagine anything worse than those are."

"Well, he got this one pair custom-made for me. It's the same picture of my face over and over again on a puke-green background. He caught me sleeping on a bench in the break room at work with my mouth open. I didn't know the photo existed until three years ago when he gave me the pajamas for my twenty-fifth birthday."

Coop laughed hard at that. "He thinks you like getting ugly pj's better than roses or candy?"

"It's just a joke. I laugh at it. As long as my parents never see them, it's all good."

"Why wouldn't your parents appreciate them? No sense of humor?"

Why had she even mentioned her parents? "No. I think I told you they're both physicians, and they are dead serious about their work. Me being caught on camera like that wouldn't be funny to them at all. They're obsessed with being perfect. Being caught looking like that is not okay when you're their daughter." She stopped herself, already saying too much. "But I like these pajamas and the others."

He just stared at her for a moment, then asked her a question that had nothing to do with her parents. "What do you give Boone for his birthdays?"

"The ugliest, most garish ties I can find. The last one I gave him had a huge macaw on it, all bright green and yellow and orange."

He shook his head and laughed.

When he stopped laughing and looked at her, she said, "I've decided that I'm not going to hike today. My leg muscles are still tight."

"So, what are you gonna do?"

"I'm going to go see Boone and the clinic he's so proud of."

"I haven't seen Boone since my parents' anniversary party last Christmas Eve, and that was just for a couple of minutes. I've missed him. If you wouldn't mind, could I tag along? His house is pretty secluded, and if he's at the clinic, I know the private entrance he uses at the back to get in without running into anyone. But if that's a bad idea, just tell me. No hard feelings."

She was silent for a long moment, thinking she wouldn't mind him coming with her, and she was pretty certain that Boone would love to spend time with Cooper, too.

Before she could tell him that, he said, "Not a good idea, huh? You know what? Forget it. You two should have time alone."

She almost laughed at that insinuation that was still hovering in the air around them— that there had to be more to their relationship than just being good friends. "No, I think it's a good idea. You can surprise him."

"When do you want to leave?"

"How about in half an hour?"

"Works for me."

"Okay, I'll get ready and meet you on the

porch then, and I'll call Boone and let him know I'm coming."

"Okay, see you on the bench."

HALF AN HOUR LATER, they were heading down Twin Arrows to the highway. Mc-Kenna had called Boone, and they had arranged for her to meet him at his house. She hadn't mentioned Cooper. She was excited about seeing Boone again. It had been almost two years, and she'd missed him a lot. She was driving the car again, and Cooper sat back in the passenger seat not talking. She figured that he was a man who spoke when he had something to say, and if he didn't have something to say, he let the silence go on.

As they neared the town, he finally spoke up. "Watch for Twin Pines Road. Boone's place is at the end of it. It's on the south end of town, and you take a left on it."

The town was quiet as she drove along Clayton Way, and just when she thought she'd missed the street as the town limit sign came into sight, she spotted Twin Pines. The street was narrow, barely wide enough for two cars to pass each other. Boone's place was the only house at the far end. The two-story farmhouse painted a pale yellow with white trim had a wide porch and sat back from the road with a gravel driveway leading up to it.

"Keep going by the house and follow the drive to park behind it."

She finally stopped where Cooper had told her to, and before she could get out, the door to a screened-in part of the porch swung open. Boone was there, dressed more casually than she'd been used to, but he still looked good in jeans, a button-down white shirt and Western boots. The man always looked pretty near perfect.

He flashed her a smile as he hurried down the stairs and across the grass to grab her into a smothering hug before she could even shut the car door. He lifted her off her feet and swung her around before he put her back down. "You look great!"

"So do you," she said and hugged him again when she saw Cooper getting out of the car and coming up behind Boone.

Boone jumped when Cooper came closer and said, "Break it up!"

The two men faced each other, then gave each other man hugs and slaps on the back.

Boone looked pretty pleased with everything, and so was McKenna. It was interesting seeing the two men interact. Then Boone turned to her and said, "Let's go inside," slipping his arm around her shoulder and pulling her close to him.

"Is the clinic close by?" McKenna asked as the three of them walked toward the enclosed porch.

"Close enough for me to get there in three minutes but far enough that I can have privacy here."

Cooper kept quiet, but she couldn't read his face. "That's good that you can get away, sort of, when you need to."

"Yes, but sometimes I don't see the house for days and days."

They took the steps into the screened-in porch, which held a glider and a potted plant that had been dead long enough to look mummified. "I wouldn't let anyone see that plant if I were you. A doctor who kills plants is probably not a good idea," she joked.

Boone laughed and let her go ahead so she could precede him and Cooper into the house. "I'll have to let Agnes rest in peace, I guess."

She turned to him as he came through the door. "You named your plant Agnes? Really?"

He was grinning. "You bet," he said, then turned to Cooper. "I have another one named Bozo."

The surprise Cooper showed at those two names was priceless. He swung the door shut before he said, "No, not Bozo."

Before he could say any more, Boone spoke up, watching Cooper, but talking to McKenna. "He did some clowning at the kids' rodeos when he was a teenager."

"Dad asked me to."

"I know, but you're the one who got stuck in the barrel, and it took three men to get you out."

"It was small, and I was almost six foot by then."

"Yeah, that's what you told me when you got out."

Boone was enjoying himself, but Cooper simply responded, "Hmmm." Then he looked at McKenna and winked before he said, "You have a good memory," which she was quite certain was not what he'd really wanted to say.

When there was a moment's silence, Boone spoke up again. "How 'bout I make the three of us some coffee, and we can talk, then go to Elaine's for a late breakfast or early lunch?"

McKenna saw the moment Boone's plans registered on Cooper. It wasn't more than a few seconds before he got it, and no time lagged before he said, "I hadn't planned on staying. I just came to see you for a few minutes, then Max can give me ride back home. He's at the substation today."

"Oh, come on, Coop. It's been way too long, and now you're taking off after you barely said hello?"

"I'll be around longer in July, and we can catch up then. Listen, I'll let you two have your alone time. The last thing you all need is a third wheel. Max can get me coffee and a ride."

McKenna cut in. "You don't have to do that."

"I do. I want to. Since we made our deal, it's been shelved, and I really do want to be alone up there today. I'll be gone in a few days, and time's short."

She felt heat in her face. Their deal. She'd almost forgotten about it. "I'm sorry. I didn't think about that."

McKenna felt mortified that she'd so easily let herself forget about their deal again. Now he couldn't wait to get away. "Boone, are your guests still here?"

"No, it didn't work out."

McKenna looked at Cooper. "Then I can stay here in town until you leave. The house is all yours."

His eyes narrowed on her. "Darlin', I didn't say I wanted that. I made a deal, and I'll live up to it." He took out his phone and punched in his brother's number. All he said to Max was that he needed a ride back home from Boone's house. When he ended the call, he said, "He'll be here in five minutes."

Cooper looked at McKenna for a moment. "I'll see you when I see you. Enjoy your visit, okay?"

"Okay. I'll either be back to hike in the afternoon, or I'll be back by dark."

"Take your time," he said, then tapped the brim of his hat and went back outside.

When the door shut behind Cooper, Boone said, "You'd better tell me what that was all about."

She didn't fully understand what had just happened, so she stated the obvious, "Our deal was to see as little of each other as possible, and that hasn't been happening, mostly because of me. I even went with him to his friend's place last night and helped with an abused horse."

"You went to Luke's?"

"He called Cooper because he needed help, and I asked to go along."

"McKenna, sit down and let's talk."

She sat by the huge wood table in the center of the kitchen and looked out the windows above a farm sink that was so large that she could have taken a bath in it. The house felt comfortable, but she felt edgy.

"I'll stand, at least until Max picks Cooper up."

"Okay, being the great doctor that you are, you can stand and talk at the same time."

He was going for a very poor joke, and she tried to manage a bit of a smile. "I have skills," she murmured.

"Now, tell me about how you and Coop are doing," Boone said.

MAX ARRIVED IN under five minutes, driving a very plain black truck with heavily tinted windows, and he didn't ask Coop any specific questions until they were driving along the main street of town. "Max, do you have any contact with Jimmer Stucky?"

"Not a lot, but I see him around town, and a few months ago, Dad bought a picnic table from him. It's real nice. He's handy with wood."

"Could you call him for me?"

Max made a turn Cooper didn't expect. He pulled the truck off the main street and into the parking lot behind the sheriff's substation. He stopped and turned to Coop. "What's going on?"

"I don't want anyone, especially Danny's kid, to know I'm around town. I've only got a handful of days before I'm leaving again, and I need to get something for the old house."

"Man, I thought you were in some kind of trouble, sneaking around town. What do you want from Jimmer?"

He'd come to a decision while he'd trailed Boone and McKenna through the porch and into the house. They'd passed an old glider, and he'd remembered McKenna's suggestion that a glider would be great on the porch with pillows.

"Quick version. I want to get a glider to put up at Grandpa's house and need to know if Jimmer makes gliders and if he has any available right now. If he only does custom, it won't work. I want it here and set up by the time I have to head back on the circuit."

"Lillian should have Jimmer's number."

He put a call in over the radio, and his dispatcher answered. "Lil, I need a number for Jimmer Stucky." He grinned. "No, he's doing good—not in any trouble as far as I know. I just need to ask him something." He listened, then said, "Send it to my cell phone."

The number came to Max's cell in under a minute. "Dang, that woman's good."

He put in a call to Jimmer. "Hey, Jimmer, it's Max Donovan—" He cut off, then said, "No, nothing like that, unless you want to confess to something." Coop heard the laughter on the other end of the line. "I just want to find out about your new business, the outdoor furniture you're making."

Max put the call on speaker so Coop could listen. It went well, and Jimmer had three gliders ready to go. He had a dark wood glider with horse heads carved into the armrests, but it was a glider on chains that you attached to the ceiling or framework like a swing. The other two were more plain. Jimmer offered same-day delivery, including setup. He'd add free cushions with any purchase.

Max hit the mute button. "Which one?"

"The horse head with chains and tell him I need really nice red seat cushions."

Max tied up the deal for delivery to the ranch in one hour, and he made it in cash. Then he drove Coop up to the old ranch. When Jimmer showed up, Coop stayed inside until the delivery was complete and the payment made. After Jimmer had driven off, Coop came out to look at his purchase, and the reality of the glider was even better than he'd hoped for.

A box stood unopened beside the glider. "What's that?" Coop asked.

"Oh, the red cushions. He said they're the best he had."

Coop smiled. "Perfect."

WHEN MCKENNA AND Boone stepped out of the Over the Moon Diner around noon, she was feeling good. The visit with Boone had been great, catching up on everything and hearing about his plans to build a hospital in Eclipse. He'd asked again about her maybe wanting to partner with him, but she didn't see that happening, at least not for a long while. She loved the rhythm of the town that was partly built for tourists—people looking for a Western experience or a nature getaway—but whose rhythm seemed to come from the base of the population—people who had worked the land for years and years, who were born and raised here, generation after generation. People who loved it. But she had her life back in Boston.

McKenna drove back to the ranch while Boone went to work. She was thinking of a short hike, maybe just on the Donovan land. The day had been great so far—if she took out the fact that Cooper had left so abruptly that morning. She hadn't understood why he'd done that, not when he'd asked to come along.

As she got closer to Twin Arrows, she found herself hoping that Cooper would be at the house. She wanted to tell him about her visit, about Boone's plans, and she wanted to figure out why he'd acted the way had. She slowed and made the turn onto Twin Arrows. There were a few shallow puddles in the dirt, but the road had dried out since early morning, and the muddy puddles that had been there had drained away. The sky was vivid blue, and not a cloud was in sight.

Oddly, she felt as if she were going home, and as that thought solidified, she slowed the car without thinking about it. *Home?* After a handful of days? She laughed, a slightly nervous sound, and something caught her attention. Slowing, she saw movement in the coarse grass above a shallow ditch near the road. She caught a flash of white fur as she went by and realized it was a small white dog lying on the ground.

McKenna decided to pull over and got out. Cautiously, she approached the animal on foot. It wasn't moving. Another step, and she could make out black floppy ears and an irregular black circle around one eye.

"Hey, sweetie, hey," she said softly as she crouched down and tried to brush the weeds and grass away from the tiny body. The pup looked young and appeared half dead.

McKenna reached out to gently touch the dog's side, and she could feel faint, uneven breaths. "It's okay, it's okay," she said. "You're going to be okay."

The dog shocked her when it trembled, then sighed, its eyes never opening. Maybe it had been hit, but there was no blood, and although there was no mud around the spot, the puppy was smeared with it.

She looked around, scanning the area, but there wasn't a sign of another vehicle or even a house. She wondered if this land was Donovan land, too. A soft whimper drew her attention back to the dog, and she knew she wasn't going to leave it here. It would die for sure. She got up and went to the car, rummaged around, found an old T-shirt then went back.

She kneeled by the dog and gently rolled the pup on its side, pushed the cotton T-shirt under it, then rolled it back and swaddled it.

"Okay, baby," she said softly. "I'm going to take you to a nice house where you can get better. Trust me."

She got to her feet, cradling the puppy to her chest and hurried back to the car. She climbed in, laid the dog on the passenger seat and was grateful they only had a short distance to go.

She drove slowly. As they approached the gates, she was relieved they were open so she could drive right through and up the long access road to the house. No other car was there, but there were tire marks. Once she was by the porch, she jumped out and went around to retrieve the puppy. She cuddled it to her and whispered encouragement, as much for herself as for the dog.

"Just hold on, sweetie. I'll do anything I can to help you." She was relieved when she felt the animal move, settling closer against her body. "Good, good," she whispered the way she did constantly with a sick child. It seemed to work for the puppy, too.

She climbed onto the porch, saw something on it that hadn't been there before, but went right past it and into the house. She crossed to the couch and the hearth, calling out, "Cooper! Cooper!"

There was no response, and she wished so much he was there. "I guess it's just you and me, kid," she said and sat down cross-legged on the floor in front of the hearth cradling the puppy in her lap. "Let's just sit here and think what to do."

Then she had an idea and found Luke's phone number. She called, and he answered on the second ring.

"Dr. Luke Patton."

"Luke, it's McKenna Walker. I have a problem."

She laid out what had happened and how she came to bring the puppy home with her. He walked her through an examination of the puppy, and she sent him pictures. He diagnosed exhaustion and hunger, probable dehydration. He said he'd make up a box for her with what she'd need for the puppy, and she could pick it up anytime. He estimated her age to be about five months.

By the time she got off the phone, McKenna was feeling better, and the puppy was starting to stir. She slowly opened her eyes, looked around, and went back to sleep on a sigh.

McKenna just wished Cooper was there.

Like an answer to her wish, she heard Cooper call her name as the front door swung open and thudded against the wall.

"Over here," she called. "I'm so glad you're back."

"I thought you'd be gone longer," he said. "I went to get my bedding from the stable. I wanted to be here when you saw…" His words trailed off as he came to stand over her. "What've you got there?"

"A puppy. I found her on the side of the road, and I thought she was dead, but she's not."

"You didn't hit her, did you?"

"No, she was just there, and I couldn't leave her."

"Of course not."

He sat down on the floor beside her as she told him about her call with Luke. "I'm going to go down and pick up some stuff he put together for her, but first, she needs a name," she said. "Any ideas?"

"I don't know. Have you ever had a dog?"

"One. She was cute, and I could tell her anything. She was my only best friend."

"What was her name?"

"Scout. I named her after the girl in the Harper Lee book."

"Then why don't you call her Scout, after your old dog?"

"Scout." She tried out the name and nodded. "Yes."

"Good. Now that that's settled, I'll run and get the stuff from Luke. I'll get back as quick as I can," he said as he stood up.

"No, you can't go into town again."

"If I'm careful, I won't be noticed driving your rental, and to be truthful, I'm at a point where I almost don't care if someone sees me. I'm leaving soon, and if people show up at the gates or try to get onto the property, my folks have it covered."

CHAPTER TEN

COOP GAZED DOWN at McKenna holding the puppy in her arms. When it brought back its head and licked her chin, she was startled, and her laughter was like music to him. The smile that accompanied it touched something in him that he tried to ignore. He collected himself, and said, "I think she's gonna fall in love with you the way Bravo has."

He didn't add that he didn't blame the puppy or the horse. He didn't quite get how Boone could just be friends with her. Or maybe Boone actually did love McKenna but knew better than to push for anything more than friendship.

"I'll see you soon," he said and walked out the door into the clear afternoon.

He glanced at the glider that he'd been so anxious to show to McKenna, which she hadn't seemed to notice yet. The puppy had been her total focus. He ran a finger along the smooth wood of a carved horse's head on the armrest. It was the best combination of a glider and a swing. The brass chains that were bolted into the beams of the porch roof were impressive, and the red pillows looked great. Still, he'd felt a little bad relegating the old bench to the other side of the house. It held a lot of memories.

He went to the rental and headed out. When he got to the highway, he called Luke.

"Hey, just leaving to pick up the kit for the dog. It's breathing better, its eyes are open, and it licked McKenna's face," he said, remembering McKenna's laugh.

"That sounds good. I've got the box put together, and it has everything you'll need."

"Great. See you soon."

Coop made the round trip to Luke's and back in just under an hour, and by the time he was at the gates to the ranch, he was anxious. McKenna hadn't called him, and he hoped that was good news for the pup. Then, as he crested the access driveway and saw the house, he smiled. McKenna hadn't just found the glider, she was sitting on it with what he knew had to be the puppy wrapped in white on her lap.

He pulled in and parked by the porch. When he got out, McKenna didn't move, but she smiled over at him.

"Good, you're back."

"Is everything okay?" he asked a bit reluctantly because the white bundle in her lap wasn't moving.

"Very good," she said. "Scout's sleeping, but she's so much better now. Her breathing's good and she's warmed up."

That was a huge relief. "That's good news. I'll get the box from Luke."

"This is a beautiful glider you got, by the way," she said, smiling up at him. "It's really wonderful, like having a swing and a glider all in one. The carvings are so well done, and the wood feels like satin when I run my fingers over it."

He turned to get the box off the passenger seat in car, lifted it then looked back at McKenna as he nudged the door shut with his shoulder.

"I have a story about the glider, but I'll save it until we get the pup settled." He wanted to see her face when she heard where it had come from.

"Okay, I'd love to hear it," she said as she slowly stood and carried the puppy inside.

He followed and put the box down by the table while she went over to his bed and laid Scout on it.

"I hope it's okay for her to sleep there," she said as she turned toward him, looking expectant.

There was no way he'd tell her to get the dog off his bed. "That's fine."

"Good," she said on a sigh and crossed to the kitchen. "Why don't I make us some coffee, and we can sit down for a minute now that Scout seems more comfortable? I'd say she she's doing pretty good, actually. She drank some water out of a bowl while you were gone." McKenna almost glowed with what he knew had to be relief.

"Sounds good, darlin'," he said.

Sitting across from McKenna at his old wooden dining table, drinking coffee and talking with her about things he'd never thought about before seemed the perfect way to spend his last days on the ranch.

They drank their coffee and chatted. McKenna checked on the puppy a few times, finding it sleeping peacefully.

When he was almost finished his coffee, Coop remembered something Max had given him earlier: one of the special Flaming Coop D hats that his mother had introduced into his merchandise line. She'd pushed him to make women's hats, and he'd listened. They'd sold like hotcakes when they'd been introduced, and his mother handed out the hats to women who might need them.

He got up and said, "I almost forgot something. I'll be right back." Then he went outside, closing the door behind him. He broke into a jog after he took the porch step in one long stride, and he found the hat right where he'd left it in the stable by the hay bales.

When he got back to the house, McKenna had washed the coffee mugs in the sink and was drying her hands on a small towel. "Where did you go?" she asked.

"To the stables to get this." He held up the hat.

She tossed the towel on the sink counter, then came over to Coop. "You left your hat?"

"No, I left *your* hat."

"That's not mine. It's like one of the hats Farley showed me that day, and I saw the price tag. It definitely isn't mine."

"Let me explain. My mom has this thing she does with hats like this." He told Mc-Kenna about her gifting them to special women she'd met or heard about. It touched her. He held the hat out to her. "She wants you to have this one."

She stared at the hat, then took it and ran the tips of her fingers over the suede brim and touched the leather band wound around the crown. "It's lovely," she said.

"It's yours. She thought you might like to try it when you hike to block the sun in your face and on the back of your neck. She wears one all the time."

She put it on and looked at him. "It feels like it fits me, but I've never really worn one before. Well, yours at the canyon, but it was big."

"It fits you, but do me a favor and check and see where the tag is when you have it on."

"What tag?"

"The Flaming Coop D tag is burnished in the crown's lining at the back of the hat."

She slipped off the hat, turned it over and looked at it. Then she rolled her eyes. "I put it on backwards, didn't I? I had the tag at the front."

"Yeah, you did, and I thought I should tell you so you won't wear it like that in front of the wrong person."

"You saved me from embarrassment! Thank you for being so kind," she said and put it back on the right way this time. "How's that?"

"You got it."

"Good," she said. "Thank your mother for me, but I'm curious about something. I saw the price of the hat on the tag at Farley's. How much do you make on a hat? Like, what do you get from the sale of each hat?"

"Nothing. All the proceeds from my merchandise sales go to different charities."

She studied him and surprised him when she said, "You have a big heart, cowboy."

He tried to wave that off. "I make enough money from my work and this ranch, so I can give the proceeds away to help people who really need it, and I still have more money than I'll ever need." He felt embarrassed even saying that. "Please don't spread that around. I paid you a whole dollar to keep what I tell you between the two of us."

She smiled—a soft expression that made him feel awkward for a moment. "Cooper, I was talking to you about your heart, and as far as I know, that brings this conversation under the umbrella of patient/doctor confidentiality. So I won't tell anyone. Cross my heart and hope to—" She cut off her own words. "You get the idea."

He certainly did, and he trusted her to keep her promise. "I do."

When the puppy whimpered, McKenna was on her feet and by the bed before Coop could turn and look over his shoulder at her getting down on her knees. He heard her whisper softly, "It's okay, little girl. You're safe now. I promise."

When she slowly stood, he could see the puppy was stretched on her side and had apparently fallen back asleep. It seemed that McKenna had a good bedside manner, not only with children but with small dirty dogs that someone probably dropped by the side of the road and left to die.

When she came back to sit down across from him again, Cooper asked, "Is everything okay?"

She nodded. "I think so. She sure seems comfortable, but I hope it's okay that all she wants to do is sleep."

"Luke said to let her sleep as much as she wants, but to make sure you offer her the water he sent and to try to get her to eat."

"When she wakes up, I'll try to get more liquids in her and some food," she said. "She sure seems resilient. I didn't think she'd survive the short ride up here, actually."

"She's a fighter," he murmured.

McKenna got out of the chair, knelt by the box and reached inside. She took out a large plastic bag with medication in it, along with an oral syringe.

She looked up at Cooper. "Why the antibiotics?"

"Luke said it's just cautionary. He said to watch and, if she develops a fever, to use them according to the label."

"Thank goodness," she said, more to herself than to Cooper.

He watched as she pulled out jar after jar of pureed baby food, along with bottles of electrolyte water for infants, and a red dog collar that looked about right for Scout. A doggie sweater was in the mix—white knit with red hearts on it—along with a stainless steel bowl with embossed paw prints ringing its sides.

"Nice," she said and turned it over. Her expression turned to one of surprise. "Ha!" she exclaimed and held up the bowl for Cooper to see.

He leaned closer and saw "Scout's Equipment" stenciled on the bottom of the bowl by the supplier.

"How ironic," he murmured as she set it on the table.

The last item was a package of puppy training pads for the floor.

"Luke thought of everything," he said.

McKenna looked past Cooper and saw the puppy starting to sit up. "She's waking up," she said as she went over to the bed to pick up Scout. "Hello, sweetheart," she said, and he watched her put her hand on the pup's chest. "Her heart feels strong." She kissed the puppy's nose. "No fever. Perfect," she said.

Cooper made a suggestion. "Put her down and see what she does."

She gently set Scout on the floor. There seemed to be no weakness in her legs, but she shook slightly. She turned her soft brown eyes up to McKenna.

"What now?" Cooper asked.

"Water and food." McKenna turned to him. "I'll get a bowl for water, then try to see if she might eat? Maybe while I do that, she could sort of take her time getting used to the house, if you'll keep an eye on her."

"Of course."

He watched Scout start to slowly wander around the main room, and the more she moved, the more stable she looked. Her shakiness was gone quickly, and she seemed intent on sniffing every object she got close to.

McKenna finally went into the kitchen, retrieved the water bowl she'd used earlier, then went back to put the bowl on the floor by the table. She opened a water bottle Luke sent and filled the dish. Then she reached for a jar of baby food and read the label: "Chicken."

She looked at Cooper. "Do you think it's easier on her stomach to eat chicken, or would beef be better? There's iron in beef."

"Whatever one she'll eat, chicken or beef."

The puppy had circled back toward McKenna as she spoke to Cooper, and she stood very still, waiting to see if Scout would come to her on her own.

"Sweetie, how about some water?"

McKenna bent to put her forefinger in the water bowl and swirled the liquid to get the puppy's attention. Scout was three feet away when she stopped and sat down, cocking her head to one side.

"Water. It's good for you." McKenna clicked her tongue.

The puppy cocked her head from side to side, then abruptly stood and went straight to the bowl. With just a slight hesitation, she put head down in it and started drinking.

McKenna glanced up at Cooper. "She's so smart, isn't she?"

He shrugged. "Well, drinking water is pretty much a survival instinct."

"Buzzkill," she said and smiled. "She's intelligent." With that, McKenna turned back to watch Scout. As the puppy's drinking slowed, McKenna spoke to Cooper without taking her eyes off Scout. "I want to take her with me when I leave. Is that okay?"

"Sure, but I hate to point this out—how do we know she doesn't belong to someone and didn't just run away?"

She closed her eyes for a moment, then

looked right at Cooper. "Super buzzkill, cowboy," she said.

As she reached for the jar of food and opened it with a pop, he said, "I prefer 're-alist' to 'buzzkill.'"

She spooned some chicken puree into the feeding bowl. As it fell into the dish, she said, "I apologize. You're right." She looked at the dog. "Scout, how about some food?"

The puppy stopped drinking but didn't look at McKenna.

"Scout?" she said again. "Scout, sweetie. Chicken. It's good."

She nudged the bowl toward the dog. She'd barely moved it a few inches before the puppy came to the bowl. Scout sniffed and sniffed. Then she cautiously licked the chicken mush before she started to eat. She seemed to have her muzzle almost buried in the food, but whatever worked was fine as long as she ate.

"She's starved," McKenna said.

"I hope she doesn't bloat up from eating so fast," Cooper said.

"You're right again," she said, and got up on her knees to scooch closer, then reached for the metal dish. She was too late. The mush that smelled so awful had almost disappeared. "Shoot," she muttered and picked up the bowl.

The puppy turned toward her and suddenly dove at her, hitting her in the chest and literally pushing her back onto the floor. Then she climbed on top of her and started licking her face like crazy.

Cooper reached and scooped Scout up in one arm then stood, looking down at McKenna. "Small but mighty," he said with a wry expression. "She took you out." He held out his free hand to her. "Come on, darlin'. I'll take care of Scout while you clean up."

She grimaced. "I had no idea how bad that baby food would smell."

She took his hand, and he easily leveraged her up and onto her feet. Scout was content to be held by Cooper, who was the one to grimace now.

"There's definitely baby food in your hair."

"Great. I'll take a quick shower." McKenna reached to stroke the fur between the puppy's floppy ears. "Scout, you be good for Cooper," she said before she headed to the bathroom.

COOP CARRIED THE dog to the kitchen to get some paper napkins and tried to wipe her muzzle clean. She didn't seem to mind at all, and actually helped him by licking around her mouth and nose. Tossing the napkins in a waste basket beside the sink, he took the puppy over to the couch with him to sit down. With Scout on his lap, he stared at the bathroom door and listened to the shower running. Lightly stroking the puppy's back, he closed his eyes and whispered, "You're one lucky pup to have McKenna care so much about you."

There was no response because Scout was asleep again.

When Coop heard the faint squeak of the bathroom door, he opened his eyes. McKenna had stopped in the doorway, wearing her pajama bottoms and a tank top. Her hair was damp and combed back from her face. When she smiled, he thought he felt his heart lurch—not in an unpleasant way but in a way he didn't understand and figured he'd imagined it. A beautiful woman had stopped him in his tracks before, but this was different, and he pushed it aside.

"What a great picture you two make," she said. "Don't move."

She turned to go back into the bathroom and came out seconds later with her phone in her hand. She stopped a couple of feet from the couch, lifted the phone and took a picture, then a second one.

When she looked down at her phone, she grinned. "It's perfect."

She took a seat on the couch beside Coop. He would have rather taken a picture of McKenna in her pajama bottoms that were every bit as ugly as the others. Purple cows wearing bright pink tutus glided over full moons with cartoon faces. Her feet were bare, and with her hair slicked back like that, it accentuated her cheekbones. He liked it…a lot, along with the faint fragrance of flowers he caught in the air.

Tucking her feet under her, she reached to gently touch Scout's head. "How did she do?" she asked in a whisper.

"She went to sleep pretty quickly," he said, watching her stroke the puppy gently.

If the dog could have, she would have been purring. He looked at McKenna's slender, almost delicate hands and compared them with his own rough, calloused hands. McKenna's hands held life or death in them, making a huge difference every day in the world, but what was he doing? Making money. Making fans. Making some sort of a difference for eight seconds where he thrilled people, but that was gone as soon as the crowds filed out of the arena.

"Are you all right?" she asked.

"Sure, just appreciating Boone's taste."

When he looked up at McKenna, her green eyes narrowed on him. "Do you know that if you hold in laughter, you can have any number of medical problems?"

Coop shifted to face her a bit more directly without disturbing the dog. "Why would you tell me that?"

"I've never seen someone try so hard to not laugh as you were a moment ago."

He bet she could read her patients, even the babies, really well. He cleared his throat. "What medical problems?"

"Hiccups or headaches or ulcers, but worst of all, you can develop a very bad attitude that's accompanied by seriously terrible mood swings." Her eyes were twinkling now.

"Darlin', you had me until you threw in

the attitude and bad mood. That was over-kill."

She shrugged. "Okay, I added that at the last minute, but not laughing is a very bad thing for human beings. So just get it over with, Mr. Rodeo Champ."

He sighed heavily. "My name's Coop, just Coop, and now I can't laugh. I've never been a man who could laugh on command." He eyed the pajama bottoms again. "But looking at what you're wearing, I might chuckle. Not as funny as the others but worth a smile."

"It was Boone's first attempt years ago. Boone has a great sense of humor, and I love that about him. I'm really sorry for the af-front to your sense of taste."

Boone had a side to him that Coop had apparently never seen before. "I don't think I remember that type of humor from Boone."

"You missed out, then. He's all leather-jacketed, custom-booted, hair-styled-just-so handsome that he could stop any woman in her tracks, but he does have a strange sense of humor."

Coop finally laughed. "He's hidden it well."

Scout stirred in Coop's lap. She slowly sat up, looked around, then scrambled over to go to McKenna, who reached for her and cuddled her to her chest.

"Even during my internship, Boone could make me laugh when I needed it."

Coop raised an eyebrow in question. "He's pretty perfect."

"No, if only he hiked, he'd be perfect," she murmured.

He decided to ask her something he wondered about. "If Boone's nearly perfect, why did you two break up?"

She bent to kiss the puppy's head before she sat back and met his gaze. "I've told you that it just seems I don't have whatever it takes to be more than good friends. When Dalton ended our—whatever it was—you know, I was relieved. I finally got it. I'm good at being friends, but that's it."

"Hmm," Coop said before he caught himself. Quickly, he asked, "What else do you do for fun besides hiking?"

"Fun?" She said it as if she didn't know the definition of the word. "Um, I go out to dinner sometimes with friends, and I… I like to read—a lot—and I love old Western movies."

"That's it?"

"What do you do for fun? And don't tell me it's getting on the back of a crazed horse that wants to destroy you."

"Well, that sort of describes it. But I've always had other ways to have fun, although I've curtailed some of that to concentrate on what I need to do."

"You're not married, and you haven't mentioned a significant other, so I guess you've curtailed some things, but I doubt you aren't dating."

"Now, darlin', this is getting too personal," he said with as much of a smile as he could muster. "You don't really know me."

She was quiet for a moment, then shrugged. "I guess not, but I do know some things about you."

"Oh, is that right?"

"I think I know you're a kind person."

"I am?"

"You're letting me stay for the full two weeks. You didn't have to do that. This place is all yours. You call the shots. You could have given me the bum's rush."

"Run that by me again?"

"You could have kicked me off your property if you'd wanted to."

He wouldn't dispute that. "Well, sure, but that'd be downright against the cowboy rule of treating a lady like a lady and never cussing around her."

She smiled. "You made that up, didn't you?"

"Not exactly. It's something my dad told us was in the official cowboy code."

Her phone chimed, and she shifted to pick it up from the cushion beside her. After a glance at the screen, she looked at Coop with her eyes wide. "Danny."

He'd totally forgotten to tell her about where the glider came from. "There was some—" he started to say before she answered the call and cut him off.

CHAPTER ELEVEN

McKenna took the call. "Hello?"

"Hey, Danny here. I wanted to let you know that the trails are finally open, except for the Broken Wing route. So, you're welcome back anytime you want to come."

Cooper was watching her, and even Scout had turned to look at her quizzically. "That's good news. Thanks for letting me know."

"It's my job." She was relieved she could get off the phone with him now, but that didn't happen. He kept talking. "One other thing—are you busy tonight? I'd sure like to get you and Jimmer in the same room. I know you and him'd spark to each other real good."

She rolled her eyes. "I can't tonight, I'm busy. Sorry."

"Well, if you can't tonight, maybe we can talk about it when you get up here tomorrow."

"Thanks again for letting me know about the trails."

"You bet. Be seeing you soon," he said before he ended the call.

She sank back into the cushions, resting her head against the couch back and stared up at the ceiling. "Danny wants me and Jimmer in a room together so we can spark, or he can, or maybe I can. I don't know. It's like his mission in life to make sure we meet."

Coop chuckled roughly at that. "He means well."

"I'm not going to spark with anyone, much less a man named Jimmer with Danny Stucky as a father. For Pete's sake, what would Jimmer and I have in common?"

"Well, that's kind of what I wanted to tell you. I forgot about it when you showed up with Scout, but you have one thing in common with Danny's son."

"Oh, no, I don't," she said as she closed her eyes, trying to figure out how to get past good old Danny when she got to the gates in the morning.

"Yes, you do. Today after Max and I left Boone's, Max tracked down the glider I wanted for the porch. It was delivered and set up around noon."

She opened her eyes and cautiously turned to look at Cooper. "What do you think that Jimmer and I have in common?"

"The glider. I got it because you thought one would be nice on the porch, and Jimmer made it, delivered it and installed it on the porch."

She sat up straighter and blinked. "Is there a punchline coming?"

He shook his head. "No, it's not a joke. I had no idea the guy was so talented. All he thought about when he was a kid was playing football. He's a big guy. Who knew he'd be able to make something so intricate?"

"So, he knows you're here?"

"No, Max contacted him for me, paid for it and met him here for the delivery. They both left without Jimmer knowing I was in the house. All he knows is it was bought for use up here."

She let out a breath. She hadn't realized how tense she'd started to feel after Danny's call, but now that it was over, she wanted to be outside. It was near sunset, but there was enough daylight left for her to walk with Scout.

"I think I'll take Scout outside and see how she does."

At the mention of her name, Scout looked up. Then she turned and jumped off the couch. She hesitated for a moment before crossing to the puppy pad by the bathroom door. Stepping onto it, she made two circles, then squatted and did her business.

McKenna almost clapped but controlled herself. She was impressed, but she didn't want to scare Scout, so she settled for saying, "Good, good, Scout. Good girl."

She turned to Cooper. "Did you see that? I told you she's smart." She grinned and watched Scout start to make the trip around the room the way she had the first time she'd been placed on the floor.

Cooper drew her attention. "So, I take it you're going hiking in the morning."

When he mentioned it, she realized there was no way she could take off for an entire day to hike. "I told Danny that, but I can't go. I can't take Scout, and she can't be left alone."

"She won't be. I'll be here. I'll keep track of her."

His offer was unexpected, and she wished she could accept. Cooper had been great ever since she'd brought Scout to the house, but she didn't want to leave him to puppy sit. "I really appreciate the offer, but I can't leave."

"I've worked with Dad and my brothers around animals a lot. Believe me, with her, it's simple—eat, drink, sleep. She's no two-thousand-pound horse."

McKenna almost took his offer, then realized she didn't want to be away from Scout for too long. "I appreciate that offer, I really do, so maybe I'll do a morning hike, then take the afternoon off."

"If that works for you. I just thought some hiking therapy might be good."

She was a bit surprised that he remembered. "There's a short trail that looks interesting. Maybe I can do that. For now, I'll take Scout out to see how she does."

Abruptly, the puppy stood up and jumped down off the couch. But it wasn't for another visit to the pad. Scout looked around, then started across the floor toward the front of the house.

"She seems strong enough, despite what she went through. I mean, it's like a miracle, but I know a long walk wouldn't be possible with her."

McKenna heard a soft whine and turned to look over at Scout, who was standing by the door looking back at them, her tail wagging furiously.

"Do you think she wants out?" McKenna asked Cooper.

"It looks like it. Maybe she heard the word walk, and that triggered her to go to the door."

McKenna had been ignoring what Cooper had said earlier about Scout possibly being a runaway and having family who were worried about her. Getting attached had been too easy for McKenna, but she knew she had to consider that someone might be looking for her and do the right thing.

"It would save potty pads," she murmured. "I'll go and watch her for a bit," she said.

"Okay, I'll go and check the horses," he said as he stood.

She scrambled to her feet, wanting to say she and Scout would tag along with him, but he'd probably had his fill of both of them for the day. She went over to the door while Cooper picked up two apples. When she opened the door, the puppy hesitated, then cautiously stepped out onto the porch to sit down and take in the strange place she'd never seen from the outside.

Coop went past them, saying, "Keep her close," over his shoulder as he jumped the single step down onto the ground to start off in the direction of the stable.

McKenna sat on the glider and didn't think about Jimmer one time as she watched Scout finally start to slowly walk around the porch. When she stopped at the single step, she sat down again and looked at McKenna. For some reason, she wouldn't take the step down.

"Okay, sweetie, I'll help you."

She realized she hadn't put on her boots and walking on the rough ground through grass and weeds wouldn't work. She hurried back into the house to grab her boots and carried them outside.

She stopped when she saw Scout had gone

down the step after all. Now she was sitting on the ground doing the same thing she had earlier, just looking around. A cautious animal. McKenna quickly put on her boots, and Scout looked up at her when she arrived at her side.

"Brave girl, Scout," she said, bending to pat her head.

By the time McKenna saw Cooper coming back, Scout had explored an ever-expanding area in front of the house, and the sun had dipped below the horizon. Shadows were gathering, but the sky was coming alive with stars and a moon that looked almost full. Its light bathed the land in a silvery glow, showing details but a lack of color. It was beautiful.

"Luke called," Coop said as he got close to them. "He wanted an update on Scout."

The puppy was sitting down again, watching the two of them.

"What did he say?"

"He's very happy. He figures there wasn't abuse, or she would have been a lot weaker and would have taken much longer to get up and walk around. It looks like she just wore herself out trying to get somewhere."

"So, she's just lost?"

"Probably. He said he knows about most of the animals that go missing, but so far he hasn't heard about a dog that matches her description. But he'll ask around. He asked if you could send him a picture of her so he could put it up in town."

McKenna was hoping that no one would turn up to claim Scout before she left so that Scout could go with her to Boston. But that also meant someone who cared about the puppy might never see her again.

"I have the picture I took of you two."

She opened her phone and pulled it up. It was even better than she'd thought, with Cooper's big hand laying gently on the small puppy's back. He wasn't smiling, but there was a softness in his eyes that she was pretty sure wasn't part of his Flaming Coop D image. She wouldn't share it.

"I need to take a picture of Scout that shows her body and markings. Where do you think would be best to do it?"

Cooper picked the puppy up, took her to the porch and set her down on the glider's red cushions. She sat there looking up at him, then turned her attention to McKenna as she stepped up on the porch.

"She'll show up really well against the red and the dark wood."

"If she stays there." McKenna went closer. "Maybe you could sit by her."

"As long as I'm not in the picture."

"I'll crop off your head," she said.

"Said no woman ever to me."

McKenna smiled as Cooper sat down beside Scout. "I'll take your word for it."

When the puppy looked up at Cooper, McKenna saw the expression in his eyes that she liked so much in the first photo. She liked it that he liked Scout. She quickly took the picture. The white dog showed up perfectly against the dark wood background. But Cooper was definitely in the shot. She studied the photo.

"This is a good one," she said and quickly edited the picture to center it on Scout without Cooper showing. She saved it as a second photo, leaving the original intact, and sent it to Luke.

When she looked up, Scout had shifted closer to Cooper, resting her head on his thigh with her eyes closed. McKenna went up to sit by Scout and showed Cooper the edited photo.

"You'd never know she was the same puppy you found hours ago," he said. "Even her fur looks cleaner."

"I'll clean her up more tomorrow when she's more used to this place."

McKenna put her phone away, and as she leaned back, Cooper started the glider moving slowly.

"This is just perfect," McKenna said on a happy sigh. "I can't believe you retired the old bench and got this in its place. I'll really enjoy it while I'm here."

"It'll be waiting for you for whenever you come back."

"Oh, no, I've intruded on you too much as it is." She looked out over the land "You're very fortunate to have all this."

"You're welcome to come back here whenever you need to make sense out of your life. It sure does that for me."

She couldn't believe he was making an offer that might just go beyond the last offer she'd accepted, to stay here for the full two weeks. The idea of being able to take off and come here whenever she needed to recharge was beyond being kind.

"I appreciate you being so generous, but I don't think I'd be able to do that."

"Keep it in mind?"

She nodded, but not very emphatically. She'd always remember the ranch, but life had a way of getting in the way of wishes. "If I lived around here, I'd jump at it. Shoot, I'd help Simply Sanctuary muck stalls if they needed it. It's such a wonderful thing Luke and you are doing."

That brought a slow smile from Cooper. "Too bad Boston's so far away. Luke would sure take you up on that."

She couldn't take her eyes off him. "I imagine you do a whole lot more for Luke than you'll admit to, beyond helping out financially, like sneaking into town to help him with a horse."

His smile faded and she regretted that. "I do what I can, but I'm on the road for long stretches during the year, and the burden's on him."

She had a thought that she realized had been nudging at her, and right then, it became a rational idea that she actually felt a touch of excitement about sharing. "You mentioned before that Luke could use more space for the rescued horses."

"Yeah, Luke has land around his place, but it's a small plot, and when there's a lot of traffic in town, the noise carries. It's not very peaceful for the horses."

"What would it take to turn this place into a sanctuary for the horses during their rehab? That would expand the available space, and no one really lives up here."

He stared at her hard, then blinked. "Here?"

"It's so quiet and calm. I can almost feel the peace just by stepping onto the land. Don't you think an animal could feel it, too?" He didn't respond, and she kept talking. "I'm sorry, I don't have a clue how much money it would take to start that up here, or even if your family would want that sort of thing on this land. It's just an idea."

"I think they'd be on board," he finally said. "The money, it could be expensive, but I know a lot of people around here who would cut the costs a lot by making donations or volunteering."

"Then you think it could work?"

Scout stirred, lifted her head to look around, then turned and scooted closer to McKenna. With a sigh, the puppy stretched out and laid her head on her front paws.

Cooper didn't answer right away but sat forward to rest his forearms on his knees and cast her a sideways look. "It's a possibility."

"Honestly?"

"Yes, but I'd have to clear things with my family and Luke."

"Of course, I understand. It's their land and their home."

Coop saw the glow of excitement in McKenna's eyes and wanted to give her a definitive answer, which would have been a resounding yes if only he were involved in the decision. "This is mine. This is my home, my getaway for when I need one, and it never occurred to me to use this land that way. But it would be the answer to any number of problems affecting Simply Sanctuary. You've been here a matter of days, and you saw it clearly. It's a brilliant idea."

She exhaled, and then a smile came, a beautiful expression that lit up her eyes. "Brilliant? You think so?"

He knew he was staring at her, but he didn't want to look away. "Yes, I do."

Her eyes widened. "So, you'll think about talking to your parents and whoever else has a say in this land?"

"This land up here is Caleb's, Max's and mine. We inherited it when my grandparents passed. I can tell you without having to talk to the two of them, they'll agree to using it for the sanctuary. Mom and Dad will get behind it, too."

"Gosh, that's great. I want to help, but since I'll be heading back to Boston soon, maybe I can help monetarily."

"No, that's not going to be a problem."

"If it's needed, I have a good investment portfolio, thanks to my parents, and I'm not planning on retiring for a very long time. If the money could help, it's available."

He loved that she'd made that offer, but he wouldn't take money from her. There were a few things he felt he should explain.

"How much do you think this land, the way it is, is worth?"

She shrugged her slender shoulders as she started to stroke Scout's back. "I don't know. How much land is it?"

"Around a thousand acres up here. Grandpa got out of the Army after the Second World War, headed here and got this land by making a deal with the family that owned what became our main ranch down below. The deal was that he would work all the land, then split the profits from breeding cattle or horses, and any crops he raised. In ten years, he made an offer on the whole parcel, and it was accepted. He paid forty thousand dollars, and that was a fortune back then. He kept his family up here in the house for as long as it took to get below and build a bigger house for his boys and his wife."

McKenna appeared fascinated as he told the story that he'd heard so often over the years. She said, "I already thought your grandpa was an incredible man. Now I know I was right."

"Yes, he was," he murmured, memories of his grandpa flooding over him, and for the first time in a very long time, he felt the weight of what the man had done for his family and what he'd left behind for them when he was gone. "We've had offers from developers for this land that would let all of us retire right now and never have to work again. But it won't ever be sold. I know Grandpa would love the idea of rescued horses roaming it in peace and safety."

He was taken aback when he saw McKenna swipe at her eyes. "If you ever need me to do anything to help, please let me know," she said. "Scout and I owe you."

At the sound of her name, the puppy stirred and looked up at McKenna. She whined, and McKenna picked her up to cuddle her to her chest. "Would it be okay if I call every once in a while and see how things are going with the sanctuary?"

"Sure, but Luke's the one who'll know what's going on. He'd be the one to call."

The puppy she'd rescued would never understand what the gentle woman holding her had done for her. But he was pretty sure she'd love McKenna for as long as they were together. He exhaled. It was pretty easy to imagine a life with McKenna. If things were different, maybe he and McKenna could have had something.

But he knew when she left here, that connection wouldn't survive. She seemed pretty adamant about relationships being out of the question. Honestly, he had to admit that was his position, too, as long as he was on the circuit. He wouldn't bring anyone into his life without a clear understanding between them that anything they had could be no more than temporary. He'd learned the hard way it was easier to just keep his eyes down and do the best job he could.

She bent to kiss the puppy on its head, then looked at him. "Can I ask you a favor?"

Her auburn hair was still a bit damp, and a single curl was clinging to her cheek. He had the urge to reach out and gently tuck it behind her ears. But he didn't.

"What favor?" he asked without moving.

"I need to get dinner started. If you could watch her, I'd appreciate it."

No matter what she would have asked, he would have said yes. "Sure."

Sitting outside on the glider with Scout was just fine by him. In fact, maybe being alone with the puppy would be a good thing. He could breathe and relax and get his thoughts in line without McKenna close by.

"We'll stay out here and bond." When he saw just a flicker of amusement in her light green eyes, he knew staying outside for a while really was best for him. "I'll keep a good eye on her."

"How does meatloaf sound, with some vegetables and rolls?"

"That sounds good."

She glanced around at the night that was turning silvery in the glow from the moon. "I think the horses will do well up here," she said.

"I know they will, thanks to you."

"You and Luke are the ones who'll make it happen if it does."

"One way or the other, we'll try," he said.

"I know you both will, and I'm incredibly happy about that. Maybe you can send me some pictures of the sanctuary when it's up and running."

That wasn't what he wanted, just pictures and a few phone calls. "Why don't you come back to see for yourself? Then stay to hike. If you get to keep Scout, bring her, too, and let her run."

Whatever hint of a smile he thought he'd seen in her eyes was gone, and she looked sad. "You think Luke will find her real owners if they're out there?"

"He'll do his best."

She exhaled and her voice was just above a whisper. "That's what I thought." She looked down at Scout, the sadness still in her expression, and then she turned to head toward the door and disappeared inside the house.

She was sad. He knew why. She was upset about the possibility of the dog being claimed by someone else. In a few short hours, she'd already invested so much in Scout. It was a love at first sight kind of thing between her and the puppy. But if someone didn't claim Scout, McKenna wouldn't be able to go on her hikes after he left. There was no one to take care of the dog while she was still here, and Scout couldn't stay alone.

Coop heard McKenna moving around in the house as he stared out at the night. Hiking was why she came, because she needed her "therapy." He figured Boone knew her better than anyone and understood how much she needed this time for herself with her hiking.

When his cell phone rang in his jeans pocket, he tried to shift to retrieve it without waking Scout. He did and saw the caller ID. The name Big Matt came up, the nickname he'd given to Matt Arness years ago when Coop had signed with him to be his manager and agent. The small icon by the name showed the face of a fifty something guy with a handlebar mustache as red as what little hair he had left on his head.

"Hey, Matt. What's happening?"

Matt had come into the picture when Coop was within breathing distance of his first championship and had stuck with him ever since. He was the main reason for most of Coop's financial success and for building his image.

"How are those ribs?" Matt asked without a preamble. "Givin' you any more trouble?"

"Nope. No pain at all and full range of movement."

Matt exhaled. "Just what I wanted to hear."

"Is that why you called?"

"I need to talk business."

"Okay, but make it brief."

Matt started talking quickly, the way he did when he was enthusiastic about making more money. "I just got off a call with Donny Jackson from the T. S. Gunmen Rodeo in Fort Collins, Colorado. He's opting to have his big show the week before the Fourth of July but well before Cheyenne."

Jackson ran one of the oldest and best rodeos on the circuit. "Why did he call you?"

"To make you a last-minute offer. He wants you there to be the draw for the saddle bronc ride that's the big finale on the last day." Matt named the dates, then said, "He's willing to pay for whatever prep you need to get ready, any extra practice and any needed equipment. But he needs you to be there early for PR, and that means full media access to you from beginning to end."

"Who else is competing?"

"Wheeler and Brand are on the ticket—terrific crowd magnets."

Wheeler was a veteran bull rider with more than a few championship wins and was older than Coop by two years. He'd heard of Brand, who was younger, starting to get a lot of good word of mouth about his bareback bronc riding. He was becoming the golden boy of the moment.

"What's my package worth?"

Matt gave him a summary of the money involved, and it was a very good deal. Also, there was a prospective sponsor who wanted to sign him. The money was better than nice.

"Check it all out, and if it's real, make the deal for the sponsorship and with Jackson," he told Matt.

"Money designation?" Matt asked.

"First, I need a new account set up with Luke Patton having full access. Name it Sanctuary Two. I'll talk to you about it when I see you."

"None of the usual split between charities?"

"Not this time. You take your cut, and everything else goes into that account once, then back to the usual splits."

"Okay, get packed up, and I'll meet you in Fort Collins tomorrow afternoon for signatures and to get your PR schedule going."

As Matt said that, Coop knew what he was going to do, and it wasn't leaving tomorrow. He'd promised McKenna to help her with Scout, and he'd keep that promise. "No, I can't meet you in Fort Collins tomorrow. The earliest I can meet is in two more days."

"That makes everything tight. Why can't you do it sooner?" Matt asked.

"It's personal. I just can't leave early. That's not negotiable, so don't even try."

Matt knew when to give in, and he did. "Okay, I'll meet you in Colorado in two days, but swear that you staying there's got nothing to do with an injury."

"Nothing to do with my physical condition."

He heard Matt exhale over the line. "Okay, okay, okay, I'll tighten up your schedule for when you arrive to make sure you make the date."

"I'll call when I'm leaving," Coop said as he heard the door open with a soft creak.

He glanced over at McKenna standing in the doorway. The light from inside seemed to halo her loose hair, making her look almost ethereal, as if he'd blink and she'd be gone.

Despite their deal that started with him wanting her to leave, now he was deliberately sticking to their deal of the whole week to help her with Scout. That was true, but he knew it was also for himself if he was being totally honest. If things could be different, he might have even ignored the early rodeo and stayed longer. But they weren't different.

"Dinner's ready," she said. "I hope you like it."

He gathered Scout up in his arms, then stood to go to McKenna. "I'm sure I will."

"I hope so. I'd really hate to disappoint you."

Coop thought that she hadn't disappointed him once so far, a rarity amongst the women who'd come and gone in his life over the years.

"Darlin', if the food tastes as good as it smells, you've got a winner."

CHAPTER TWELVE

SCOUT SLEPT UNDER the table all through dinner, resting her head on Cooper's boot while he and McKenna talked mostly about the idea of the old ranch being repurposed and turned into the second Simply Sanctuary. During that time, McKenna had a vague sense that he had something on his mind, but by the time they were done, he'd grown quiet, focusing on his food. She just hoped he hadn't spoken to Luke while he'd been outside. If that was the case, he could be holding back the news that Scout's owner was coming to get her. Why he wouldn't just come out and tell her, she didn't know.

Cooper reached to stack their empty plates and put the two mugs on them, along with the silverware. "If you'll get Scout off my foot, I'll clean up while you go out and enjoy the glider for a while."

She needed to know before she went outside. "Did Luke call you about Scout?"

"Nope."

"I guess no news is good news," she said.

"You really don't want someone to be out there looking for her, do you?"

That was so to the point that she didn't know what to say for a moment. But she wouldn't lie. "You're right, but I know the chances are that's what's going to happen."

"Maybe it's for the best."

"I know. The real owner deserves to get her back."

"Yes, they do, and if she stays here with you, how are you going to keep hiking?"

She slowly sank back down on the chair, and he hated himself for saying that. She looked stricken, and he wondered how she could get so attached to Scout in such a short time.

"I'll...figure it out."

"Don't worry about it for the next two days. That gives Luke time to talk to people, and I'll be here that long to watch her for you."

"Aren't you leaving the day after tomorrow?"

"I talked to my agent, and I don't have to leave until late in the day two days from now. Scheduling, you know. Maybe when I do leave, things will be settled with Scout."

Scout came out from under the table and looked up before she headed to McKenna, who quickly scooped her up into her arms.

"That's great news," she said as Scout started to lick her chin. "Yes, you're a good girl," she murmured to the puppy. At least McKenna had her for now, and that was all good.

"Go on out and enjoy yourself."

McKenna went out into the night with Scout and sank down on the glider. Again, Cooper had come up with something that helped her but cost him his time alone. She settled on the red cushions, but Scout squirmed to get loose. Reluctantly, she set the dog down by her, but Scout had other ideas. She jumped off onto the porch floor without missing a beat, then stopped, looked around and crossed to the step to climb down onto the ground.

McKenna stood up quickly, afraid the puppy would take off. But she simply went along the front of the porch, stopped, circled and did her business. Done, she headed back, going up the step and across to McKenna. Once in McKenna's lap again, Scout leaned into her chest with a sigh.

"I'll never forget you."

It seemed bittersweet to sit out there with Scout and just absorb the moment. She didn't know how long she'd been sitting there when the door opened. Scout was instantly aware of Cooper's presence and jumped down to run over to him.

"Hey, there," he said to the puppy as he crouched in front of her. "Dang, you look as if you swallowed a bug and enjoyed it."

"What does that mean?"

He straightened up and raked his fingers through his dark hair. "That she looks smugly happy, like a pig wallowing in good mud. True bliss."

"Oh, I should have known that," McKenna said as she stood up.

Scout looked from one person to the other, then went down the step again onto the ground. This time she sat down as if studying the view.

"Pretty slick getting around," Cooper murmured.

"She sure is."

Abruptly, he said, "Luke called."

She felt her chest tighten. "What did he say?"

"Scout's yours."

She thought she had to have heard wrong. "I don't understand."

"Sit and I'll tell you what Luke found out."

"No, just tell me, please."

"Okay, Luke called a few people in town, and it seems there was a family traveling through here about three days ago. They're from Texas, and apparently they stopped on the side of the highway just past Twin Arrows to check their tires. They had three puppies with them, and somehow Scout got out—probably a kid not watching closely—and they didn't realize they only had two puppies until they got into town. I guess they came back to look but couldn't find her, then they had to leave. They talked to Lillian at the sheriff substation and left their name and address in case the puppy was found."

"Oh," was all McKenna could say. "The poor people. They must have been frantic."

"I'm sure they were, but they were so happy to hear she was okay. Luke told them all about you, what you did for her and how much you care about her—that you probably saved her life. They decided that you should keep her. But they'd love it if you sent them pictures of her now and then."

"Really?"

"Absolutely, and they like the name you chose. She's all yours."

McKenna moved to the glider and sank down on the red cushions. Scout leaped up beside her, then scrambled into her lap, and McKenna drew her into a hug. She felt shaky and stroked Scout's back, trying to calm herself down, not just the puppy.

Cooper took the seat beside them, then unexpectedly shifted to put his arm around her shoulders. "Listen, darlin', you're okay, Scout's okay, and the world's still turnin'."

He started the glider swinging, then with his free hand touched her cheek to brush a wisp of hair behind her ears. Their eyes met, and for some reason, McKenna felt herself holding his gaze.

Cooper looked away. "I think I might

sleep out here tonight while I have a chance before I leave."

"Wild animals won't be roaming around, will they?"

"They'll mostly give this a place a pass."

She looked at him. "You're either a brave man or a crazy person. I'm not sure which."

"I've been called both, so take your pick," he said with a crooked grin that made him look younger in some way.

Scout sat up, then jumped off the glider and down on the porch.

"That's how she got away," McKenna said. Cooper still had his arm around her, and she let herself rest her head against his shoulder. "I'm so thankful how this worked out—the hiking, this place and now Scout. It's nothing I ever dreamed of but everything I would have dreamed of if I'd thought about it."

He shook his head. "That's another dog chasing its tail explanation, no offense to Scout."

"But what I said makes sense. What doesn't make sense is a dog chasing its own tail or a dog chasing a car. Tell me what a dog is going to do if it ever catches up with its tail or with a car? He can't drive a car, or bury it, and he sure can't eat it."

Cooper slipped his hand off her shoulder and sat forward to cast her a sideways glance. "That's a pretty fine question to just throw out there, darlin'," he said with an exaggerated twang.

She found herself smiling at him. "Dagnab it, you catch on quick, you old buckaroo."

Both of them laughed at the same time, a welcome sound on the night air. When the laughter drifted away, Cooper was smiling at her.

"If we had a lot of time, we could have a weekend binge-watching old Westerns."

"That sounds like a lot of fun," McKenna said as she stood. "I'll take Scout in and get us settled for the night."

His dark eyes studied her with an appraising look. "You know what? You look real happy."

"I am," she said. "This has been a great day all around."

"It has," he said, then surprised her when he simply said, "Hmm."

"What?" she said right away. "Don't do that. Tell me what you were going to say."

He stood up right in front of her. "Uh, okay, you asked for it. I was going to say to get in there, get your sleep. You look as tired as an old dog who has chased his tail too long."

"Wow, that's terribly offensive," she said in a mock sarcastic tone.

He touched her chin with the tip of his forefinger and murmured, "I'll take care of checking on the horses, and you take care of yourself and your new family member."

His eyes seemed so warm, matching his voice, and she stood very still. "I will," she said just above a whisper.

"See that you do," Cooper said, then turned and jumped over the single step down onto the ground and headed toward the stables.

McKenna stood there for a moment, wondering why Cooper Donovan was still single, or at least wasn't seeing anyone.

"What a waste," she muttered.

BY THE TIME Coop returned to the house, he'd been gone a couple of hours. He'd called his brothers and his parents while he'd been in the stable and told them about McKenna's idea. They'd gone through the pros and cons, and in the end, there were no cons. They all agreed to lease the property for a dollar a year to Simply Sanctuary. The development was his and Luke's territory. One stipulation was the old house was off limits—it would always be just for family.

Then he'd called Luke and gone over it all again. When he'd finished, Luke's silence was deafening.

"Luke, are you still there?"

He heard the man clear his throat, then say in a tone rougher than normal for him, "Yep, sure am. I'm just blown away by the offer."

"You're taking it, aren't you?"

"You bet. It'll make things so much better." He cleared his throat again. "I don't know how to thank you all."

"The only thanks the family needs is for you to keep doing what you're doing. Also, Dad mentioned that he wants to donate the construction of a new barn and stable. He'll talk to you about what you need them to be."

"No, he can't do that."

"He can and he will. We can also amp up the publicity so more people will know what you're doing and donate. The other thing is helping hands. You'll have them—volunteers and whatever specialists you need to do your work."

"Coop, I can't even imagine the difference this will make in what we'll have the capability to do."

When he'd made it back to the house, he'd hoped McKenna would still be awake. He had so much he wanted to tell her. But when he stepped into the shadows of the big room, nothing was stirring, not McKenna or Scout.

He heel-and-toed his boots off, then padded over to the couch just to check. Both McKenna and Scout looked sound asleep, McKenna on her side facing the fireplace and the puppy cuddled up to her chest with McKenna's right arm holding the dog to her.

He turned away, then went into the bathroom, quietly closing the door after him. When he came back out, the woman and the dog hadn't moved. He went closer and looked down at them. He almost turned and went to the bed, but he found himself whispering, "Are you asleep?"

Her eyes fluttered open, and she looked up at him. "Is something wrong with the horses?"

Shaking his head, he said, "No."

"You were gone so long."

He moved back to sit on the raised hearth so he could be closer to eye level with her. "I was on the phone."

He kept his voice low. He told her about everything, and she never interrupted. By the time he was telling her about Luke's reaction, he heard her sniffle softly.

"So, it's really going to happen?"

"Yep, but it's going to take time. If they can get the basic structures up and roofed before the snow comes, they can do all the construction inside over the winter. Hopefully, it can be open late next spring."

"I wish I could be here to see it all happen," she said in a slightly husky voice. "But just knowing it's going to save lives, that's enough."

"You're welcome here anytime."

"I know," she said, but didn't say if she'd come back to check it out.

"I told my mother that you came up with the idea. She said, and I quote, 'She really deserves that hat and so much more.'"

She sniffled again, and he stood and looked down at her. "You get your rest so you have energy for your hike."

"I hate to leave Scout, but I'm so thankful you'll be here."

He was, too. "Sweet dreams."

"They won't be any sweeter than right now," she murmured.

She was right. Having her here, talking to her in the semidarkness and knowing that he'd made her happy was pretty sweet for him, too.

As he settled in bed, he stretched out and clasped his hands behind his head. His life had taken a new direction from the moment McKenna had stepped out of the trees by the pond. The center of everything had shifted from him and his work in favor of a woman he hadn't even known a week—and her dog. With that thought, he closed his eyes and lay there in the silence, wondering why everything had happened the way it had.

COOP KNEW HE was asleep, but a voice was there, soft and gentle. "Oh, sweetheart, you're so wonderful." A soft chuckle ran across his nerves in the most pleasant way. "I love you so much. You're the best surprise, ever."

He didn't know who was saying that to

him, but he liked it. He liked being thought of as wonderful and the best surprise. Then something else was there, the voice saying, "Oh, no, no, no," and then someone was licking his face. Sleep was gone, and he knew exactly who the licker was and who the voice belonged to. He knew that voice hadn't been talking about him but about one small dog that was lucky enough to be loved by McKenna.

He opened his eyes as he rolled away from the licking and finally propped himself up on one arm. McKenna was lifting Scout up and off the bed, and he realized that it was still dark outside. As she moved back and put Scout down, he threw off the sheet and stood up.

In jeans, a red tank top and her hiking boots already on, she looked ready to leave.

"I already fed Scout and put fresh water in the bowl. Also, the pad by the bathroom is changed."

He raked his hair back off his face. "You're leaving now?"

"Yes. I was going to wake you up, but Scout saved me the trouble. There's a cell signal on most of the trails, so call me if there's a problem."

Cooper rotated his neck to work out some stiffness from the way he'd slept. "Sure. But things'll be fine."

The puppy had wandered over to the kitchen, then suddenly turned and ran at McKenna. But when she got close, she darted past her, then past Coop and jumped up onto the bed, stopping when she got to the pillow and flopping down on the sheets.

"You should get going. It's almost dawn."

"You're right." She hesitated, then came close to him and the dog. "You be good," she said and leaned in to kiss the Scout on her head. Then she stood back. "Thanks again."

"Glad to do it," Coop said and picked up Scout to carry her as he walked to the door with McKenna. She went out and across the porch to get to her car, and Coop watched until she was out of sight, heading for the gates.

"Well, it's just you and me, buddy. Be kind to me and behave yourself, and I'll do the same for you." Scout looked up at him and whined softly. "I know, you miss her. So do I."

MCKENNA HEADED BACK to the old ranch just after high noon, smiling to herself. The day had started out well when Danny Stucky hadn't been anywhere in sight while she logged in, then headed to Soaring Heart Trail. The hiking had been hard but worth it when she got to the halfway mark. The trail's name was perfect. When she'd found the turnout and gone another hundred feet up a steep incline, she'd stepped out into the blueness of the sky and a clear view of the world laid out far beneath her feet. She had that old feeling of being a conqueror fighting for the privilege of getting to where she hadn't been certain she could.

"I made it!" she'd yelled.

Things settled in her, and now in the car approaching the open gates to the ranch, she slowed for the turn. It almost felt like coming home, but it wasn't that. It was knowing that Cooper and Scout were going to be there to welcome her. She drove up the long road, and as she crested the rise, she saw the house. She was surprised Blaze and a pinto were secured to the hitching post. No human or puppy was in sight.

She parked the car at the end of the porch,

then went over to get a good look at the pinto. It was a beautiful horse, and she was pretty sure that a woman had been riding it. The saddle was different than the one on Blaze, maybe a bit smaller and fussier, with silver trimming the horn. A leather bag clipped to a metal ring on the back of the saddle had a fancy lock on it, and the leather was tooled with what looked like roses. Surely not something a cowboy would have used.

A lady friend, she surmised, feeling decidedly like an intruder. The thought of leaving and coming back later came to her, but she didn't want to do it. She wanted to see Scout, and if Cooper had a lady friend, she'd take the puppy and get out of his way. First, she had to find Cooper. She went up the step and to the door, almost knocking on it first but deciding to just open it. The door swung inward, and McKenna faced an empty room. No man, no visitor and no puppy.

She called out, "Cooper, I'm back," but there was no response.

They couldn't be too far away, probably at the stable or the pond. She'd guess the pond since the horses were left at the house. On her way down to the pond, she was anxious to see how Scout had done.

When she was about to step out of the trees into the open to look across at the pond, she heard laughter—a woman's laughter. It stopped her in her tracks. The truth hit her. Cooper had offered to keep Scout while she hiked so he could have the woman come up here, where they wouldn't be seen together. The two of them were sitting on the top step down to the dock, and the woman, with her back to the trees, was holding Scout up and laughing.

"She's precious," the woman was saying. From what McKenna could make out, she wore jeans, a denim shirt, a red Western hat, and she was enjoying Scout.

Maybe that was why McKenna didn't turn and retreat. She started across to them, called out, "Cooper!" When he turned at the sound of her voice, Scout squirmed out of the woman's hands, then pushed between the woman and Cooper to come flying toward her.

McKenna crouched, and Scout leaped at her, barely giving her time to catch her and hold her to her chest while the puppy began to frantically lick her chin. "Hey, sweetie, I missed you so much."

"She missed you, too," she heard Cooper say.

She looked up at him standing over her, wearing a white T-shirt and jeans, along with his familiar boots and hat.

Then the woman came up beside him, a slender woman with the brim of the red hat shadowing her dark eyes. "Oh, you must be the doctor," she said and smiled, showing fine lines at her eyes. She took off her hat, and McKenna could see that her dark hair confined in a braid was streaked with gray. She was older than Cooper, but her smile was radiant and warm.

"You really look lovely in that hat," the woman said.

"I love it. It's perfect for hiking."

Then Cooper spoke again. "I was hoping you'd get back in time. McKenna, this is my mom, Ruby Donovan. Mom, this is Dr. McKenna Walker."

She'd known the lady was his mother as soon as she'd seen her and noticed the resemblance: the high cheekbones, tanned skin and the eyes, darker than his but just as compelling. But the hat comment...that sealed it for her.

"It's so nice to meet you, Mrs. Donovan," she said, thankful that Scout had given up licking her face and had settled on resting in her hold. "Thank you so much for my hat."

"Ruby—call me Ruby. You deserve the hat. I wish you'd arrived fifteen minutes ago before Coop's father had to leave."

"They came up to talk to us about the plans for the second sanctuary."

"And we wanted to meet you, too, Doctor," Ruby said. "You were only here a few days, and we've been here on this land all of our lives, and not one of us thought about doing that until you did."

"I was fascinated by how tranquil it was up here and about Luke saying how peace and quiet was what the horses needed for the second half of their healing process. This ranch has all of that. It sounded like a good fit."

Ruby nodded. "It does, and hopefully we can get things started soon."

"I hope it goes well. I asked Cooper to send me pictures of the progress as it's being built and to let me know when it's going to open."

"You just come on back here and see for yourself."

"Mom, I told her that, but she's pretty busy back in Boston." McKenna glanced at Cooper to find his dark eyes on her and a slight smile touching his lips. "I have the impression this is the first vacation she's had in a very long time. She needs to do the vacation thing more often and not expect so much of herself."

Ruby hooked her arm with Cooper's. "Coop, my dear son, that sounds like you talking about yourself, sort of the kettle calling the pot black." She looked over at McKenna. "Ask Coop when he last took a vacation. Coming home to heal up or coming back here the morning of his brother's wedding and leaving that same night to go back on the circuit doesn't count."

"Mom, that's enough. Remember, you told Dad you'd be down soon, and he's waiting."

"Right. I'll go back to the house to get Jiggers, and then I'll head on down."

"I'll walk back with you," he said.

"The more the merrier," Ruby said and started for the trees.

Cooper reached to take Scout from McKenna and motioned her to follow Ruby.

"Your horse's name is Jiggers?" McKenna asked as they walked.

"Jiggers, because the mare was so nervous when we first brought her to the ranch, and Grandpa Donovan had a saying about having the jiggers when someone was really nervous. It fit then, but now she's calmer."

Coop's arm brushed hers as he walked on her other side, and she liked the idea of him being close. "Grandpa told her to rename Jiggers, but Mom didn't want to."

"No, I didn't. I wanted to keep the name to remember how she'd changed since being here."

As they approached the horses patiently waiting for them, Ruby stopped by Jiggers. "If you need someone to puppy-sit when Coop's gone, just ask. I'm always around down below."

"Thank you. I might take you up on that."

"You're very welcome to." She glanced at Cooper. "Don't take off without one last goodbye before you leave, you hear me?"

"Yes, ma'am, I sure do," he said.

Ruby mounted the horse in one graceful motion, then rode away toward the switchback.

"Safe ride, Mom," he called over to her, then went to the glider and sat down. He released Scout on the porch.

"I'm hungry," McKenna announced.

"How about I do bacon and eggs again, and you come and sit down while I make them? You can rest and tell me all about your hike."

That was the first time anyone had deliberately asked for details about her hiking, and for some reason, it seemed right that the person was Cooper. There wasn't anyone else she'd rather share with. That made her frown, because it was so true. Just one more day after today. That was it, and then whatever she was feeling, it would be over.

CHAPTER THIRTEEN

COOP SAT ON the glider as the afternoon dragged by. He was alone by choice, but he hadn't expected to miss McKenna and the puppy after they'd left to go to Luke's for Scout to get started on her shots. He'd thought he'd go for a ride while they were gone but ended up grooming both horses instead. He'd thought about swimming, but took a shower instead, and then he'd come out to sit on the glider before he did something else. Scout and McKenna had been gone for a lot longer than it took to get some shots.

He finally picked up his phone and made a call. It rang four times before McKenna answered.

"Hi, Cooper."

"So, how's it going down there?"

"Great. I got here just in time to watch a horse graduate from Simply Sanctuary. It's going up to Twin Bridges to its forever home. I suggested that Luke keep a list of every horse that makes it out of here and put it up for people to see, with the graduation date beside their name and picture."

"That's a good idea. How's Scout doing?"

"She's great. She's chasing balls with bells in them, and she can't figure them out. But she will."

"Yes, she will," he agreed, grinning to himself.

"I was going to pick up something for dinner before I come home. Is there anything you'd like from the diner?"

"I'm easy. You pick," he said.

"Okay, I'm getting ready to leave. I'm waiting on Luke to sign a card for the airline so Scout can ride in the cabin with me when I fly back to Boston."

"Then I'll see you when I see you, darlin'."

He hung up and sat there. He'd admitted pretty early on that he could fall for McKenna if he let himself do it, but now he knew he was teetering at the line he'd promised himself he wouldn't cross. So he wouldn't mess up what little time he had left with her up here.

He finally went back inside and saw the

old coffee percolator sitting on the stove. He filled it halfway, turned on the propane then went into the bathroom to get his razor and shaving soap. When the water began to boil, he stood in front of the old mirror at the kitchen sink.

"Time for a change," he said to his reflection, then lathered up. Ten minutes later, the man in the mirror was clean-shaven.

He heard the sound of a car engine off in the distance that gradually grew louder as it came closer to the house. He sat down at the table and stared out the window, watching the rental car pull up by the porch step. Making himself stay where he was, he saw McKenna get out, then open the back door and take out an animal carrier.

She was speaking, and although he couldn't make out her words, her smile said it all. The conversation with the puppy seemed to amuse her, and when the door finally swung open, he heard her say, "You're a car dog, and soon to be an airplane dog."

McKenna, in her blue tank top with jeans, set the carrier down on the floor and unsnapped the latch for the gate. Scout nudged it open and stepped out. When McKenna looked up, she spotted Coop at the table, and she seemed pleased he was there. That felt good, too good, and something settled in him. Getting tangled up in her had never been in his plans, and he'd leave while he still could without too many regrets.

"How did it go?" he asked, keeping any other questions to himself.

"Great! Luke's place is fascinating." Scout made her way over to her water. "He vaccinated Scout and signed the airline card so she could fly with me. He says she's in good condition, just a bit underweight, and he gave her a bubble bath."

Scout was back by them, and McKenna picked her up, then went closer to hand her to him. "Smell her," she said, and he caught the scent of what he thought might be cotton candy.

Taking her from McKenna, he held her up in front of him. "Cotton candy? Really?"

McKenna smiled. "You got it."

He put the puppy down, and she made a beeline to the pad by the bathroom door. "No clapping," he said to McKenna.

She looked at him. "I was thinking of one of the puppy treats that Luke sent back with me. He also gave me the carrier and a chew toy. He wouldn't let me pay for anything. Is there something we could get him?"

"Well, he is partial to bolo ties, red ones especially."

She sat down on the nearest chair by the table and took off her boots. "I'll see if I can find one before I leave."

"So, are you going straight back to Boston after your vacation's over?"

"I have to." She looked over at Scout, who was lying down by the carrier now. "Oh, by the way, Luke thinks Scout's a terrier with something else mixed in there."

"That sounds like as good of a guess as any."

"Whatever she is, she's sure smart and cute." She looked at Coop, and then her smile turned to a frown.

"What's wrong?"

"Nothing. I just realized you'd shaved."

"Uh, yeah, I shave every once in a while."

"I didn't realize you had a scar on your chin."

"Now, if you were a fan, you'd know I did, and you'd know that I got it from Caleb betting me I couldn't jump a water trough."

"Oh, sorry. You didn't make it."

"Of course I did. But I didn't land right and hit my chin. There was blood everywhere, but I won the bet, and he had to make both our beds for a week. Caleb said the scar was a great way for people to tell us apart."

"I don't imagine anyone who really knows the two of you would have trouble telling you apart."

"Mom and Dad always knew. We couldn't fool them."

"How about Boone?"

He chuckled at that. "We got him a few times. Did you pick up the food from Elaine's?"

"Yes, it's in a Styrofoam box on the passenger seat. It should still be hot. She assumed I was buying it for myself and Boone. Seems she knows Danny, and Danny mentioned me hiking up there and told her Boone and I were…you know."

"Yeah, I know." He got up and went to the door. "I'll go and bring it in."

When he came back inside, he was carrying the box, and McKenna was in the kitchen making coffee. He put the box on the table, and when he lifted the lid, the fragrance of barbeque rose in the air.

"This smells great."

"I was hoping you'd like it, because Elaine insisted I get it for Boone, along with coleslaw and corn. She threw in cornbread, too, because Boone likes cornbread."

"This is one time Boone and I agree on our taste," he said.

He took out a large container and put it on the table along with two smaller containers. While he put the box on the floor under the table, McKenna brought over plates and cutlery. He set the table and McKenna went back to get their coffee and some napkins.

When they were both seated and Scout had settled under the table by the box, McKenna opened the large container and nudged it over to Coop.

"Help yourself," she said, and when she looked at him, her eyes seemed overly bright, as if tears were close to the surface.

He didn't understand that at all. She'd been so happy when she got back, and he'd been happy to see her. Things had changed in the blink of an eye.

He took some ribs and some of both sides,

then looked down at the food on his plate. His appetite was fading, but he made himself start to eat.

The cell phone in his pocket rang, and he sat back and saw Luke was calling. He took the call. "Hey, Luke."

"Coop, I forgot to give McKenna my private number. I knew you'd have it, so you can pass it on to her. She wants to keep up with the progress of the new construction. I want her kept in the loop."

"I'll pass it on to McKenna," he said.

"Okay, I gotta go. Tell her I enjoyed her being here, and she's welcome anytime."

"I will." He ended the call and looked at her. "Luke forgot to give you his number."

"I have it. I took one of his business cards."

"No, his private number." He had McKenna's number in his phone, so he quickly texted Luke's number to her. Her phone chimed almost immediately. "That's it," he said. "He wants you to keep in touch."

"I really want to keep in touch with him."

"So, when you get back to Boston you're going straight back to work."

"Yes, I am." Eating ribs left sauce on her fingers and some on her chin. "I've been thinking that I'm not sure I want to keep doing what I do now. I love helping kids. But it's always emergencies, and I never really get to know them or their parents. It can be hectic, and it's life and death. When it all sorts out, I don't know if I want that to be my future."

"Maybe you're just suffering from a bit of burnout."

She was silent as she put her half-eaten rib down and reached for the napkins. "You know, maybe you're right." With her clean hands, she picked up her coffee mug, blew on it and took a sip. "I've never taken much time off."

"Why not?"

She put her mug down, then fiddled with her food, only taking small bites. "I remember my parents always talking about perfection when a life was at stake, that good enough wasn't good enough, and if a doctor couldn't hold up that standard, they didn't deserve to be a doctor. It really is life and death. I can't afford to not be better than good."

"In a different world, maybe everyone would be perfect, but we're in the real world. We're human. Believe me I want a win every time I'm in the arena, but I get bucked off...a lot. All you can do is your best. That's all any of us can do."

"That's easy to say," she said, an unexpected touch of sarcasm in her voice.

He could see the tension in her just talking about her parents, and he sort of understood why she seemed to be so hard on herself. Measuring up to her parents' expectations seemed to be her number one driver in life, maybe more so than personal satisfaction.

"I'm sure your parents are very proud of you." He hoped that was right.

She carefully set her fork on the edge of the plate and looked down at her remaining food. "I guess they are, as long as I keep the Walker name on the 'best in my specialty' list of pediatricians."

That wasn't what he wanted to hear, but before he could think of what else to say, she wiped her hands and finally, the spot on her chin, then tossed the napkin by her plate.

"I think I'll go to the trails around noon tomorrow. There's one closer that I hear is great and really challenging. It's called Split Moon. Is it okay with you to watch Scout in the afternoon?"

"That's okay," he said. His phone rang, he glanced at it then took the call. "Hey, Mom."

"Your dad and I have been talking, and we'd like you and McKenna to come down tonight for a barbeque. He's on his way back from Delany's Ranch, he wants to see you again before you have to leave, and he wants to meet McKenna. Tell her to bring Scout. Your brothers will be here, too, and I think Joy would like Scout."

"Hold on a minute," he said and pressed the mute button. "Mom's inviting us both down for dinner around seven. She really wants everyone to meet you, and she's inviting Scout, too. How about it?"

"We just ate," she said, a partial lie because half of her meal still sat on her plate. "I don't want to intrude on family."

"You won't be intruding. You'll be as welcome as summer rain."

She lifted both finely arched eyebrows. "That's so much better than being likened to a pothole."

"I love summer rain." His words were out before he realized what he'd actually said. "I mean, you'll be very welcome at the ranch."

"I'm flattered, and I really like summer rain so much more than a pothole."

He chuckled with just a bit of relief. "I'll never do that again. Promise."

"Okay, then I'll come along, although I probably won't eat much."

"Then fake it, okay? Dad's big on being the barbeque champ. Don't take his belt buckle away from him."

"I'll eat a bit so I don't offend him."

"Good plan. You'll also get to meet Caleb. He'll be the one with no scar cutting across his chin and soft hands from being a paper pusher for so long. Max is going to be there, too. You really should meet the county sheriff."

"I'm looking forward to it."

He unmuted his phone, let his mother know they'd be there and ended the call. "So, do you want to drive or go by horse and take the switchback?"

"That would be dangerous, wouldn't it?"

"No, it's all good. I know it like the back of my hand, and Bravo's been on it before when Mom was riding him during his therapy with Luke. He's good on the switchback. So, drive or ride?"

It took her a moment before she said, "I'd love to ride, but what about Scout? I guess we should drive."

She didn't seem happy with her decision, so he offered her an option that could work. "She's tiny enough for me to tuck her into the front of my shirt and let her peek her head out so she can see what's going on."

"You think so?"

"Yes, I carried small animals around like that back in the day. It works."

"Okay. Or I could do it in my shirt."

He glanced at her tank top. "I don't think so. The switchback isn't dangerous. We've all used it for a very long time, and nothing's happened. But if you're riding it for the first time, you shouldn't be distracted."

"Okay, point taken. What time should we leave?"

He checked his watch. "If you want to look around down there before dinner, we can leave as soon as you're ready."

"I don't have any nice clothes with me."

He chuckled at that. "Darlin', it's a barbeque on a ranch with a family where dressing up is wearing a button-down instead of a T-shirt."

"I can do that." McKenna stood. "I'll clear this up, then I'll get ready."

"No, go and do your thing, I'll put this stuff away. But, one thing, and it's important. Remember not to mention these ribs."

"Ribs, what ribs?" she said with a smile and went to get ready.

Coop quickly cleared the table and put away the remaining food. When McKenna stepped out of the bathroom, she turned toward him with her arms out wide.

"Is this acceptable barbeque attire?" She did a full turn to show off her slim jeans, boots and a dark green sleeveless top with silver buttons. She'd left her hair down and tucked behind her ears.

He took so long to answer, just taking in her image, that she asked, "It's wrong, isn't it?"

"No, no, it's very right. You look great."

She let out a sigh. "Thank you."

He finally moved, brushing past her to go into the bathroom. "Give me five," he said before he shut the door behind him.

McKenna almost backed out of riding down the switchback when she actually saw it from her saddle on Bravo. Cooper had Scout tucked in his buttoned-up red Western shirt with only her head and front paws showing. She looked perfectly content, which was a far cry from what McKenna was feeling. Cooper had laid out his rules for the ride: stay behind him, take it easy, don't rush, give Bravo her head and enjoy. He didn't seem to anticipate her abject terror at the idea of riding any horse down the packed dirt-and-rock path.

"McKenna?"

She heard Cooper but couldn't take her eyes away from where he expected her to ride with him.

"Let's go back and take the car."

"This is dangerous, isn't it?"

"We'll take the car," he said, and the next thing she knew, Cooper had Bravo's reins in his hand, leading the horse and McKenna back to the house.

McKenna let Cooper put the horses back in the stable while she sat on the porch step wondering how she could apologize for what she'd done while Scout ran about through the grass. When Cooper showed up, he walked over to her, his shadow falling on her as he stood there. "Are you okay?"

She kept her eyes down on her hands clasped tightly in her lap. "I'm sorry. I couldn't do it. I just couldn't."

"Hey, it's no big deal. Forget about it."

That hit a nerve. "The way you also had to forget about my freak-out during the thunderstorm? I'll never forget that."

He crouched in front of her, and she was startled when he gently cupped her chin and eased her head up until she either had to look at him or close her eyes. "You're okay, and this isn't anything. Come with me. I promise you'll have a good time. It doesn't matter how we get there."

He stood, letting go of her, and extended his hand to her. "Come on. Please."

She wanted to take his hand and never let go. But she slowly stood on her own, steadied herself, then looked at Cooper. "I don't know," she said.

He rested his hands lightly on her shoulders. "It's just between you and me. Remember, what happens here, stays here."

"You're so kind," she said.

He was very still, then he leaned toward her and touched his lips to hers. There was warmth and gentleness there, something so real yet beyond her comprehension.

She felt as if everything was put on hold at that moment, until his lips moved from hers, touched her cheek, then her forehead, before he gathered her into his arms and just held her. She leaned against him, wrapped her arms around his waist and felt his heart beating against her cheek.

A phone rang, Cooper's phone, and she felt his hesitation. He moved back and let her go, but his eyes were on her as he answered.

"Hello? Oh, Mom, sure. We'll be on our way in five minutes."

He ended the call and slipped his phone into his back pocket. "That's Mom. They're all there, even Luke. Will you come down with me?"

McKenna couldn't move for a minute, then she nodded and started for the car.

CHAPTER FOURTEEN

McKenna had worried that she wouldn't fit in at the barbeque, but the Donovan family had welcomed her and Scout with open arms. She saw another side of Cooper, watching his interaction with his brothers and the easy way he had around his parents. Dash Donovan turned out to be a big man with thick gray hair, strong shoulders and a smooth deep voice. He had to be in his sixties, but he looked as fit as a young man. What caught her attention was his connection to Ruby, his wife.

The two of them could have been newlyweds the way they stayed close, smiling at each other with some silent messages being exchanged between them. That was love, real love, and she envied them. She'd never know it. Love hurt too much, even getting close to it.

She sat down on a wooden slat bench and

glanced over at Cooper. He and his twin, Caleb, were talking about some horse their dad had just purchased, a white gelding named Streak. The two men looked alike side by side, but to McKenna, Caleb was less defined than Cooper, without that hard edge his twin had. She could tell them apart easily even without the chin scar.

Max was with his dad at the barbeque, wearing his uniform shirt and his badge on his belt. He was big like the Donovan men seemed to be, but with hazel eyes, and his hair was a dark brown. She'd been introduced, and he made a joke about his name being 911.

"Call me if you ever need me. You've got my number."

She laughed because it was funny, but Cooper kind of groaned.

Ruby was over with Harmony in a lounge area on a smooth rock patio that ran along the back of the large adobe brick house. The barbeque wasn't just a barbeque. It was a beautifully fashioned rock structure with two stoves, a double refrigerator, an open spit and a pizza oven built into it with seat-ing and two tables that could have held thirty people.

Caleb's wife, a blonde with flyaway short hair and beautiful blue eyes, and their daughter, Joy, were watching Scout running and playing, skidding to a stop, then taking off again.

The puppy made a break for her, and Joy, a toddler, clapped her hands and ran after her. The tiny girl stopped when Scout jumped up into McKenna's lap and pointed a finger at Scout.

"Pretty baby," she said, her blue eyes on Scout.

Caleb trailed after his daughter, then swept her up and onto his shoulder. "She's crazy about your puppy," he said, so much like Cooper but so much different. "It's real nice you're enjoying the old house. The whole Sanctuary thing is going to be terrific."

"I hope so. You have beautiful daughter."

"She is a beauty, isn't she? She kind of looks like her mother."

His wife, Harmony, came up beside her husband and looked at her daughter, who appeared to be playing a drum on Caleb's head. "Joy, don't beat up Daddy."

The little girl stopped, grinned then started again. Her parents gave each other a look that said it all. They loved her and they loved each other.

Harmony spoke to McKenna. "She's crazy about her daddy."

"I can tell. You have a great family."

"Thanks," they both said together and laughed.

Luke came up and asked, "Is it a good joke you want to share?"

She shrugged. "Joy's good entertainment."

Scout started to wiggle, wanting down, and she set her on the patio. Scout ran off, and Joy squealed with delight while both parents went after her.

Luke sat down by her. "Just wanted to make sure you have my private number."

"Yes, Cooper gave it me. Thanks so much. I'll keep in touch."

"Safe ride, McKenna," he said as he stood and smiled at her. "You're terrific." With that, he headed over toward the barbeque area.

She looked down at her hands. This family had the thing that her family hadn't. It was an intangible she hadn't been gifted with: they just plain loved each other.

"Can I sit down here?"

She looked up at Cooper. "Of course," she said.

He was beside her, but she felt a distance between them since the kiss. It had scrambled her thoughts, and then Cooper had acted as if it had never happened. She didn't understand why she'd reacted so deeply to a kiss, to him holding her hand, to him smiling at her. Now he was being polite, and she hated that.

"So, how are you doing?"

"I'm okay. Everyone's so nice. I'm glad I came."

He stretched his legs out in front of him. "Me, too. I love being here. The land changes and shifts as time goes by, but it's always there and always home."

She truly envied him. "Boston changes, too. I have a panoramic view of the city from the windows in my loft with a view of all the new construction."

His chuckle made her more edgy. "Were you born there?"

"Yes, and raised there. My parents' grants kept them there, so that was it. Then they divorced, and I was on my own while they went on with their separate lives. It was numbing seeing two people who should have loved each other tear each other apart. Ugly."

She made a face and continued. "I started hiking to get away from them. A friend had talked me into hiking for exercise, but what I found was victory. The minute I reached the top of the trail and the world was at my feet, I felt better than I had in a long time."

He listened to her, then said, "I see why you like it."

She looked up and saw Dash at the grill next to Ruby. He leaned down to kiss her cheek and smiled at her before he turned back to the grill.

"You know, I never saw my parents kiss or hold hands."

"My folks used to embarrass me when they'd kiss in public or hold hands in church."

He chuckled and gave her a crooked smile that that ran over her nerves in a unique way—not a bad way but a way that made her feel as if something else was going to happen. She'd never felt that before and was annoyed that her heart was beating faster.

She hesitated, then said, "I have my baggage, for good or bad, and some of it comes

from me not giving up easily. But I have to
say, when I know I should cut and run, I do
it. I've done it before."

"Not with your career."

"No, I meant personally. I'd never do that
with my career. No matter where I am, I'll
still be a pediatrician who really does love
what I do. I'm what I told you before—bad
at relationships. I don't understand them,
and I can't make them work."

"Maybe you never met the right person."

She looked down at her hands clasped
tightly in her lap. She knew in that moment
she'd met a man who could have been the
right one, or at least as close as she'd ever
get. The moment she'd met him at the pond,
with his hair damp and his dark eyes narrowed on her, something had changed. She'd
found a rodeo superstar who was anything
but self-centered, who was kind and giving and safe, even fun to be around, like
on their canyon trip. But he'd made it clear
he wasn't interested in anything near com-
mitment, and she was broken. She couldn't
do it.

"I probably wouldn't know it if I did, and

even if I did, I'd wreck it. I'm like a gardener
with a brown thumb."

"I've told you, you're too hard on yourself.
I get it that your folks weren't models of love
and caring, that they drummed perfection
into you until you can't see any other options
in your life. That's a huge burden on you."

"Even worse is it hurts too much when everything tumbles down on me, and it hurts
me to hurt other people. I'm all about healing them, not breaking them."

Ruby came over to them. "Come on, you
two. Talk later. Eat now. We have the best
tri-tip steak you ever tasted, and it's ready."

One of the tables in the barbeque area
was laid out upwind from the massive grill.
Cooper touched McKenna's arm and she got
up. She planned to make sure she wasn't sitting by Cooper at the table, but that's exactly
where the leather place card with her name
on it was positioned. Scout was curled up
under Joy's highchair.

The food was wonderful, and the conversation was funny and light. McKenna enjoyed it and the fact that Cooper said very
little to her until the meal was over. Caleb
and Harmony excused themselves to get

Joy home. Max had come around to talk to them, and she liked him a lot.

"It's been wonderful meeting you, McKenna, and thanks again for coming up with the idea for Simply Sanctuary Two." Before Max could say anything else, he received a call, then said, "Gotta go. Someone's throwing rocks at the windows of an empty house near the general store. Safe ride, McKenna," he said with a smile that almost matched Cooper's.

He shouted over to his parents at the barbeque, "Got a call. Love you both!" and then he took off.

When Dash and Ruby came over to Cooper and her, they were holding hands. "McKenna, so glad you came tonight," Dash said. "Coop says you're staying for another week, and we're having a junior rodeo event for young kids. I think you might enjoy it if you want to come on down to watch. Love to have you there so you can see how my boys all started out. Coop was the one who—"

"Dad, no," Cooper cut in. "No old stories. There's enough of them around already."

Dash laughed. "Okay, I understand, son."

Ruby spoke up. "McKenna's going to be

leaving Scout with me in the afternoons so she can hike, so she'll be around when you have the junior competition."

"I'd love to check it out," McKenna said. "Thank you both for everything. I have never had a better tri-tip. It was wonderful."

"I think you are a lady with very good taste," Dash said.

They laughed at that, and then Cooper said, "We're heading up. I'll be seeing you both in July."

Ruby let go of Dash to give Cooper a hug, and then Dash held out his hand to Cooper. The men shook hands before they had a man hug.

"Safe ride, son," Dash said as he put his arm around Ruby's shoulders to pull her tightly to his side. "Safe ride, McKenna," he added, and then the couple walked off toward the house.

The ride back up was quiet, each person lost in their own thoughts. McKenna had never been in a situation like the barbeque. She almost wished she hadn't gone to see how the other half lived: a family who loved each other, parents who cared, their kids growing up so close to them. It made her heart ache a little.

When they arrived back at the house, McKenna let Scout run, and she sat on the glider. Coop went in the house, then came back out without his hat and sat on the porch step. The night was beautiful, the air clear with a hint of sweetness and earth to it.

"What's that sweet scent in the air?" she asked.

"Wildflowers," he said to her over his shoulder. "They don't bloom long, but when they do, you notice them." He stood up and stretched.

"How are your ribs?"

"Aces," he said. "Tomorrow, you're doing the afternoon hike?"

"Yes. Ruby said she'd take Scout every afternoon after you leave if I need her to. I'll just drive Scout down there before going to the gates. Your mom's so nice."

"I can tell she and Dad like you. I'll make a bet you won't have to cook any dinners before you leave."

"Why wouldn't I?"

"Because you'll get there to pick up Scout,

and dinner will coincidentally be ready, so Mom'll ask you to stay."

"I can't let her do that."

"Darlin'," he said with a bit more of a twang in his tone, "for your own sake, say thank you and stay. Trust me."

She did trust him.

WHEN EVERYONE WAS settled for the night, Coop lay in his bed trying to figure out why he'd kissed McKenna, but nothing was clear to him. He was attracted to her, for sure, and he'd had some thoughts about having more with her than friendship. He figured that was normal, but it hadn't felt normal. He'd wanted her to stop beating herself up because her parents had made her believe that she'd never be perfect. She was terrified of not living up to that goal.

He tried to slam the door on his thoughts. He'd walk away from all of this—he knew that. He'd go on with his life—he knew that. But he also knew it would be a long time, if ever, before he could let go and forget the week he'd just had.

Scout surprised him when she jumped up onto the bed, barely missing hitting him in the face. After circling once, she plopped down and settled with a sigh.

"Promise me to take care of her when you get to Boston, and try to help her find some guy who will really love her and who she can love," he whispered to Scout.

There was no response, not that he expected one, but he really did want that for McKenna. He wanted her to find someone who would love her and who she would be capable of loving back.

Even though he knew that it couldn't be him.

McKENNA FACED AN empty house when she woke the next morning. She got dressed quickly in jeans and a denim shirt she left untucked, then gathered up Scout and headed to the stable. Blaze was still in his stall beside Bravo, and both horses nickered when they saw McKenna. She put the puppy down and checked both stalls, then laid out fresh hay for them and gave them fresh water. She didn't know how much grain to give each horse, so she didn't. She'd let Cooper do that when he came back.

"Well," she said to Scout, who was sitting

on a hay bale by her. "How about we take a walk to get me warmed up for my hike today? I'll get us both some food, then take off."

The puppy stared at her, blinked, then lay down.

So much for communication, she thought as she picked her up and headed back to the house.

After eating, she was getting ready to leave when her phone signaled a text had come in. It was from Cooper.

See you at the house by noon. That was it.

She typed one word, Okay, then sent it.

She and Scout spent the rest of the morning exploring around the pond. She tried to skip rocks the way she had as a kid at a summer camp her parents had put her in while they went to a medical conference in Canada. She'd been able to make up to four skips with one stone back then, which had felt pretty good for a ten-year-old who was so shy she hid from the other campers.

When noon came, McKenna was on the glider while Scout slept off the long walk they'd taken. As she waited for Cooper, she went over yesterday's kiss, trying to set it in perspective—that it was just a kiss and nothing more. She heard a car's engine in the distance, but then it either passed by or kept going as the sound died off. She rocked the glider slowly back and forth, a soothing motion for her.

Then Scout woke suddenly, sat up and stared in the direction of the long access drive. She jumped off the glider and took off, moving faster than she ever had since being found.

McKenna was on her feet, ready to run after the puppy, but stopped at the single step down when Cooper walked into sight at the rise in the driveway coming from the direction of the gates.

Scout was almost to him, then she jumped, and Cooper literally caught her in his hands, letting her lick his face before he set her back down.

When he looked up, McKenna knew he saw her even though he didn't acknowledge it and kept walking. Never looking away from him, she felt her heart racing, and as he got closer, she saw that he wasn't smiling. She'd hoped he would be, that he'd forgotten about the kiss so she could, but he looked serious, with his eyes shaded by his hat brim. He also looked tired.

He climbed up onto the porch and sat down beside her. "Howdy."

"I'm all ready to go whenever you're ready. Scout's eaten, so don't bother with that."

"I have to leave earlier today," he said. "It's my last day, and now that Mom's okay with looking after Scout, you'll have time to hike to your heart's content. I'm heading to Fort Collins, Colorado, and the guy that runs the rodeo there needs me to be on the ground today for some publicity thing, so I have to be there."

"Oh, I see," she said, wondering why she was suddenly having trouble breathing. She stopped the rocking motion of the glider and sat still. She knew what she should say, and she hoped she could say it. "I hope it works out for you and that you do well."

"That's the plan," he murmured. "I need a favor from you, if you can do it?"

"Of course."

"It would be a big help if you could let me drive you to the gates, drop you off, then I'll drive to the house to leave Scout with Mom, and she'll pick you up when you get back to the gates after your hike."

"I don't see why I couldn't do that. I'll drive her back down when she picks me up."

"Good," he said, his voice slightly flat.

Scout was busy trying to catch what looked like a dragonfly, but she missed, then tried again and again.

"Where do you go after Colorado?"

"I'm not sure yet about my schedule, but I have to be in Cheyenne for a big celebration over the last week of July. I have to be available every day there for PR and interviews so I won't be home again until it's done."

"You're sure your ribs are okay?"

"Just fine, darlin'."

She closed her eyes when he called her darlin', and she felt a wave of sadness that she'd never hear him call her that again after he left. When she opened her eyes and looked at Cooper, he was watching her.

She didn't expect him to say, "You look kind of sad."

Sad? Maybe she was, but she was mostly feeling alone, even though Cooper hadn't left yet. Her phone rang this time, and she took it out of her shirt pocket and looked at the screen. It was a number she recognized right away, one used by a nurse she'd worked with at the ER more than once. She took the call.

"Hi, Helena. This is a surprise."

"Well, I knew how upset you were before you left, and I wanted to pass on some news I thought you needed to know."

"Good news?" she asked.

"Yes, good news. A friend of yours in the NICU wanted me to tell you that Dr. Hill signed off on your preliminary diagnosis of that thirty-week preemie you were called in on for a second opinion. The baby's prognosis is excellent. He'll be released when he reaches his goal weight, but other than that, he's doing great."

McKenna pressed her hand to her mouth and closed her eyes.

"McKenna? Are you still there?"

She slowly took her hand down and opened her eyes. "Yes, yes, I'm here. That's the best news ever. Thank you so much for letting me know."

They said their goodbyes, then McKenna sat back and started the glider moving again.

"Good news, huh?"

"Excellent news," she said and told him briefly what it was about. "I tried to make a diagnosis, but some of the tests were still at the lab and Dr. Hill wouldn't let me wait for the results. I'm guessing the imaging machine backed up my diagnosis." She exhaled. "I'm so relieved."

Cooper silently listened to her, then smiled that slow smile he had. "I don't understand much of that, but I do understand that you're grinning from ear to ear, so it must be good."

She couldn't stop smiling. "Very, very good."

"So, you want to get going?" he asked.

"Sure, just give me a minute," she said.

She got up and tossed her backpack over her shoulder as she went into the house. A minute later, she returned with her things and an insulated bottle of water.

"Ready," she said as she stood in front of Cooper.

He got up. "I reckon I am, too."

Cooper used two seat belts to attach Scout's carrier to the middle armrest of the car so the dog could see outside.

"Tell your mother that I'll be back at the ranger station as close to four o'clock as I can be. I'll call her when I'm within five minutes from the gates. Hopefully, Danny won't be planted by them today. You know, I actually like him, but I wish he'd stop throwing suggestions my way about going out with Jimmer."

"Now that I'm leaving, I don't care who sees me around here. It won't matter, so let me take care of Danny for you, okay?"

"No, I can—"

"Take another week of Danny?" he finished for her.

"No, I don't want to. I'll have to tell him I'm not interested, but I don't want to upset him."

"I won't hurt him," he said firmly. "Just go along with me no matter what I say, okay?"

That would take some of the stress off her, and she agreed to whatever he wanted to do about Danny. "Okay."

The gates came into view and were open, and Danny was standing there talking to a man who looked as if he'd just come off the trails.

"If I didn't have to check in, I could get by him. I know where I'm going."

"Just take it easy," Cooper said as he pulled

to park to the left of the gates. He got out quickly and went around to open the door for McKenna, then he helped her put on her backpack and walked her straight toward Danny as the other hiker left.

"Well, the sun does rise in the east, don't it?" Danny said and reached out his hand when Cooper was close enough to him. "Coop or Caleb?" he asked on a chuckle.

"Coop." They shook hands. "By the way, thank Jimmer for that terrific glider. It's amazing. Max got it for McKenna," Cooper said.

"It's so beautiful," she said. "I love it, and the carvings are incredible."

"Well," Danny said, and she could literally see him push out his chest a bit. "Now you mention Jimmer..."

Cooper cut in. "Just make sure you tell him she's real happy with it, and so am I. He's a real artist."

"Sure will when I see him again." Danny looked over at McKenna, a touch of confusion in his expression. "I thought you said you didn't really know the Donovans?"

She stayed as close to the truth as she could. "You know I'm staying there, and

Coo… Coop was back for a few days, and we met."

"Oh, sure, I see." He smiled. "You two just met."

Cooper unexpectedly put his arm around her shoulders, and she froze for a second. "It's only been days, but you know what they say when you find your soul mate. It's not the time that counts, it's…" He shrugged. "You know."

When Cooper looked at her, she felt overwhelmed by the look in his dark eyes and the heat of his body against her side. She'd thought he'd planned on just being there, letting Danny think what he would, but he seemed to be having fun playing it up for the man's benefit.

McKenna couldn't look at Danny at all, so she glanced down at her boots instead and murmured, "It just happened."

"I took McKenna on a ride to the Split Rock Canyon on our land." She felt his hold on her tighten slightly, and when she looked up, he was smiling at Danny. "It's kind of romantic with the legend of the star-crossed lovers doing their version of *Romeo and Juliet*, don't you think?"

Danny stroked his mustache. "Yeah, things can get crazy when parents don't like their kids' choices in dating, let alone marrying someone."

That brought a low chuckle from Cooper. "Yeah, they sure can."

Danny's eyes held his for a moment, then he turned to McKenna. "I've known Coop since way back when he was wreaking havoc on the town, him and his brothers, long before he took off on the circuit. He's always been hard to get. Go figure. A few days, huh?"

Cooper turned his head and looked at her. "Three days, but love's love, and there aren't any rules for how it works." Then he leaned closer. She felt the warmth of his breath brush her face, then his lips found hers, and she almost forgot to breathe.

She had never been more aware of another person in her life. She felt his heart beating against hers, the heat of his body so close and a sense of losing herself, as if she could just melt into him. Then Cooper slowly drew back, and his eyes met hers, echoing her shock.

"We're getting to know each other," Cooper said in a half whisper, his eyes never leaving hers until Danny spoke.

"Dang, ain't that a pretty picture?" Both of them looked over at him, and he wasn't smiling. He was frowning as if he was watching his hopes for Jimmer swirling down the drain. "Boone must be licking his wounds."

Cooper exhaled with a scoffing sound. "Nah, he's doing okay." McKenna hadn't realized how she was leaning into Cooper for support until she felt his hold on her lessen. "Thanks for taking care of McKenna. I feel better about her going off alone on the trails knowing you're around."

A rueful smile showed under the older man's mustache. "That's my job. I take it seriously."

Cooper's hand moved to find hers, and he laced his fingers with hers for a moment. "Good, because she's one of a kind."

Danny nodded. "You got good taste, Coop, real good taste."

"Coming from you, I'll take that as a great compliment." She couldn't help but feel as if Cooper really meant what he was saying and that it wasn't just him conning Danny.

His dark eyes turned on McKenna again.

His hold on her hand tightened as he actually winked at her before he let go. "Have fun out there, darlin'."

Her breath hitched when he called her that, then he turned to Danny. "Have a good day and take care of my girl."

With that, he took off toward the SUV and stopped as he opened the door and looked back. He tapped the brim of his hat with his forefinger, then got in and drove away, leaving dust motes hanging in the still morning air.

McKenna watched until the car was out of sight and Danny spoke again. "Sorry about Jimmer and all. I had no idea that you and Coop were sparkin'."

"I'd sure appreciate it if you didn't mention this to anyone around here. He's going back on the circuit today, and I'm heading back home in a week, so this is kind of it. But I'd sure hate to be the subject of a rumor around here. I've had such a good time, and that would surely spoil it."

"Oh, don't you worry. I'll keep this real quiet. Rumors around here can get out of control. There's always gossip floating around about Coop. I guess he don't need no more."

EVEN THOUGH THE day had been beautiful and
the trail had taken her into land she'd never
challenged the likes of before, all McKenna
could think about was Cooper talking about
her in front of Danny. A kiss to back up lies.
He was leaving and just in time. She knew
how very close she'd come to thinking they
might have something different. But she'd
thought that three other times and been dead
wrong.

He wanted to be friends, and they'd trade
pictures, but she'd never come back here.
After that kiss, she was way too close to falling for Cooper. She wouldn't let that happen.
She couldn't, not when she knew she'd end
up making a real mess of everything again
and hurting him. She couldn't hurt him.

It was ten minutes before four thirty, and
the sun was dipping toward the western horizon. She'd lost count of time sitting at the
halfway point on the trail, her target for the
day. Massive rocks marked the resting point,
and she'd sat there just thinking, trying to
make sense of everything. That didn't happen, but she did feel more settled going back
knowing she wouldn't have to see Cooper
again.

The kiss had been a kiss. That was that, and she didn't want to go over it anymore, especially not with him. So she'd apologize to Ruby Donovan for being late, thank her for taking care of Scout and try to settle into the old house with just Scout there with her. That's what she'd wanted, and now she'd have it. That was good, even if she felt a sense of loss that Cooper wouldn't be around to talk to or ride with or just sit and have a meal with.

When she reached the turn to the ranger station and had cell reception, she sent a text to Ruby. I'll be at the gates in five minutes. Sorry for being late.

A text came back almost immediately. Be right there. When she got closer, there was no one around, just two trucks parked outside the open gates. No Danny Stucky waiting for her to get back. After logging out, she went to the gate to wait for her ride.

She saw dust motes rising in the air down the road first, and then the rental car came into sight. The slanted sun rays reflected off the windshield, making it impossible for her to see who was driving. As it came closer and slowed, she tipped the brim of her new hat farther down to shade her eyes and managed to see the driver. She felt a zing of shock followed by momentary joy at seeing Cooper behind the wheel. And then her heart fell.

He was coming for her, and she didn't know what she was going to do. She spent so much time on the hike getting leveled, putting things in perspective and feeling safe that Cooper was gone. Now that all collapsed, and the only thing she could think to do was to keep her distance from him as much as possible until she understood why he hadn't left.

CHAPTER FIFTEEN

McKENNA HURRIED TO the passenger-side front door after the car came to a full stop in front of her. Avoiding looking at Cooper, she climbed inside and tossed her backpack on the back seat by the animal carrier. Scout was pushing her nose against the mesh safety gate, trying to either get out or see McKenna better.

"Hi, sweetheart, I missed you so much."

Scout didn't move, and if a dog had been able to give a human the stink eye, Scout was as close as possible to doing that.

"I'm sorry, I had to go, but I'm back."

The look lingered, and McKenna settled in the seat snapping her seat belt around her.

"She's kind of mad at me," she said as she finally looked over at Cooper.

He looked semi dressed up in a white shirt with a black leather vest with turquoise stud buttons set in silver, black jeans and black tooled leather boots with red stitching around the soles. There was dust on them but they looked new. Even his hat was changed to a brushed black one with a silver rope at the crown and an embedded turquoise where the band came together at the front.

"Good timing," he said to her without looking at her as he made a wide U-turn to drive away.

She was about to ask why he was still around, but the puppy barked. It was the first time she'd barked since she'd been found.

"Oh my gosh, she just barked."

"She learned from my uncle Abel's new puppy, Tinder. They took to each other."

"Maybe they can have playdates."

He glanced at her as they left dust in their wake. "So, did Danny leave the whole Jimmer thing alone?"

"Yes, he did. He believed what you were trying to get him to believe. I asked him not to tell anyone about it, that you'd be gone today. Seems I was wrong about that. I thought you'd be in Fort Collins by now. Did they cancel the rodeo or something?"

"No, nothing like that. The ranch's plane was having its yearly inspection, and a part wasn't available until early tomorrow morning. Caleb was going to fly me down to Fort Collins, then stop in Cheyenne to pick up some things Harmony needed from her office there. We'll take off as soon as the plane's signed off."

He'd only be around less than a day; she could do that. She *would* do it. "Oh, good," she said since her mind couldn't come up with anything else at the moment.

"If you want your peace and quiet, I can go down to the main house for the night."

There it was, his last gift to her, if she took it, but she couldn't say, "I do want you to go down there," so, she answered, "If you want to go or stay, it's your choice. It's your home."

He didn't respond, just slowed at the gates that had been left open and drove up the long access driveway. As they crested the rise, the small house was ahead of them. His home. He brought the car to a stop by the hitching posts, then turned to McKenna before she could get out.

"I'll stay up here, but I'll keep out of your way. I have some phone calls to make, and I'll take care of the horses. I'll leave premeasured grain in some small empty cans in the tack area. Just give it to each horse once a day."

She should have been thankful he planned on staying at a distance. That's what she wanted, but she also wanted to tell him about her hike. She exhaled, keeping the story to herself. "Okay, I'm going to make a pot of some sort of stew for dinner. If you want some, help yourself."

"Mom fed me…and fed me while I was down there, so I'm not hungry. I'll park the car here and call down below to get a ride in the morning."

"I'm thinking of going out on the trails in the morning, and I'll have to drive Scout down to your mother's. I mean, if she can take her then. I was planning on leaving about seven o'clock, so I can take you down with me."

"That sounds like a plan," he said and opened his door.

She got out and went to get Scout out of her carrier. Then she closed the car door and carried Scout up onto the porch. The puppy began to squirm in her hold. *She isn't going to forgive easily*, McKenna thought as she set her down.

As Cooper came around the front of the car, the dog ran right to him and started jumping up and down.

"Careful, she's going to ruin your new pants and boots."

He bent to pick her up, then held her football style on his arm, where she settled and threw a look right at McKenna that said, *What are you going to do?*

"It's not a problem." He came close to where McKenna stood and handed the puppy off to her. "Make amends with her, and I'll be up and ready to drive down with you by seven in the morning. Sweet dreams," he said, then turned and walked off toward the stables.

McKenna barely slept and was thankful when dawn broke and she could get up and take Cooper to the main house for Caleb to fly him to Fort Collins. Scout wasn't sleeping with her, and she got to her knees to look over the back of the couch. There she was, sleeping with Cooper, snuggling into his chest. She was still holding a grudge.

McKenna quietly went into the bathroom and got dressed in the type of clothes she'd worn every day since she'd arrived at the ranch: jeans, a tank top—pink today—and her boots. She went out into the great room and was surprised to see Cooper coming toward her.

"Good morning," she said.

He muttered, "Morning," as he went past her and into the bathroom, shutting the door with a click.

She had coffee brewed when Cooper came out in faded jeans and a denim shirt, unbuttoned and untucked. He almost looked hungover.

"Coffee?" she asked him.

"Yep," he said and went past her to go and get his boots.

She poured two mugs and took them to the table.

Coop picked his up, cupping it between both hands, blew on it to disperse the steam into the air then cautiously took a drink. "Mmmmm." He sighed.

"So, are you hungover or what?"

He made a scoffing sound. "I don't drink, and I was awake most of the night. Now I have to fly and face the media. Things could be better. Thanks for the coffee."

His beard shadow was coming back, and McKenna thought she liked it better than the clean-shaven look. "There's more where that came from. Are you in trouble for not getting there yesterday?"

"Yeah, but it was what it was," he murmured and took another drink.

"I didn't know you have a plane at the ranch."

"Caleb does. He and Dad fly, and Harmony owns a business in Cheyenne and another up in Cody, so Caleb flies her back and forth when he needs to."

The small talk was getting on McKenna's nerves, but she didn't want to talk about yesterday with Danny, so she stayed silent and drank her coffee. She glanced over at Cooper's bed, and it looked like Scout had taken it over. She was sleeping on his pillow.

"So, are you still leaving today?"

"They got the part in late last night, and the plane just needs the sign off." He shifted in his chair and put down his mug. "I guess this is it," he said.

"I guess so."

He smoothed the handle of his mug with a forefinger. "I've been thinking—which isn't always a good thing—since the performance for Danny, I'm not so sure that…um, being friends with you is what I want."

"You don't have to be," she said.

"That's not what I mean." He sat forward, ignoring his coffee now. "You know what I mean. I saw it in your eyes when I kissed you in front of Danny. I was playing a role, trying to bug the guy and get him off your back, then I kissed you. I mean, I *kissed* you."

She got up and went to the sink to rinse out her coffee mug and stood there staring at herself in the mottled mirror over the sink. She looked pale, and then she saw Cooper getting up and coming over to her.

"Don't…" She couldn't get the words out. Then he was there, right behind her, and she literally felt his body heat. "I… I can't. You know I can't."

"I can't just walk away like it means nothing to me. I lied to you. The plane was fine for flying, but I couldn't get on it. All I could think of was you, that I was walking away, and we'd probably never see each other again, and I couldn't do it."

McKenna felt sadder than she could ever remember feeling in her life. She slowly lowered the mug into the sink and turned to Cooper. "If I was different, and if you were different, I don't know… But we are who we are. You're heading off for the circuit, and I'm heading back to Boston. What's between us up here is all there can be. I've explained my problems before. I can't keep doing it."

He stared at her, and she didn't miss the pain in his eyes, pain because she couldn't be what he wanted. "I don't know if this will count for anything with you, but I think I'm starting to really care, darlin'."

"No, no," she said. Those words hurt her more than she could stand. "I can't."

"Are you sure?"

She wasn't sure of anything except she could barely breathe. "I can't. I wish I could. I've tried, and poor Dalton, even though he was a doctor, he…couldn't deal with my work coming first, and…it was awful."

He brushed his knuckles gently along her jawline, then drew back. "If you ever find out who you really are and not what your parents convinced you you are, look for Flaming Coop D, and he might tell you where to find me." He turned and walked to the table. "Go hiking whenever you want to today. I'll walk down to the main house."

"No, you don't have to."

"Yes, I do," he said and picked up his hat. He put it on, opened the door then looked over at her. "So long, darlin'."

Scout must have sensed something going on, because she came over to McKenna and sat at her feet. As the door shut behind Coop, Scout whined softly.

"I know," McKenna said and bit her bottom lip. "I already miss him."

CHAPTER SIXTEEN

IN THE FOLLOWING DAYS, McKenna had what she'd wanted when she'd arrived at the old ranch: peace, quiet, solitude and as much time as she wanted on the trails. Ruby loved having Scout with her, and Scout was happy to stay down below while McKenna was gone. The stink eye was a thing of the past, and the puppy was thriving.

Her time alone had been perfect, except for the fact that when she and Scout went back to the old ranch in the evening, there was no cowboy sitting on the glider to greet them. When she went riding with Scout snuggled in her shirt, there was no cowboy riding beside her. Boone had come up for a visit and had gone to the canyon with her, but all she'd noticed was no cowboy was there holding her hand. At night, she was lonely sitting outside under the starry sky with no cowboy to share the beauty with.

Saying goodbye to Bravo and Blaze before she left had been harder than she'd imagined it would be. Saying goodbye to Boone, Luke and the other Donovans had been even harder. But she'd gotten through it, and all she had to do on her last day was to pack her things and close up the house.

She was sitting on the porch step while Scout slept on the glider when her phone chimed. She expected Boone to be checking to see if she'd already left for the airport, but she didn't recognized the caller ID, Arness Enterprises, or the area code. But she answered in case it was someone from the hospital.

"This is Doctor Walker."

"Doctor Walker." Cooper's voice echoed her name back at her.

McKenna closed her eyes so tightly that colors flashed behind her eyelids as her world tipped precariously close to the edge.

When she hadn't responded, his voice came again. "McKenna? Are you there?"

"Yes, yes," she said.

"I didn't know if you're flying out today or tomorrow."

"Actually, I'm going to the airport now."

"I won't keep you too long. I was just wondering if you got to hike all the trails you wanted to."

She opened her eyes and stared straight ahead at nothing. "I did, and it was incredible."

"What about the canyon? Did you go back?"

"Boone came up and we rode there. No picnic, though, because an emergency came up and he had to leave." She wouldn't add that she'd stayed behind at the canyon but had finally left when the memories started to hurt too much.

"How about Danny? Any problems with him or Jimmer?"

She'd totally forgotten about those two. The day after Cooper had left, she'd driven up to the gates for the trails, and two men had been waiting for her: Danny and his son.

"Danny actually met me at the gates one morning to introduce me to Jimmer."

"That old codger," Coop muttered.

"You never told me that Jimmer looks a lot like Danny, minus the gray hair, the mustache and the deep tan. He's really a nice guy, actually."

"So, you went out with him?"

"He never asked me, and as you well know, I'm done with dating. Besides, he barely spoke at all. I honestly think he was embarrassed by Danny."

"How's Scout doing?" he asked, changing topics.

She almost said, "She misses you," but kept that to herself because she was afraid she'd finish with, "I miss you, too." So she simply said, "She's good. She's really active and sleeps well at night and eats a lot."

"Have you gone swimming?"

She hadn't gone near the pond since he'd left, not intentionally, but because she had other things to do. "No, I didn't manage to go swimming."

She hated this small talk when all she wanted to do was ask if he was okay. So she decided to ask in a roundabout way. "How is it being back on the circuit?"

"The same as it was before. The finals for saddle bronc riding are tonight. Then I leave Fort Collins and go straight to the Live Wire Rodeo in New Mexico four days after the Fourth of July."

"Are you winning?"

"I'm on the leader board tonight, but the competition's real heavy. The horse I drew is a big black monster named Sledge. He'll be a real challenge."

"I wish you all the luck in the world, but I need to go."

"I'll call you when I get to New Mexico… to check on Scout."

She couldn't let that happen. She'd constantly be wondering when he'd call, when she'd pick up the phone and hear that voice. That meant her focus would be way off center for everything else. She could already see her attention shifting from him calling now.

"Cooper, I'm not meaning to be rude, and I'm sorry, but I don't think you should call me again."

He was silent for so long she thought he'd hung up on her. Then she heard him exhale. "Why not? I figured we'd keep in touch, maybe talk on the phone sometimes, at least. I was hoping…" He sighed. "Never mind. I won't bother you again. Goodbye, McKenna."

There was no "darlin'." McKenna buried her face in her hands as her phone dropped down on the ground between her feet. She wished Cooper had never called. She'd get on with her life, but the thing was, she wasn't at all certain there would ever be a day when she didn't think about Cooper.

FORT COLLINS CAME and went with Coop winning the saddle bronc riding and with a heck of good press following it. Then he made his way to the Live Wire Rodeo in New Mexico. He drove, hoping the time getting there would give him a chance to get his balance. McKenna had made herself clear that she didn't want to hear from him again, but he'd received a photo of Scout just before he was headed to the chute. The puppy looked good in it, a far cry from the puppy McKenna had saved. Sprawled out on dark plank flooring, her head rested on her paws and her eyes shut. All he could see of McKenna in the photo was the toe of a hot pink running shoe.

As he'd finished his victory lap in New Mexico, he did a very Flaming Coop D thing. He tapped the front brim of his hat and made it flip up off his head. It twisted in the air, he caught it. He took a bow from the saddle, then headed to the presentation area, where he accepted the belt buckle and trophy. He held them up in the air for the fans to see.

As he stood there, he realized he was doing everything he'd dreamed about so many years ago, yet he might as well be all alone in the world. All he wanted was to get back to the old ranch as soon as he could to find some semblance of peace again.

TWO WEEKS LATER, McKenna had three more hours on her shift and was impatient to leave the hospital and pick up Scout. As she left the neonatal ICU, a tall man—slender, partially bald and still in his scrubs—was coming down the hall.

Dr. George Hill called out to her. "Dr. Walker! A minute please?"

He looked exhausted as he tugged his mask down under his chin. "I was looking for you downstairs."

She didn't want problems, not now and not from the doctor who had ordered her off the floor what seemed like an eternity ago. "What do you need?"

"I wanted to let you know, I signed off on the Talbot boy to go home tomorrow with in-home therapy. Because you were there when they brought him in and made a good call quickly, he's doing really well."

For the first time ever, McKenna didn't recognize the patient's name immediately, even though it had only been four days since he'd been brought into the ER. That scared her. That had nothing to do with burnout, just plain distraction. She knew where that came from, and that scared her, too.

"That's very good news. Thanks so much for letting me know. I'll drop by his room later when I get off."

"I noticed that you've pulled some long hours since you came back from your vacation. Why don't you go home after you visit your patient? I'll get someone to cover the end of your shift."

The same man who had made her so angry and frustrated that night before she left for Wyoming was doing a kindness for her that she was very grateful for. All she genuinely wanted was to go home with Scout and try to figure out what was going on with her. She didn't have to even think about taking his offer.

"Thank you, I will."

When she finally arrived at her loft with Scout, she felt an uneasiness. Then as she went into the high-ceilinged space and looked around, she suddenly understood everything. The space was empty except for the puppy excitedly running around finding the toys she had a habit of hiding under the couch and the low coffee table. McKenna stood dead still, letting herself accept a truth that she knew had been there for a long time but that she'd never let herself admit.

She could feel the emptiness, and the reason for it was Cooper wasn't there. It was insane because he'd never been in her loft—but not any more insane than the idea that she might be in love with him. She wasn't sure what she was supposed to feel, but emptiness had to be part of it. She simply felt empty.

Slipping out of her pink running shoes, she went into the bedroom to get her laptop, then climbed up on the bed and sat back against the pillows while the computer booted up. When the welcome screen showed, she used her search engine and typed in "Flaming Coop D."

In a flash, there was an overload of hits

for Cooper, and she picked a blog devoted to rodeo action. As it opened, she saw a picture of Cooper dressed like he'd been in the huge poster at Farley's. Black and red, all Flaming Sky Ranch, all Flaming Coop D in his element. He was holding a huge silver belt buckle over his head with one hand and a trophy with the other. The banner on the page read, "Flaming Coop D chasing after number 6!!!"

He was smiling into the camera, and she almost cried. Just seeing him touched her, made her heart speed up and tears start to burn behind her eyes. Was that love? If it was, it was miserable. Closing the computer, she sat back. She needed to do something, but she didn't know what. Then she had an idea. Taking her cell phone out, she put in a call, and when Boone answered, there was music and people cheering in the background.

"Hey, McKenna. Hold on while I go into the private room behind the seats." She waited, then there was the sound of a door closing and the other noises reduced to muffed sounds. "What's going on?"

"I just wanted to talk, but you sound as if you're at a party. I won't bother you."

"Hey, hold on. It's no bother, and I'm at Cheyenne Frontier Days, at the rodeo waiting for Coop to show up. I managed to get away from work and flew down to see him before he rides again. So, what's going on?"

She bit her lip, then told him the truth. "I'm back at work, and I'm back to working long hours. Today I didn't recognize a patient's name, a little boy I'd taken care of when he first came into the ER. That's never happened before."

"I hate to bang the same drum, but you need to reconsider private practice. You'll actually get to know the patients, not just their names. You'll see them grow up. It's different, McKenna, and for you, I think it would be better. It's a good way to practice medicine. I found that out when I came back here."

She closed her eyes. "Boone, are all the Donovans there in Cheyenne?"

"You bet. It's a constant celebration around here. With Coop in the running for his sixth championship, it's crazy. I'm trying to get someone to cover for me so I can come back for the finals. He'll make history."

"Is he there now?"

"Sure is. He's everywhere. Lots of PR going on, and some family things, too. Dash is a guest judge in the bull riding events. I wish you were here to see it all. I'll pay for your plane ticket if you can get the time off work."

"Thanks, but no."

"Think about it. I can get you a room nearby. If things go as planned, Coop's going to be riding for the championship on the last day. It should be pretty exciting."

Her stomach was knotting again. "I don't know why people want to watch others putting their life on the line to outlast a horse. Cooper's crazy for doing it. I wouldn't want to watch."

"Hey, McKenna, why would you…?" His voice trailed off and McKenna wished she could take that comment back. "Oh, boy, that's what's going on."

"What?"

"You and Coop. It's not a problem for you that you *could* like him, because you do like him."

"Okay, I do. That's why I can't come back there, why I can't keep…that connection when it can't go anywhere."

"That's your choice, and if it's what you have to do, do it and just forget about Coop."

That hit her like a brick. *Forget him.* She swallowed hard. She didn't know how to forget him. She'd been trying ever since he'd kissed her, then left.

"Say, McKenna, I have to go. I'm being paged."

"Oh, sure. Of course."

"You do what's right for you, but be very sure that's the case. I love you, and I worry about you."

"Don't worry about me. I love you, too."

The call ended, and McKenna just felt empty again. She craved what she'd found at the old ranch—the peace, the safety and Cooper. That came out of nowhere, but she knew it was true. She was homesick for him, not the ranch. It seemed impossible, but she was starting to think this misery was a part of being in love. After speaking to Cooper on the phone, she'd felt broken and alone. That couldn't be love. Or maybe it was. She'd never known it, so how could she recognize if she found it?

She lay there alone until she gave up the internal fight she was having about wanting to go back to the ranch one last time and leave the last connection she had to Cooper there. She knew where his lucky dollar was, still in the side pocket of her medical bag. She thought of mailing it to him, but she felt an inexplicable need to return to the ranch. She wanted to bring his silver dollar back to him, where it belonged.

She knew that wasn't totally rational, but she had to do it. With the whole family staying down in Cheyenne for the celebration, and with Cooper having told her himself that he'd have to be on-site and available for the entire time, he wouldn't be anywhere near the ranch. She'd take a chance and go.

MCKENNA FLEW INTO Cody two days later just after the noon hour and drove directly to the old ranch in a small bright red SUV with Scout in her carrier on the back seat. The drive had seemed endless until she finally spotted the turn for Twin Arrows and pulled off the highway onto the packed dirt road. She passed the place she'd found Scout. When she neared the entry to the old ranch, she was surprised to see the chain was hanging from the gate support and the padlock was gone.

She looked around when she got out to push the unlocked gates open. Maybe someone forgot to lock up, but just in case someone was at the house, she drove slowly up the long driveway to the crest, then stopped. She looked around the area ahead at the house where the sunlight glinted off the windows. Nothing stirred, just the rippling of the dried grass as a warm breeze swept across the land.

She continued forward, stopping in front of the porch and turning the car off. The summer sun was warm on her skin, and a feeling of peace surrounded her. She opened the back passenger door to get Scout out of her carrier.

Scout had been really good on the flight and the drive to the ranch, but the minute her paws touched the ground, she took off. She darted in a straight line to the far side of the house, then turned and started to run in wide circles.

McKenna smiled at the puppy flying through the grass, then she took the single step up onto the porch and sat down on the glider to keep an eye on Scout. Slowly, she started it moving, and things just seemed to fall into place. *Home.* She envied every one of the Donovans who had sat out on this porch at night and known they were home. She couldn't remember any single place in her life that had been a real home. And now she would leave this all behind.

She figured she had a couple of hours here before she had to get back to Cody for her return flight. Two hours to do what she wanted, to break whatever bond she had with the ranch and leave, never looking back. Scout came toward her, jumped up onto the porch, then jumped again onto the glider. She cuddled into McKenna's side and sighed. McKenna thought that Scout was happy to be back here, too.

McKenna sat there just looking out at the land around her, feeling the balmy air brushing her skin and thinking about how everything had happened. Scout startled her when she abruptly sat up, then stood and jumped down off the glider. The puppy stood very still as if waiting for something, then she twisted around and ran down off the porch and in the opposite direction from the stable. As McKenna stood, she realized Scout was darting toward the trees and the path through them to get to the pond.

McKenna ran after her and watched her stop at the tree line. Scout seldom barked, but she barked right then as a man leading a horse stepped out of the trees. Cooper bent down to pick up Scout who started frantically licking his chin.

He was speaking softly to the puppy and looked up at McKenna. His dark eyes met hers, and her heart lurched. In that moment, she knew why she came—not to say goodbye to everything or to return a worn old silver dollar. This was the only place on earth that she could feel close to Cooper. She'd expected that to come from memories, not from the man himself, and she was at a loss for what to do.

"You…you're supposed to be in Cheyenne. I didn't know you'd be here," she said pathetically.

He was wearing a modified version of the outfit in his poster: black on black with red trim, but no patches from sponsors and no chaps. His lucky hat shaded his eyes.

"This *is* my place."

Scout was starting to wiggle, and Cooper crouched and set the puppy free. But she didn't run off this time, she stayed right by his black boots.

"You said you had to be in Cheyenne the whole time."

"Well, I had a problem, and Caleb did me the huge favor of flying me up here, where I could have some peace and quiet for a few hours. I had no idea anyone would be here."

A thought came to her that made her feel sick. "You're hurt again, aren't you?"

"No," he said. "I'm not hurt, and I don't need my doctor to check me out. So why are you here?"

She reached in her jeans pocket and took out his lucky charm, then moved closer to hold it out to him, trying to ignore the un-steadiness in her hand. She hadn't expected to give it to him in person.

"I never gave this back to you."

He stared at it lying flat on her palm, then looked up at her, his eyes narrowed. "Is that why you're up here?"

"Just take it, please."

He shook his head. "Not until I can give you a paper dollar for it."

She closed her hand around the coin and drew back. "Okay, I'll leave it on the table inside the house."

"Keep it," he said.

"No, you're the one who needs good luck. I'm not getting on some crazy horse anytime soon. I'm leaving it for you. It's yours."

She could barely look at Cooper without wanting to just touch his face, to feel his beard stubble against her fingertips. Her hand tightened around the coin enough to press it into her skin and make her stop.

"Goodbye," she said as she turned to go back toward the house. It seemed like forever before she got to the entry, intending to go inside and leave the coin on the table.

She was surprised when she heard Cooper's boots on the wood planks of the porch behind her and even more surprised when he took her by her upper arm as she approached the door. She jerked free and turned to face him.

"What do you want?" she asked, not caring it was said harshly. Him touching her couldn't happen again. She was sick about coming here and seeing him. She just wanted to leave.

Cooper tucked the tips of his fingers into his jeans pockets and rocked slightly forward on the balls of his feet. Any protective space she thought she had was now gone.

"McKenna, I'm not sure what I've done, but I thought even if we weren't friends, we wouldn't be enemies. Whatever you think I did, I apologize." He took a breath and shook his head. "No, I don't apologize for kissing you, if that's what this attitude is about."

It was nothing to do with attitude and everything to do with her finally falling in love but knowing she'd destroy it sooner or later and lose everything. She couldn't be this close to Cooper, seeing the fine lines at the corners of his eyes and the tightness in his jaw when he looked at her. It hurt her, and there was nothing she could do to make things better.

"It's me, not you."

"Oh, yeah, of course. Isn't that the way most people break up when they don't want a mess on their hands? It's you, not me, so I'll leave feeling virtuous, and you'll leave knowing you lied?"

She moved away from him to open the door and went inside. The room was still and as soon as Scout followed her, she started making her usual circles around the space. Quickly, McKenna put the coin on the table, then called to Scout, and the puppy followed her back out.

Coop was still there leaning against the porch post, his hat in one hand. Going past him quickly to get to the car was her goal, but she didn't make it.

"Just hold on, darlin'," he said in a low voice that still had the power to freeze her in her tracks.

"Don't call me 'darlin'," she whispered. "I'm leaving."

"You can go, but I think you owe it to me to at least listen to what I want to say."

"I don't have the time. I have to get back to Cody for my return flight to Boston," she said and started to go past him, but she accidentally stepped on Scout's paw and the puppy yapped sharply.

"Oh my gosh," McKenna said, crouching down to pick her up. "I'm sorry, so sorry," she cooed as she examined the puppy's paw, then kissed it.

"She okay?" Cooper asked.

"Yes, she's fine."

"That's good. Now will you let me speak?"

She could see he was serious, and she decided she owed him that much. "Okay, but I have to—"

"I know, be in Cody for your flight out. Five minutes." He smiled at her, and she felt her legs get weak. "I promise."

She turned and sat on the glider, burying her head in her hands. She started to shake. Then Cooper moved so close that she could feel the air stir around her. When she slowly dropped her hands to her lap, he was crouched in front of her.

"Okay," she said. "Five minutes."

Coop stood up to take the seat by her on the glider. Laying his hat on the cushion beside him, he shifted so he could look right at her. He wanted to tell the truth, that Caleb had done him a favor by flying him up here, but it was because Boone had told him McKenna would be at the ranch today and that she wasn't in good shape. Boone never wanted her to know he'd told Coop.

At first, seeing her again wasn't something he was sure he wanted to do—he didn't know if he wanted to start back where they were when she'd first stepped out of the trees while he was in the pond. She was lost, trying to find herself, and all he'd seemed to do was make it harder on her. He hadn't helped her, but that wasn't because he hadn't wanted to. In fact, he'd come pretty close to doing something stupid, like falling in love with her. He'd never tell her that now. He was still trying to figure out what that meant and how to get past it.

But now she was right in front of him, and it hurt him to see her clasp her hands tightly in her lap. She was looking down at them, not up at him.

"I'll just be blunt because we don't have time to knock that squirrel out of a tree."

He'd thought that might have made her at least look up at him, but it didn't.

"Okay, here goes. Before you showed up here the first time, I was fine with the way I was living my life, then you arrived, and it took me very little time to figure out that you were special. I didn't want to admit that, because that put me between a rock and a hard place."

"I don't see how this is important now," she said so softly that he could barely make out her words.

"Let's strip it down further. When Boone talked to me about you, he said you were lost, and he hoped you'd find what you needed up here. He sold me on it, and that's probably what made me let you stay. Against my better judgment, I did it, and you know what?"

"No, and it doesn't matter."

She kept her head down, and he reached out to lightly cup her chin with his hand and eased her head up so he could look right into her eyes. "I was lost, but didn't know it, then you were there, and bit by bit, you got to me in ways I never knew anyone could. Then I had to leave, and being away from you, all I wanted was to be around you again."

McKenna was very still, looking at him but almost blankly. "I have to go."

"Didn't you hear anything I said?"

She moved her head to break their contact, and he drew his hand back. "I heard you," she said. "I told you I can't do it. I can't. I told you and told you." She moved to get up and called out, "Scout! Scout!"

"McKenna," he said, "you've told me about your 'DNA' and how you can't make relationships work. You owe that to your folks. I understand. I mean, I don't agree, but I get it. But you've never asked me what I wanted."

McKenna finally met his eyes again. "What do you want?"

He said simply, "I want you."

She exhaled. "I'm sorry. I need to go."

His frustration grew. "You know what? You're a coward. You're so scared of making a mistake, of not being good enough, of giving another person a space in your life that you put yourself down, claim to be unable to love anyone, and you blame your parents for it." He hadn't meant to say any of that, but there it was, his awful words hanging between them.

"Stop," she said, then reached down to pick up Scout, who was right at her feet, then turned, took the stair down and went to the back passenger side of her rental.

Coop watched her put Scout into her carrier. Then without another word, she got in behind the wheel. He hurried over to the driver's side and rapped on the window. She flinched at the sound but reluctantly slid the widow between them down.

"Cooper, please don't."

He felt an ache that defied description spreading through him. He took a breath, then just said the plain truth that he honestly had never said to any other woman who had been in his life.

"I'm confused and empty, and it's because of me meeting you at the pond that first day. Now I know it's because I love you, darlin'. Stay or go, it's up to you. Take me or leave me. I won't fight you anymore. But know that I love you."

She stared straight ahead, then started the car and put it in Reverse.

As Coop watched her start to back up, he saw a tear running down her cheek, then the window went up. He moved out of the way when she made a U-turn and drove away. The air around him was warm, but he felt colder than he had ever been in his life.

CHAPTER SEVENTEEN

McKENNA WAS HALFWAY to Cody when Boone called her. She pulled over on the gravel side of the highway and answered.

"Hello."

"McKenna, where are you?" he asked without any greeting.

"On the way to the airport."

"Why?"

"Why wouldn't I be, Boone? I told you I was flying up for a reason, but I never told you what it was." She explained about the silver dollar and finding Cooper there. "Why did you call me?" she asked, swiping at her damp cheeks.

"You're going to hate me, but I guess it's worth the risk."

"I couldn't hate you for anything."

"I won't hold you to that," he said. "But if you're leaving, it won't mean much anyway."

Raw nerves gave her no space for patience,

even with Boone. "Just say what you want to say."

She heard him take a deep breath. "Okay, it's about Coop."

"What about Coop?"

"I told him you'd be at the ranch today, and the next I knew, I found out he'd had Caleb fly him up there. I really... I didn't mean for that to happen."

"Well, it did. Thank you very much! And I'm leaving, so no hard feelings. I have to. I don't want to miss my flight." It seemed she was saying that more than anything else today.

"Hold your horses. At least ask me why I told him you'd be up there."

She swiped at her damp face, then closed her eyes. "Tell me."

"McKenna, I just spoke to Coop, and he said straight out that he'd told you he loved you, and you drove away. That's the bottom line. You left him there, and you never even tried to figure out if you loved him or not."

She opened her eyes and drove on to the highway and kept going to Cody. "What if I do?" she asked in a low voice. "I couldn't make it work. I'd hurt him when everything fell apart, and I couldn't survive doing that to him."

"So you do love him."

"Yes, okay, I love him. But I never guessed loving someone could hurt so much, and I know it would never have a happy ending." She was so mad she was crying again and she pulled back off the road. "I can't do that to Cooper. I won't… I… I…won't."

He had the nerve to chuckle at that. "So, you care so much for Coop that you'll suffer so he won't suffer?"

"I… I guess so."

"That sounds very noble," Boone said. "Except the reason you're doing it is because you can't bear the thought of failing again. Three times you've failed, and now, you see number four, and it scares you to death, so you'd rather run than stay and see what could happen. You're a brilliant doctor, but when it comes to your love life, you're a wimp. You'd rather toss him away than take a chance of finding out what's really between you two. Your biggest fear from the first time I met you on rounds has been that you'll fail. If you don't take a leap of faith, you'll never know if you were right or wrong, and that's going to eat at you for the rest of your life. Unless you can just forget Coop exists."

His last sentence hit her right in her heart. Forget about Cooper? She never could. She knew that as clearly as she knew that she'd love Cooper for the rest of her life. The tears wouldn't stop, and she sniffed before she could answer Boone.

"I have to go. My flight... I don't want to miss it."

"Okay, fine, but you don't sound as if you're in any shape to fly. I accept your decisions about your life, but I don't want you leaving in tears. I wish you'd turn around and come back to Eclipse. You know where my house is. Come back and spend the night. I'll take you to the airport tomorrow when I fly back down to Cheyenne for the finals tomorrow night."

All she wanted to do was climb into bed and pull the blankets up over her head.

As if he'd read her mind, Boone added, "If you don't want to talk, that's fine. Just get into bed and get some rest. I'll take care of Scout for you."

"Thank you," she said knowing her voice sounded choked.

"I'll be here when you get here."

She waited for a couple of cars to pass before she made a wide U-turn and headed south toward Eclipse and Boone's house.

COOP HAD BARELY made the finals with a score of seventy-seven in the semifinals earlier in the day. He'd done all he could to settle down, even agreeing to get a massage before the competition started at seven that night. The horse he drew was a good one to make points on but a hard one to stay on for eight seconds. It was a challenge, and Coop knew that for that eight seconds, he couldn't be thinking about what had happened at the old ranch the day before.

He'd felt numb after McKenna had left and had barely spoken to Caleb on the return flight to Cheyenne. Caleb was used to his brother shutting down when he was facing a hard ride. Perfect focus was everything, and Coop was thankful Caleb assumed it was his competition persona. The talk with McKenna hadn't been what he'd rehearsed on the flight over to the ranch. Actually, it hadn't gone at all the way he'd planned, except for the part where he'd told her that he loved her.

He stood off to the side in the wide concrete-floored passage, letting some riders go past, acknowledging them with a nod of his head. He hoped his smile didn't look as bad as he felt it did. He had on his regular riding outfit—all done in black and red with fringe—along with his gold-studded boots, a vest and chaps. He looked overdone, but it was his trademark, and he saw more than a few kids walking around the rodeo dressed a lot like him.

He moved closer to the chutes and set eyes on Sampson the Terrible, the horse that had been drawn for him. The muscular roan had an unbroken string of not letting any rider last for eight seconds. He watched Sampson being coaxed into the chute as he fought the handlers every inch of the way. Finally, he was secured, but not a bit less feisty. Cooper knew a make-or-break horse when one showed up, and one had shown up for him.

He closed his eyes and was instantly bombarded with memories of McKenna. He quickly opened them again.

Coop slowly approached his adversary:

Sampson weighed in at over 1,500 pounds of muscle and bone. He hoped the animal would have a bad day and he'd have a good ride. Just eight seconds in the saddle. As he climbed to the top rail of the metal enclosure to get the saddle in place, he looked Sampson in the eye. He tried to focus, to blank out everything around him and make it about the horse and him, period.

But that failed when he had another flash of when McKenna had left. Seeing her start to cry had almost undone him. He just hoped she was okay back in Boston, doing what she loved.

Then Sampson swung his head toward Coop, and he barely missed the impact because he hadn't focused. Dang, he had to concentrate. Just eight seconds. He could do it. He had to do it. Then he could figure out his life.

It was a struggle to get Sampson readied, but it happened, and Coop only took two attempts to climb on the animal's back. He shifted and tested how the saddle felt with the width of Sampson between his thighs. Then he twisted the harness rein about his left hand three times before it felt secure.

His grip on the thick rope was too important to rush until he was totally satisfied at how it would affect the horse and him.

With a nod to the handlers, he said, "Got it."

Someone said, "Safe ride, cowboy," and then the announcer who had been filling in a bit while he waited for the go-ahead signal said, "For the last competition of this rodeo and the saddle bronc finals, from the Flaming Sky Ranch, sitting on the back of Sampson the Terrible, a mass of pure meanness, a local boy out of Eclipse. Safe ride, Cooooooooop Donovan!"

The cheers were deafening as Coop nodded and released his grip on the top metal rail of the chute. A handler immediately opened the gate, and Coop felt the expected tightening in the animal's muscles as he charged out into the freedom of the arena with seven seconds to throw Coop off his back before the clock ticked to eight.

Coop owned the horse and the saddle for nine seconds, and then the pickup riders were there alongside, getting him off cleanly. As they protected him from Sampson, he jogged over to the gate and went inside to wait behind the barrier for the other rides to post. As soon as the last rider posted in third, Coop was the only one in first.

As he mounted a horse for his victory ride, he realized the rush he'd always felt from being up against the best of the best and beating them seemed flat. When the crowd started chanting his name, he started his ride, but everything felt off-kilter to him.

He scanned the sea of faces in the packed arena even though he knew exactly where his family and friends were seated. Then he saw a woman jumping up and down cheering. She was wearing a bright yellow baseball cap, and for a fleeting moment, he thought he'd spotted McKenna in the stands. The next moment, he knew he was wrong. She didn't look like her at all.

McKenna was who he wanted to see then, more than anything. But the woman he'd fallen in love with was in Boston taking care of scared, sick children. Meanwhile, he was in Cheyenne, coming within two points of setting a world record in saddle bronc riding, taking his sixth championship, getting his belt buckle, the trophy and money, and he'd give it all up to just see McKenna right then.

McKenna was alone in Boone's house when the clock chimed midnight. Boone had talked her into staying for two nights to calm down and refocus before she headed back to Boston. She'd called into work and arranged to have two more days off. The new day was starting, and she was leaving on an eight o'clock flight out of Cody. She'd already packed, and there were no goodbyes to say. No one even knew she hadn't left as planned, except Boone, and she'd almost made him swear a blood oath that he wouldn't mention her name to Cooper when he saw him in Cheyenne on the last night of the rodeo. They'd said their goodbyes earlier in the day before Boone flew down for the grand finale.

Scout was sleeping in her bed in the guest room at the old farmhouse. McKenna stood in the middle of the living room, then went to the door and stepped out into the cool midnight air. Wearing a blue tank top and denim shorts, she went back in to get her phone, then padded barefoot to the front door and went out onto the porch.

Leaving the door ajar in case Scout woke up, she crossed to the steps and sat down on the top one. The night air gently brushed across her arms and legs and teased her hair, which she'd left down. She didn't know what happened in Cheyenne earlier and fought off every urge that came to her to search the results of the rodeo. The sooner she left, the better.

Her phone was still in her hand and buzzed as a new text came in. When she looked down at the screen, she moaned softly. *Cooper.* She couldn't do it. But the idea that he might be hurt flashed in her mind. Before she overthought it, she touched the screen to open the text. When she started to read it, she was thankful she was sitting down.

McKenna, please read this before you delete it.

Her heart was pounding when she kept reading, almost hearing the words in his voice in her head.

Excuse what I'm going to say, but I'm past worrying. I just need to say the truth. My first truth is I love you, I need you, and I don't want to let you go. If you think you could love me at all, I'll do the rest. I'll love you enough for the both of us. I called you a coward, but I'm the coward. Seeing my life ahead of me without you terrifies me. I need you. Darlin', I love you. Please come and save me.

She sat there with the phone in her hand. He'd been right to call her a coward. It wasn't her being scared about loving him, it was being afraid she'd fail at what other people seemed to know how to do naturally. She'd never believed she'd be able to love someone with her whole heart, that there was even a possibility. Now she hoped she'd been very wrong.

Quickly, she punched a number in her cell and called Boone. When he answered she said, "Where are you?"

"I'm here at the hotel in Cheyenne. There was a party for family and friends after Coop made his big win, and they're just shutting down."

"Coop won?"

"Big time."

"Is he at the party?"

"He never showed up. Caleb flew him back to the ranch. There was some kind of trouble at Caleb's restaurant in Cody. Some furniture was broken, and the mechanical bull was wrecked. Coop hitched a ride with him."

The ranch. McKenna smiled. "Thanks. I'm leaving now. Call you soon, and thanks for all you tried to do for me."

"Hey, sure, I'd do anything for you."

"Love you," she said and ended the call.

She gathered up her things and then, with Scout in her carrier, McKenna headed back to the ranch knowing Cooper wasn't the one who needed saving. She finally knew she did, and he was the only one who could save her.

As McKenna drove up Twin Arrows to the gates to the old ranch, she found them open and pulled onto the Donovan land. By the time she was at the rise in the driveway, she was feeling almost sick from nerves. Then she crested it, and the headlights from the rental car lit up the house. Cooper was there sitting on the glider…alone. As she slowly pulled up to the hitching post, she stopped, turned off the car and got out without any idea what to say. Cooper was watching her but didn't move to come toward her.

Her first step in his direction was the hardest step she'd ever taken in her life. She was scared, but she knew this was it. She'd found love and she didn't want to lose it. She got to the single step, stopped and clasped her hands tightly in front of her. Silence enveloped them, and she knew what she had to say.

"Cooper, I need you to save me."

That's when he moved, coming down to her in two strides. Then his hand cupped her chin, and she felt his unsteadiness there. "It'd be my pleasure, darlin'," he whispered then kissed her.

As he drew back, his arms surrounded her, pulling her into his chest, and she felt the beat of his heart against her cheek.

"I heard you won at Cheyenne."

"Yeah, but where I really won is right here, with you." A bark came from the car, and Coop smiled. "So Scout's along for the ride?"

"She sure is."

McKenna let go of Cooper to get to the car and let Scout out of the carrier. The first thing the puppy did was stop and look around. Then she dove like a bomber jet right at Cooper. He managed to scoop her up before she hit his shins head-on.

"Hey, I missed you," he said as he lifted her close enough for her to place a few licks on his chin. Then he put her back down. "Go and chase your tail," he said as he turned back to McKenna.

She reached out, needing to hold on to him, almost overwhelmed by what loving Cooper meant. "Please, just hold me," she said, and he did. "What are we going to do now?"

He surprised her by literally sweeping her off her feet, then carrying her up the single step to the glider. Gently he put her down, then sat beside her with no space between them.

"Be happy. Be incredibly happy. Then everything else falls into place."

She sighed as she turned to him, their faces just inches apart. "Yes, happy," she whispered. "But you'll have to leave soon."

"No, I told Matt to put my schedule on hold for a month."

She frowned slightly. "For a month? Why, did you get hurt?"

"No, no." He gently brushed his thumb between her eyebrows. "No frowns. I'm fine, although Sampson was seriously trying to destroy me. I figured if you wouldn't have me, I'd need some pity-party time, and if you'd have me, I wanted you-and-me time. And it would give us breathing room to figure out what we want, together."

"Very practical for a big-time risk taker," she said teasingly and loved the smile he gave her.

"Sending you that text was the biggest risk I've ever taken. I didn't know if you'd call me and tell me to leave you alone, or if you'd ignore it completely."

"How could I ignore you when I love you so much?"

He leaned close to whisper in her ear. "Thank you for loving me."

She shifted, putting her arms up around his neck and burying her face in his shoulder. "I'm so stupid. Looking back now, I think I started falling in love with you when you told me I could stay on at the house for a week after you left. It seems so obvious now, the way I tried to stay close to you instead of obeying the rules of space and quiet."

"I'm glad you broke the rules. Right now we have some negotiating to do. I figure as long as you love me, everything else is negotiable. First decision is, Boston or here? That's going to take some time."

It didn't. "Here," she said immediately. "I've actually thought about leaving Boston and coming out here to work with Boone at the clinic. I think it's the best decision for everyone, and now's the time to do it."

"Really? You'd do that?"

"Of course. He said I should go into private practice, but I think his clinic is a perfect place for me to be. We can live up here, just us, and Scout, too."

"Darlin', I think we're sparkin'."

She grinned at him. "Boy, do I like sparking."

He gave her a quick kiss. "Me, too."

"I love you," she whispered. "I love you so much. Thank you for saving me."

Cooper framed her face with his hands and smiled at her. "My pleasure, darlin'," he said, and then he kissed her.

* * * * *

*Don't miss the next book
in Mary Anne Wilson's
Flaming Sky Ranch miniseries,
coming January 2024 from
Harlequin Heartwarming.*

THE NORA ROBERTS COLLECTION

40% OFF!

Get to the heart of happily-ever-after in these Nora Roberts classics! Immerse yourself in the beauty of love by picking up this incredible collection written by, legendary author, Nora Roberts!

YES! Please send me the **Nora Roberts Collection**. Each book in this collection is 40% off the retail price! There are a total of 4 shipments in this collection. The shipments are yours for the low, members-only discount price of $23.96 U.S./$31.16 CDN. each, plus $1.99 U.S./$4.99 CDN. for shipping and handling. If I do not cancel, I will continue to receive four books a month for three more months. I'll pay just $23.96 U.S./$31.16 CDN., plus $1.99 U.S./$4.99 CDN. for shipping and handling per shipment.* I can always return a shipment and cancel at any time.

☐ 274 2595 ☐ 474 2595

Name (please print)

Address Apt. #

City State/Province Zip/Postal Code

Mail to the **Harlequin Reader Service:**
IN U.S.A.: P.O. Box 1341, Buffalo, NY 14240-8531
IN CANADA: P.O. Box 603, Fort Erie, Ontario L2A 5X3

HARLEQUIN
PLUS

Try the best multimedia
subscription service for romance
readers like you!

Read, Watch and Play.

Experience the easiest way to get
the romance content you crave.

Start your **FREE TRIAL** at
<u>www.harlequinplus.com/freetrial.</u>